SNOWFALL

AVERY BLAKE

DAVID W. WRIGHT

STERLING & STONE

SNOWFALL

ROSA AND REBECCA had been gone from The Reserve for too long, and the women were dying to get home.

The word still didn't feel right to Rosa, but Rebecca insisted everyone use it.

She never said *Home is where the heart is,* but that's only because she didn't want Rosa making fun of her, which she absolutely would have, seeing as that was one of her roles as the younger and apparently more frivolous one in their relationship.

Almost there. Until then, at least the conversation was pleasant. They were discussing nothing of consequence, and given the weight of nearly every conversation, and the darkness Rebecca was forced to adopt as the most senior ranger to both stay alive and not abandon ship, an exchange with a whole lot of nothing felt surprisingly nice.

There was silence, save for the clomping of hooves, the bears' heavy strides, and a single sigh from Rosa's horse. In that quiet, she found herself thinking the same thing she always did. *At the end of the world, at least her mother was dead.* Followed by an older thought, one she'd been having as long as she could remember, since her baby brother was still in diapers — *I have to keep Mikey safe.*

Then Rebecca broke the quiet.

"Favorite straight lesbian movie?"

"*Clarity of the Moon,*" Rosa said. "Or maybe *Thelma and Louise.*"

"*Clarity of the Moon* was … okay," Rebecca smiled. "But I did love *Thelma and Louise.*"

"How about you?"

"Mine is really old. And small. You probably haven't heard of it."

"Try me," Rosa said.

"It's called *Fried Green Tomatoes.*"

"Oh, I've heard of that!"

"You have?" Rebecca looked surprised.

"No," Rosa laughed. "It's before my time."

"It's before my time, too. I think from just before I was born. I'm not *that* old, you know."

She wasn't. A rather stunning forty-five, but she still had twenty years on Rosa, and the younger woman loved to give her "elder" a hard time about it whenever possible.

Baloo made noises behind them. That set Smokey off, who started to grumble as well.

"Think they're hungry?" Rosa asked.

"Probably. But they can eat when we get back."

Baloo was a brown bear, and Smokey a grizzly. Both were absolute beasts, but Smokey was a half-ton, outweighing Baloo by a full five-hundred pounds.

The bears were a godsend. Literally, according to a growing handful of residents inside The Reserve. People felt the same way about Kelso, the trainer, who seemed to have an almost telepathic rapport with the bears.

Rangers rounded up the bears, brought them back to The Reserve, and handed them over to Kelso. He had them trained within a month, while Baldwin made each bear a bespoke set of armor and Alegra crafted a harness to hold Simon's nodes. They were needed to keep the humans in charge. Depending on the voltage, the nodes could do anything from incapacitating the bear wearing it to turning its brain into jelly.

"Can you tell me everything Alanis is holding in her other hand?"

Rosa sighed. "I just don't get her like you do. Sorry."

"*Jagged Little Pill* is a perfect album."

"One good album … a million years ago."

"Do you know, or not?"

Rosa laughed, then rattled them off. "A high-five, flicking a cigarette, giving a peace sign, playing the piano, and haling a taxi cab."

Rebecca smiled. "See …"

"See what? Everyone knows—"

"*Shhh …*"

Sudden. Sharp. Insistent.

"Do you hear that?" Rebecca whispered.

Then she did. Humans arguing.

Without any words, they rode their horses faster, Baloo and Smokey keeping pace beside them.

They crested the next rise and saw the skirmish — an argument erupting between what looked like a couple dozen men and women, divided roughly down the middle. A fierce looking woman with silver hair, sharp features, and deep lines in her face was standing toe-to-toe with a heavyset man with shoulder length hair and a half-month of salted stubble.

They were staring at each other, neither speaking. Rosa wasn't close enough to hear what they had been saying before the group suddenly stopped talking. Maybe Rebecca had, her hearing was slightly better. But Rosa wasn't about to ask her now.

Stubble stopped staring. Drew a sawed-off shotgun from his back and put it in the woman's face.

Spears and bats and other melee weapons were raised on both sides, but several guns followed the man's lead from his side.

"What the fuck do they think they're doing?" Rosa whisper-yelled. *"We have to stop them!"*

"Not yet," Rebecca said, low but calm.

"What are we waiting for?"

"That." Rebecca pointed at the sky.

A drone dipped into view. A flash and then it was there, like Rebecca knew it was coming. What looked like a cup dropped from the bottom, then three aliens skittered out onto the snow-covered ground.

Reptars charged into one side of the skirmish, ignoring the other completely. The aliens didn't need weapons, because that's what they were — their limbs the blades of a blender, shredding Stubble and his men into bloody cabbage, ripping the heads from their shoulders with rows of razor like teeth, throats sparking with tiny bolts of blue as they ripped through their enemies.

The bears were hunched, ready to charge.

"When?" Rosa asked, wanting the answer to be *Now!*

"Not yet," Rebecca said, her jaw set.

Blood painted the snow. A haunted chorus of screams echoed in the air. Like Rosa and Rebecca, the opposite side of the conflict had been staring in horror, frozen before and only now starting to scatter.

The reptars had finished their work, turning a small mob of men into a mountain of chum.

Several of the humans braced for a battle they couldn't win, raising their weapons like prayer beads.

The aliens were already walking away, but now turned back toward the group of humans.

"*Now?*" Rosa asked, panicked. The reptars were going to rip those people apart.

"Now," Rebecca agreed.

The bears charged. Over the crest then down the hill. *Roaring.*

The aliens turned, eyes glowing, blue sparks rippling through them.

The drone whistled down to the ground, hovering about thirty feet away from the bloody snow, its hatch opening, waiting for the aliens to come home. The reptars ran, terrified of the bears, same as always.

"How much longer do you think that'll last?" Rosa asked as they galloped toward the battleground, referring to the reptars apparent fear. "Eventually they'll fight back and turn our bears to bacon before doing the same thing to us."

"That's why we always wait," Rebecca said.

"How did you know they were going to attack like that?" Rosa asked.

"I didn't know," Rebecca admitted, shaking her head. "I just did."

Rosa didn't ask anything else. She never got much of anything once Rebecca fell quiet like that.

They reached ground zero, where the bears were holding court with a dozen terrified humans standing several steps back, hands raised, palms out, eyes wide, their fellow humans lying in bloody strips all around them. The reek of metal and meat hung thick in the air.

The silver-haired woman approached them, passing Rosa's horse and extending her hand to Rebecca.

"I'm Jane. I don't know what in the hell that was, or where you got bears like that, but we'd be dead without you for sure. I don't know what to say, other than *thank you,* of course."

Rebecca pointed to Jane's group, specifically at a man who looked like a scarecrow, and who Rosa had seen raising his spear at the aliens. "They were going to leave you alone because the threat was over. Your people started it again."

The truth hit them all like a falling piano.

Rosa said, "What was that about? And tell us the whole story, not just your side of it."

Jane looked from Rosa to Rebecca, her face saying *Do I really have to listen to her?*

Rebecca fixed her gaze on Rosa, deferring.

So Jane said, "We were having a difference of opinion when it came to rights and wrongs, even in the light of an alien invasion."

"And where exactly do you draw the line at post-apocalyptic ethics?" Rosa asked.

Jane turned to look at the men and women behind her. "That we have to stand for something."

Rosa pointed to a pile of bloody brisket that was once covered in salt and pepper stubble. "And what did he stand for?"

"Whatever it took to survive. We're not innocent." The woman shook her head, a pair of poltergeists inside her eyes. "But we've done enough."

Jane didn't need to get explicit. But Rosa was a priest, and this reluctant leader was venting her confession.

"We've stolen plenty, but we've never murdered. We've had to kill, of course. Most of us came from the same neighborhood that got ransacked by some of the more organized bandits back in the first month after Astral Day. We stuck together this entire time. Lost some, gained a few, and without a home you have to lower yourself to stay alive, but we were always defending ourselves. Never killed on offense. Firth wanting to change that divided us down the middle."

Jane was crying, so were most of the people behind her.

Heavy sobs of exhaustion, full of fear, and bleeding with relief.

"Can you help us?" One of the women called from in back.

"Haven't we already?" Rebecca asked, in a voice that sometimes filled Rosa with chills. She knew Rebecca wasn't a cold woman. She was a practical one, a practicality borne of being the leader of The Reserve, borne of having to make the tough choices. Caring too much, Rebecca had once explained, would lead to weakness and mistakes. She couldn't afford to care. Rosa was lucky, perhaps, that Rebecca had let her into her heart.

"No disrespect," said someone else, a woman who looked like she might've been beautiful before fear of death carved her face into a carcass in waiting. "But everything's worse in winter. Firth would never have been willing to do any of that stuff before now. How long before we turn, too? What else are we supposed to do?"

The woman looked at the bears, well-mannered and waiting to go home. Next to their well-fed horses. Then to the heavy clothing keeping Rosa and Rebecca warm, free of rips and garish red stains. And finally to skin that looked wind-kissed instead of scorched and to postures unbroken by battle without rest and trauma without mercy — the way theirs had been shattered. "You come from The Reserve, right? In Yellowstone?"

Neither answered.

"We went there looking for help, but your people refused to let us in."

Rosa shook her head. "We had nothing to do with that."

Rebecca shot her a look then turned back to Jane. "Is there a doctor among you?"

Jane shook her head, a fresh tear falling.

A man standing slightly behind her pointed to pile of macerated human. "Colby was a doctor."

And Rebecca said, "There is a growing community from here, two-days by horse. Maybe five days walk. If you—"

"We won't make it," Jane practically mumbled. It looked like the hardest thing she'd ever pushed from her mouth. Defeat was concrete in her voice. "We're dead if you don't help us."

"We have seen people in worse shape than you."

"It wasn't winter," Jane said to Rebecca, pleading.

"Five days north. You will survive."

Rebecca pulled one of several prepared maps from her saddle and handed it to Jane. She also gave her two parcels, one cured elk and the other assorted dried fruits. Rosa wanted to give them an extra share from her bag and would have if Rebecca wasn't watching her like Smokey was watching Jane clench and unclench her fists.

The two groups said their goodbyes and thank yous, departing with nothing left to say.

Until they were alone, then Rosa had plenty.

The argument started almost immediately. They both knew it would. Same as they knew Rosa would start it.

"They could have come back with us. There weren't that many."

Patiently, as though talking to a child. "*Too* many. We're looking for a doctor. It would have been a tough sell, taking all of them back just for one doctor, but *maybe* it would have been fine. Without a doctor, absolutely not."

"That's cold, and I hate it."

"I know," Rebecca said, still sounding so perfectly reasonable. "And I'm willing to discuss it as long as that seems to be helping you. But we can't change the facts. Garvey took off with our medicine, and the pneumonia is spreading. They were thieves. *Admitted* thieves. We can't have that in our home. The Reserve comes first."

"Right. Reserve first. And we only know they were thieves because they admitted it. I'm sure we have people at *home* who've done worse."

Rosa hated that she was pouting, but it was work to keep it away from her face and out of her words, and right now the weight was too much to carry.

The age difference should have been ludicrous. Instead, Rosa saw it as a comfort. Rebecca was the opposite of her mom in every way. Maternal for starters. But also calm and collected, wise and well-mannered, amiable when she needed to be.

But there was something else Rosa was starting to see, something she could only think of as *ruthless*.

They rode most of the way back to The Reserve in silence, with Rosa breaking it only once when she just couldn't help it. "You know, maybe they wouldn't have had to steal anything if we let them in when they asked for our help."

Rebecca answered by changing the subject. "Are you still pissed at Mikey?"

"Of course I am."

But when they got back to the Reserve about an hour after that, Rosa learned something that stopped her heart for two beats in a row.

She repeated what she didn't want to hear or believe. "What do you mean, *Mikey is missing?*"

Chapter Two

Rosa stared at Matilda, waiting for her response.

But she didn't need to repeat anything. That wasn't going to help. Matilda stated everything as fact, so Rosa was really just processing the information and hoping it would change. Because Mikey had been a problem in her life since the day he was born. Not his fault, it's just the way it had always been. It was their mother's fault. Same as most things.

"Where did he go?"

"I don't know," Matilda said without lowering her notebook, still neatly recording inventory. "That's why I said he was missing."

"I mean before he went missing. Where was he before then?"

"My job is inventory, Rosa Lopez. Not managing your family members."

"It's just the one, and while I know that's true, Baldwin said Mikey was last seen coming here, so maybe you could help me."

"Sorry," she said, still not looking up, "but I cannot. I have no idea where your brother went."

"I understand that, Matilda. But you're very observant. I'm sure there's something you can tell me. Did he say anything, or was he with anyone, or—"

"He left here three hours and eleven minutes ago with Paul and Lara."

Rosa threw her hands in the air. "Why didn't you say that before?"

"You didn't ask me who he was with." Matilda finally looked up, but it was only to walk past Rosa then hang her clipboard on the wall.

Rosa sighed. No use getting upset. It was hard talking to Matilda, even though she always meant well.

"Are Paul and Lara still here in The Reserve?"

In a monotone, Matilda said, "Paul was reported missing from his latest check-in fourteen minutes after your brother, Miguel Lopez."

And you couldn't have mentioned that five minutes ago?

"And Lara?"

"I do not know where Lara Christiansen is currently located."

"Thank you for your help," Rosa said, giving her a smile, and reminding herself that it wasn't Matilda's fault.

"Okay," she said, without looking up for Rosa's gratitude or for the goodbye that she gave at the door.

Rosa left the Warehouse. She nodded at Rochester and Theo, the two armed guards assigned to watch all of their extras. The Warehouse was the only place in the Reserve that had two armed guards. Some residents saw it as overkill, but most thought it was barely enough.

The Reserve itself was a gorgeous building. Fully modern. Less than five years old, and built from a generous grant. The education wing was massive and now housed most of their headquarters and operations. The facility was blessed with a fortunate blend of skillsets, or at least that's the word Rebecca preferred to use. Rosa wasn't so sure anything was blessed these days, but she couldn't argue that they were a lot less cursed inside their refuge than most of the rest of the world. At least, from what they could gather.

It had been a long, hard half year. They were lucky to have a National Forest to make their hideaway in, but that didn't make them lucky. What did was the walled off community populated by capable citizens, lookout towers scattered throughout the woods, working radios, ample solar panels — and all state of the goddamned art, thanks to that grant.

It was a ten-minute walk to the bunks, where The Reserve once held its nature camp for children from five to eighteen, with sessions lasting anywhere from a single week to all summer. The building still had the giant Yellowstone Discovery sign on its roof, and the bunks were all filled, but now it was rangers and engineers, blacksmiths and farmers, doctors, architects, and other artisans of survival claiming every empty bed.

Rosa found Lara in her room, but not Mikey, whom she was half-expecting to be hiding under the bed.

"I swear, he's not here," Lara insisted.

"Why would he leave, and where would he go? Matilda said he was trying to talk her into extra rations."

Lara shook her head, laughing. "Yeah, I was there. Not sure how he ever thought that was going to happen. God himself couldn't talk Matilda into extra rations."

"Where is he, Lara?"

She pinched her face. Didn't want to talk about it. "He asked me not to tell you."

"Of course he did, but he also knew you were going to.

Because that's how my brother is. He wants everyone to be uncomfortable on his behalf. You uncomfortable keeping his secret, and me uncomfortable having to dig it out of you. Not fair for either of us. So please, Lara, we both know you're going to tell me. Can't we just get to that part and save all of the back and forth. I'm tired. I want to clean up and lie down. We've been back for an hour. Rebecca's probably already crashed, and here I am chasing my brother around like I have been for his—"

"He's with Paul."

"I know. Matilda told me that much. But where did they go?"

"They went off to look for Garvey."

"Are you serious?" Rosa didn't wait for her to answer because of course she was. "Fucking Christ."

"You probably shouldn't say that."

Rosa looked at her, not quite knowing how to respond. Like a lot of people in The Reserve, Lara was suddenly a lot more religious than she'd been before the invasion.

"Did my brother by any chance say *why* he would do something so idiotic?"

"He's pretty sure he knows where Garvey's hiding and thinks he can get our drugs back."

"Thanks," Rosa said, already on her way to the door.

"You're going after him, aren't you?"

"Of course."

Rosa was fuming. Garvey was a doctor. And a drug addict. Thanks to his chemically-induced moodiness, he was always getting into it with Rebecca and the others. Then he took off and hooked up with some bandits headed by a guy named Braxton. Took a bunch of The Reserve's supplies and medicine with him. Mikey hadn't cracked a mystery. Everyone knew where Garvey was "hiding" — in a posh little vacation spot about eighteen miles away.

Fortunately, there was no way Mikey or Paul had a vehicle, and they were both city kids who would have a hard time making it even a few miles on foot, but that didn't mean she wasn't going to hurry. Rosa was beyond exhausted and pissed as shit at her brother for leading her on yet another one of his selfish pursuits.

There was only one person in The Reserve she trusted right now to help her. Most of the people had written Mikey off, Rebecca included. She would tell Rosa to leave it alone, let life deliver the lessons it was dying to teach him. And she couldn't blame her, or anyone else who felt the same way. Rosa would've agreed if it wasn't her brother. But he was, and so right now, that meant she needed Solomon.

He was The Reserve's best hunter, by far. Confident, regardless of his weapon. While the area was full of men and women who never missed when pulling the trigger, their skills were like penny stocks in the market once everyone knew that their visitors didn't like guns.

Solomon was a trapper, a woodsman of merit and stature. His patience was almost porcelain. So beautiful, it made Rosa want to cry. He could go two minutes without blinking and half an hour without moving a muscle if that's what it took to execute the perfect shot.

A perfect predator, with intimate knowledge of his prey. He knew where it slept, and what it last ate. Solomon seemed lucky, but he wasn't. The man did his homework. He was The Reserve's best teacher, though as long as Rosa had known him, she'd yet to hear him speak a single word. The man was mute long before Astral Day.

Everyone had a theory, but none had any proof. When

the subject presented itself, Solomon always shook his head.

He obviously wasn't deaf or dumb. No Palsy or Down Syndrome.

But he could have been shaken as a baby. Paralysis of the larynx, or vocal folds. A skeletal defect since birth.

Injury to or disease of the brain, damage to his vocal organs, congenital issues. Psychiatric reasons.

It could have been anything, but Rosa thought the real reason Solomon never made a sound was that he didn't feel like it and had chosen not to.

He was exactly where Rosa expected, sitting in his small one room cabin, built by himself and slightly away from everything else. No bathroom or kitchen because he didn't need either. Solomon was sitting on the floor, his many weapons laid out before of him, a short spear in his lap with its handle either being fashioned for the first time or sanded down yet again, Rosa couldn't tell.

He looked up and she smiled. The question was in his eyes.

Rosa nodded. "It's Mikey. He's headed for the Slums. Left a few hours ago with Paul. I'm sure they're on foot."

Solomon grinned at the nickname. There was nothing ghetto about where they were going.

He stood, gathered his pack and a couple of weapons, joined Rosa by the door with a nod.

Then they were off. As with every other time she accompanied Solomon — or he accompanied her — Rosa just wanted to watch and observe. Soak up as much of his brilliance as she could. Unfortunately, Solomon only explained with gestures and nods, making it difficult if not impossible to divine as much as she wanted to. It tested her patience, which knowing Solomon, was probably at least part of the point.

Still, Rosa learned plenty. Humans left tracks wherever they went, and could thus be found just about anywhere. Deep forests, grassy meadows, sandy trails for sure, but also paved walkways or linoleum floors.

She had been with Solomon while he was tracking a person before. He had to learn their dialect of travel, meaning he preferred to spend time in a place where they had broken ground because by eliminating other tracks, it was easier to home in on the right one.

Solomon knew Mikey and Paul's dialect already, so it was a simple trail to follow. Rosa herself cracked the final clue, seeing where kids had climbed over a giant log, evidence courtesy of Adidas and Nike.

They found the boys walking slow and laughing loud about halfway between The Reserve and the Slums.

"Mikey!" Rosa called out.

Her brother turned. He looked neither surprised nor happy to see her. "What do you want?"

"You know what I want. This is stupid. You need to come back."

Mikey kept walking, whispering something to Paul, probably ordering his friend forward, to keep on going without looking back. Then, with no eye contact for Rosa, he said, "The only thing I have to do is get our drugs and medical supplies back from Garvey, since no one else seems interested in doing it."

"You can't do this, Mikey."

Her brother kept walking, so Rosa tried again.

"You're just a kid!"

That got him, just like she knew it would.

He reeled around, stomped seven steps in her direction, then stopped as though hitting an invisible wall. "No, Rosa. I'm *not* a kid, and I stopped being one the minute you left me alone with Mom. To be——"

"I told you, I'm sorry. I was doing my best." This time Rosa said it without emotion. The other way hurt too much.

"Well, your best left me alone with her."

Rosa sighed. "You're not with her now, Mikey. Things have changed. We're lucky to be at The Reserve. But you're not just putting yourself at risk by doing this. You're endangering all of us by provoking our enemies."

Mikey stood several feet away from his sister, the two of them eyeing each other like gunslingers. Paul stood a handful of paces behind his friend, and Solomon held guard next to Rosa, closer to her than Paul was to Mikey, but still granting her a reasonable berth.

"I don't see why we always have to do things the hard way," Mikey said.

"And what's the hard way?"

"There are plenty of bandits outside of Yellowstone, and we've done a good job of not letting them in. But now we have a group inside. They're already a threat, and one of our own has gone over there. Don't you think that's dangerous? Shouldn't we be taking back what belongs to us?"

"Maybe," Rosa said, "When it's time. I trust our leadership, and that they're making the right choices."

"Oh, do you?" Mikey sneered, and Paul smirked behind him. "Easy to say when your girlfriend's in charge."

"She's not in charge. She's on the council."

"What's the difference? She's still part of the leadership that's doing a shitty job."

"I don't know how you can say that," Rosa argued. "We're—"

"IF WE DON'T GET MEDS THEN KATRINA IS GOING TO DIE!"

It came out in an unrestrained bellow. Mikey had lost

it, the truth of his anger finally cracking through its facade. Then, his voice suddenly empty like a deflated balloon, he added, "She's sick."

A heavy worm of worry was thick in Rosa's stomach. "When was the last time you saw her?"

Mikey shrugged. "No one will tell me where she is, only that she's sick. I wish they'd never gone. Why rescue survivors if we're just going to bring their sickness back? What sense does that make? I don't know why we've gotta go around saving everyone else."

"Because," Rosa gave her usual argument, "that's how we hang on. How we rebuild."

"Well, maybe we should worry more about all the people we already have."

Then Mikey marched away from her.

As had been the case with so much of her life, Rosa was forced to follow.

Chapter Three

EAMON WAS FREEZING and trying not to show it.

His balls were like week old raspberries and his lungs felt frosted in ice. But it was hard admitting to more than a shiver when Jefferson was probably three times Eamon's age, though he'd yet to hear the old man huff or puff or wheeze in any way.

Sherry and Charlotte were back at the cabin, bonding with each other. And with a baby, who wasn't behaving much like a baby at all. In the last few days, Sweet William had been expressing himself with more clarity than ever. He could still — *Still? Ha!* — only string a few words together at once, but he was taking his time. Thinking. Working to say just the right thing. It was truly remarkable. Eamon missed it for the half day they'd been gone.

And the two parallel scars along William's right cheek still glowed like someone had glued light strips to his face. They seemed even more pronounced. Eamon let the boy's hair grow long so when they did venture outdoors, he could hide his face from people. Not that he was ashamed, but he had to hide anything that made his child different.

They now lived in a world where different would get you taken. Or killed.

"How long do you think we'll stay out here?" Eamon finally asked.

They were crouched behind a fallen tree. Jefferson turned and gave him a look that made Eamon regret asking, then went back to scanning the area. He knew it was stupid before he opened his mouth and had waited more than an hour to finally say it. Neither one of them should be wasting a breath on something so asinine.

Jefferson finished his survey, then came back down.

"Why isn't there any blood?" Eamon asked.

"Because we're not hunting deer."

"Why does that matter?" Eamon was careful to keep his voice low, not wanting the old man to yell at him again. "You saying boars don't bleed?"

"Shoot a deer and there's a blood trail immediately. Same for most animals. Shoot a boar and the snow will stay white. It takes some pumping for the blood to seep through a fatty hog. Plus, their hair soaks it up like a sponge. So, we look for blood on the brush instead of the ground."

Jefferson stood and motioned for Eamon to follow him. He did, glad the old man was letting him go without chastising—

"You'd probably know that, if you hadn't wasted so much of your life in the city."

At least Jefferson smiled to let Eamon know he was kidding.

It was fine. He could take the ribbing. It would be easier if he wasn't so damned cold. Which, Eamon supposed, was exactly Jefferson's point.

He laughed to himself, hoping the old man had missed it but knowing little if anything escaped his attention. One of the countless reasons Eamon thanked God for having run into Jefferson, which despite the dwindling population still seemed like a coincidence of apocalyptic proportions. The man saved his life, then saved it again. Apparently, he even saved it the first time when Eamon thought it was the other way around and he was sparing him from Felony.

"At least I got to live in a city. Now they're all gone," Eamon finally answered.

"That way." Jefferson pointed and changed direction like the wind.

Eamon followed. "Isn't that what you're always saying? That in a good life you experience everything, take what comes, and live without regrets."

"Something like that," Jefferson said.

"I'm not as spoiled as you think I am."

"Thou doth protest too much."

"You think I'm entitled." Maybe he was, but it still hurt to say out loud.

"Of course I do," Jefferson said with a sad little smile, "but until recently, I would have said the same about most of the world."

"Most? Really?"

Jefferson shrugged. "We have more than at any time in human history, and by an order of magnitude. Inexpensive food, no matter how terrible it is. New gadgets, the old ones ancient after only a year. Cheap clothes designed for obsolescence from day one. We have forgotten ourselves."

"And you think this is all to remind us?" Eamon looked up at the sky, not sure if he meant God or the aliens.

"I think everything is always here to remind us."

Eamon expected Jefferson to fall silent then, since sometimes conversation with him was like an exchange with the Sphinx.

"It rolls downhill and rots the bedrock. Parents are

deluged, so they offload the largesse onto their offspring. We're all spoiled, and it's been getting worse for the while. Whoever survives this will be stronger."

"How do you know any of us is going to?" It was a terrifying question, but Eamon had to ask it.

"Because I believe we're supposed to. And because I'm sure humans have survived worse than this before."

"Worse than aliens?"

But at this, Jefferson finally delivered on Eamon's expectation, walking slightly ahead and leaving him in a smiling silence. After another ten minutes or so he stopped and pointed.

"There …"

Eamon followed Jefferson's finger to the boar, a pair of arrows still protruding from its back. He wasn't about to ask any of the questions he couldn't help but think, even though he'd never get an answer and would only prove himself a city boy. He knew the biggest two.

What if you miss?

"I won't."

Are you sure about this?

"The wishes of our universe are better than my certainty."

Sometimes the old man repeated that last one like a mantra.

Jefferson had the short blade pinched between his fingers, eyes fixed on the target, steady breath going in and out. This part had already been explained. He would throw the knife because their arrows had already weakened the boar. The beast still had plenty of fight, so the old man's aim would need to be true. If it was, they'd be dragging hundreds of pounds of fresh meat through the forest, then loading it onto Olive.

He let the knife fly.

It pirouetted through the air, round and round like the silver spokes on a racing bike, before landing in the boar's neck.

The hog didn't fall, but he squealed like the devil himself was yanking its tail, thrashing about in the snow.

Steam plumed from flailing nostrils as the animal looked around, searching for something to attack.

Next blade out, he sent it flying.

THUNK!

Jefferson's second knife landed in the boar's hide.

"Now!" Jefferson yelled.

They raced over to the boar. Jefferson grabbed its front legs and Eamon took hold from behind. They flipped the animal onto its back, exposing its fleshy underside.

Jefferson took out his pig sticker — the old man swore that was the thing's official name — and plunged it down, fifteen inches of fixed blade boring past the armored plate.

They held the thrashing hog until it finished dying, sharing a quiet victory in the icy cold.

Eamon left Jefferson to prepare the boar for transport, then went as fast as he could back to the tree where they left the bright red snow sled they would use to drag their kill to Olive. He got there fast and felt proud enough to give himself a smile, but then he froze as his hand touched the sled's icy metal edge.

He looked around, wishing his heart wasn't beating so loud into the silence.

A branch snapped. His heart pounded harder.

He had his knife, but that was it. Eamon couldn't take on a boar by himself like Jefferson. Even an elk would end him and would have already if Jefferson hadn't been there to save him.

You see an elk, stay a dozen bumper cars back. Any closer, you'll provoke a response.

The elk seemed placid, or maybe Eamon just didn't listen. But it charged.

And if an elk charges you, do not stand still or play dead. Do not fight. You run as fast as you can.

Eamon hauled ass, dodging behind the nearest tree faster than the elk could pivot. But it came back, pissed as a pool full of kindergartners, and charged his way. It fell a few feet in front of him with Jefferson's arrow in its neck.

"Thanks for drawing him out," he said while yanking the projectile from the elk's body.

Eamon let the memory fade, waiting through a few long minutes of nothing before he finally decided to move, cursing the time he'd lost after getting to the sled as fast as he had.

Jefferson was right. The city had numbed him. He used to believe the city streets had made him tough, and maybe they had, but only for the city streets. Out here in the forest, he was greener than the trees. And it showed.

Even the stupid gang of children were frightening. It wasn't the clown makeup they were wearing the last time he and Jefferson had spied them, managing to steer clear undetected after he showed Eamon where the family was hiding. A long line of kids had been standing single file outside of an old motel, as if waiting to gain entry by showing what they'd pilfered that day at the door. Eamon found the makeup garish more than scary — the brats knew how to hunt and track, they were more adept at living in the wild, and according to Jefferson, they were intent on finding Eamon and Sherry. Or far worse, their baby.

"What took you so long?" Jefferson asked, while Eamon was still far enough back that the question felt like an insult.

"I thought I heard something."

"Yes, things move." Still smiling, Jefferson held out his hand for the sled.

Eamon set it on the ground then together they hefted the beast onto its back. Once it was all tied up, they started walking back toward Olive, with Eamon taking the first shift dragging the boar.

They made it less than a hundred steps before they were surrounded.

"Fuck," Eamon mumbled. *"I knew it."*

A part of him did, he just couldn't stand how paranoid the truth always made him. Now they surrounded by an ugly fence of children, looking like refugees from a circus of nightmares. Lord of the Flies, led by a ringmaster. And there she was, standing off to the side like the last time Eamon had seen her, conducting her puppets from afar.

"We've been looking for you," she called out, the victory thick in her voice. "It's getting cold. My children are planning to use your skin for new jackets."

"Really?" Eamon said. "You've been looking for us all this time and that's the best you've got? You've had to have been thinking about that for a while, and I'm sorry to tell you it sucks. It's not even clever."

"Eamon …"

He ignored Jefferson and kept on going.

"Think about how much work it would be to skin us, then sew jackets for all of you, assuming there's enough, and I'm not sure there is, for something that can't possibly keep you warm. I'm freezing now. Elk would be better, but hell, no reason you can't use that boar we were about to take home."

The mother laughed, her children closing in.

"Eamon." Jefferson tried again, his voice still placid, but now with a critical note that caused him to turn.

Jefferson said nothing, but stared into his eyes — gaze

like Eamon had never felt. He seemed to know more than feel something, and in the next second it was as if he intuited something in an instant that Jefferson would never have to explain.

"The kill is yours." Jefferson looked down at the boar, buying them time. Then he kneeled, and zen as always, methodically began to unwrap their meat from the sled while everyone stood around watching.

"It's not the boar we're after," said the oldest boy.

"This will feed you for a while. Lot of carcass, but there's still more than a hundred pounds of pork here. A fair price for letting us go, and a tax I'm happy to pay."

Jefferson kept on unwrapping the boar.

Circus Mama said, "Both of you wanna take us to where you live, then you can both keep breathing. But I don't need both of you, so I suggest you stand up and away from whatever it is you're doing down there, or we'll end one of you while the other one watches. My choice."

Jefferson looked up, still zen. Like a magnet every eye was on him.

And slowly he stood, but now everyone could see he was holding. A pairing knife, engraved with the words *Thank you for carving out some time to spend with us.* Some sort of thank you gift, once treasured then discarded, unearthed with a few other valuables from an overturned van Felony had come across on his way back from the demoralizing trip to New Hope. Made sense that Jefferson would have hidden a knife inside the boar, just in case.

If they hadn't run into the Family Circus, Eamon would've never even known.

"Like I said," Jefferson went on with his Dalai Lama smile, "fair trade. You take the kill and we walk away. I won't do anything I'll have to meditate on later."

The woman growled, "You're outnumbered and surrounded."

"Oh, absolutely. But I've survived worse than you, and even if I fail to survive this. I — *we* — will take at least two of you with us."

Eamon had knives if he needed to draw them, but his feet were rooted and his knuckles were bared. For now, that was how he preferred it.

Circus Mama looked at her children, then in an icicle voice said, "I can afford a couple. 'Specially if I replace 'em with your baby and that pretty one we can use as a lure once we teach her what to do."

"We'll be leaving now." Jefferson gave a single wave of his hand, motioning for Eamon to follow, then stepped toward the circle, holding his knife out in front of him in a surprisingly passive grip, knowing he didn't need anything more. His eyes always said enough, and the small girl standing in his way wasn't about to stop him.

On the other side of the circus, Jefferson turned and said, "Until we meet again."

They were walking fast, but nowhere near a run, when the statues behind them were animated again, and Mama Circus had finally cleared her throat enough to scream.

"Beat them both, but leave one of them alive enough that we can tie him to the sled. A torso's probably fine!"

Jefferson ran as though he knew the placement of every stick and stone in the forest. Eamon used his back as a bullseye, weaving and dodging in tandem, racing through the forest right behind him.

The spears missed, so did most of the arrows.

One didn't. Same for several of the rocks. The kid with the slingshot was steady. An arrow whistled by Eamon with less than an inch, and made an unpleasant thunk into Jefferson. But Eamon took most of the rocks.

The Jeep wasn't that far, and they were nearly there, when Jefferson mis-stepped then slid down a steep incline, frozen with packed snow. Eamon was right behind him, gulping faith without thinking like the old man taught him. He had an extra second to correct, landing battered and certainly bruised, needing a minute to collect himself and pretend every bone wasn't echoing with trauma he'd feel for a while.

But at least he wasn't dead. And was a helluva lot better than Jefferson.

He was screaming — a sound Eamon had never heard and couldn't stand. Worse than a baby crying. A proud man peeled back to raw skin and nerve, exposed bone and unprotected marrow.

The circus reached the edge of the incline but weren't nearly as eager to descend.

Both of Jefferson's legs might be broken, but pummeled as he was, Eamon's weren't. So he stood, scooped the old man into his arms, and with a strength he didn't know he had, carried him the remaining way to their vehicle.

He loaded him inside, ignored the ugly thing squeezing his insides, then started the car and raced toward the Cottage.

Chapter Four

Sherry found herself blushing. She laughed to cover it up, as though that might help.

"Oh, it gets *much* better," Jolie said, taking a sip of her tea.

They had been talking about sex for over an hour, and Sherry still felt like a little girl. It was the most adult conversation she'd ever had about the subject, and second place wasn't even close. The only time she and her mom ever talked about it was when she was yelling at Sherry and calling her a whore, or telling her that if she was gonna be a slut she should use her mouth instead. Conversations with girls her own age, give or take, weren't much better.

Jolie set her cup on the table and leaned forward like she had every other time she dropped another morsel of intimate wisdom.

"My period went out like an old lightbulb three weeks after my forty-fifth birthday. I was thrilled to leave them behind, but that's only because I had no idea sex was about to get painful. For twenty years I could do it with Jefferson for all three meals and a snack, but I suddenly found myself never wanting to have sex, since it *always* hurt so much. I was never interested in taking hormones, and Jefferson didn't want me to, anyway."

"Was he mad ... that you couldn't have sex?"

Jolie laughed. Waved a hand. "No! Of course not. I took care of him plenty, and he's a patient man. Turns out that's all it took, anyway. A few months. Then it was back to fireworks for us."

"So, you still ... you know?"

"Fuck?" Jolie grinned. "Of course we do. And like I've said, though there's nothing quite like the sex you have when you're young, it's different enough to be better after a while."

"But what about ..." Sherry didn't quite know how to say it. "When you're ..."

"Saggy?" Jolie laughed again. Sipped her tea.

"Yeah. I guess."

"Who cares? Stretch marks, crows' feet, we're all human. If that's what you're thinking about during sex, you're thinking about the wrong things. Sex is a time to become one with another person. And that's all there is to it."

Sherry lifted the tea to her lips. She didn't really like the taste, but Jolie loved it, and it always felt good to please her. After a small sip, she set it on the table just as William toddled over from where he had been putting a puzzle together. It had a thousand pieces, with maybe half of them missing. He had a hard time pinching the pieces to pick them up, but it was all he wanted to do. He was starting to put them together.

William stopped next to Sherry and tugged on her pant leg. "Where's Daddy?"

She reached down and scooped him up onto her lap. "He'll be home soon."

"How do you know?"

"Because I do," Sherry said.

William looked bothered. His face pinched with worry. It always gave her a fright when he looked like that because whether it meant her dropping a pot a few minutes later or Eamon stepping on glass, something always happened.

"What is it?" She asked.

He shook his head and went back to the puzzle. When William wasn't sure how to say what he was thinking, he rarely ever tried, preferring to take the time to think it out instead.

But the answer was crunching through the snow a few minutes later.

All three of them were at the door by the time Sherry was swinging it open and Eamon was dragging a titan-white Jefferson inside, his legs twisted in an alarming akimbo.

"What happened?" Sherry was hysterical.

But Jolie was not. His wife came over and kneeled by his side, put a hand on his shoulder and squeezed it as she said, "Everything will be okay."

William agreed. "I will help."

Jefferson argued hard both times in the last six weeks that he had cause for William to help him. Once when he cut his hand whittling by the fireplace, a skill he was only taking up now that he had so much idle time, though Sherry didn't understand after hearing so many of his stories where she got the impression that he'd been sick with time for a while. He also burned himself making coffee. But Jefferson said those injuries were nothing. Insisted, especially seeing as it took William a while to recover whenever he healed anything and Jefferson had already *lived a long life without needing to be healed by a magical baby.*

But now he was staring at the child, not even whimpering, no sounds leaving his mouth except a rasping coming from somewhere deep in his throat. Tears falling from appreciative eyes as William ran his hands across Jefferson's body.

Jolie went to his feet, gently lifted Jefferson's left leg into her hand, then gestured for Sherry to follow her lead. She stood, joined Jolie, picked up his right leg, then the two of them pulled the limbs straight.

There was no screaming, but tears of relief fell faster until Jefferson finally started to laugh.

"Thank you," Jefferson croaked, reaching up to stroke William's face. Then he turned to everyone and said, "That was like inhaling the universe."

William nodded, but the boy couldn't manage anything more. After wobbling in place, looking almost transparent as he worked to hold his smile and stay upright, he failed at both and fell to the ground.

It wasn't unexpected. Eamon scooped up his son and carried him into their bedroom, with Sherry following a half-beat behind. She closed the door as he lowered their baby into his crib. He looked sickly, already sleeping and breathing hard, but it would pass like always.

Eamon turned around and Sherry ran into his arms.

"It was scary, seeing you come in like that."

He held her, stroking Sherry's hair.

"What happened?" She asked.

He told her, then she raised a threadbare issue. "I want to go hunting with you tomorrow."

"No." He shook his head. "It isn't safe."

"It's safer for you if you have help."

"But it's not safer for William here. We've talked about this."

"We've talked about a lot of things, Eamon. Like going

back to get the rest of their stuff from The Oaks, before it was all gone."

"You make it sound like all that took was driving over and loading up. We didn't have a lot of space, and the runs are dangerous."

"Then maybe we should have stayed there," Sherry said, even though they both knew she didn't believe it. She was the one who pushed to stay hardest. Although it wasn't especially difficult. Jefferson and Jolie both went where the universe led them.

"I thought you enjoyed Jolie?"

"I do enjoy her, but I enjoy you more, and as much as I love William ... he's a lot. Mostly, I know I could be helping you out there, and you're not letting me. We need more food."

"Felony will be back soon."

"You've been saying that for a while."

"You don't think he'll be back?" Eamon looked at her, silently pleading for Sherry to agree.

"You know I'm not willing to give up, but that doesn't mean that we shouldn't start being more prepared ... in case he doesn't."

"He will," Eamon said, emphatic like always.

"How can you be so sure?"

Eamon shook his head, pinching the bridge of his nose. "It's hard to explain."

"I doubt it's that hard," Sherry said. "Why don't you give it a try."

Eamon got into bed and Sherry nestled in beside him, putting her head on his chest and waiting to hear whatever he was going to say.

"My brother has been friends with Felony forever. They've known each other since they were kids. Liam was getting in a scrap with these three older kids. I still remember their names, because two of them rhymed. Harry, Jerry, and Doug. All big and black like Felony."

"That sounds racist."

Eamon rolled his eyes. "It's a statement of fact."

"I know," she laughed, "I just think it's funny how sensitive you are."

"Anyway, Felony steps right in the middle of my brother getting tromped. Tears all three of those little fuckers right off of him. He was the same age as Liam but already bigger than the high schoolers beating up on my brother. He ripped them away like they were made of paper."

"You saw it?"

"It's family legend."

"So, he's good at protecting your brother and beating up bullies."

"The dude fought in the war instead of going to college. The only time from high school or after when he wasn't working for my father. He didn't have to go. He *wanted* to go. Wanted to learn to "bust heads better," even though I've always thought there was more to it than that. Felony's survived a bunch of shit he shouldn't have."

"Like ...?"

"Like, one time he was jumping out of a plane at nearly ten-thousand feet. His cord got tangled in the reserve and he spent forty-five of the longest seconds of anyone's life flying toward the ground at more than seventy miles per hour. He sustained three fractured ribs, a broken nose and jaw, and a punctured long. He also lost six of his teeth. All the front ones are fake."

"I get it, he's tough as—"

"No." Eamon shook his head. "Do you know why he survived that fall?"

Sherry blinked, waiting for his answer.

"Because his body was so relaxed that it didn't fight the fall. That's how chill he is, in every situation. And he's incapable of letting anyone down. Remember how he stayed with us all, long after we both thought he would've split? It was because he figured we needed him more than my brother. But the second Liam needed him, he was off. If the aliens unleash hell tomorrow, it'll be the roaches and Felony. And if he's alive, then he's also on his way."

"Fair enough. I'm sure he'll be back and I'm sorry for ever doubting it." Sherry gave Eamon what she knew he needed. "But even so, I'm going to have to learn to hunt eventually."

"Felony taught you to shoot months ago."

"There's a difference between shooting arrows outside and hunting. Stop fighting me. Jefferson and Jolie are getting older. We keep saying we're going to build a life, so we need to start thinking about our future. And I need to be doing more than cleaning the house."

"You're raising William, and we've agreed that's the most important job in the world."

"I know you appreciate me, Eamon, and that you're not trying to disrespect me. But you're not listening to me, and that's what I need from your right now. What if something happens to you? I need to know these things."

"But I'm only just learning myself. Jefferson's teaching me. I can teach you."

"Why can't he teach us both of us?"

"What if something happens to you?" Eamon asked, fear darkening his eyes.

"What if something happens to *you*? What if it's just the roaches, Felony, and us?"

Eamon laughed. "Of course you can come out with us. I'm sorry you felt like you even had to ask. It's not my place to give you permission, anyway."

She kissed him on the mouth. "I love you."

"I love you, too."

"And you know …?"

"Yeah?"

"All this talk about roaches is turning me on." She grabbed for his buckle. Pulled him toward her. Put her lips back on his mouth. And then Sherry showed Eamon exactly how much she missed him.

Chapter Five

EAMON LEFT the house that morning wanting only to take Sherry hunting and have a great time doing it.

They could go out again with Jefferson later. He told Eamon it was a solid idea, and that he was awful sorry it sounded like a girl had to think of it first. Then he laughed and threw a ball of socks at the back of Eamon's head.

"You're walking too close to the tracks," Sherry said, laughing as she tugged his shirt. It was his third reminder. She was clearly taking to her lessons and parroting them back. "Walk *near* the tracks, not on them."

Eamon laughed. "Ha-ha."

They were only tracking for the fun of it, following a cougar they didn't want to catch. The sled was gone for good, and Eamon didn't want to take on anything with fangs or anger.

They crunched in the snow for a few quiet moments until they halted in tandem, four ears perked and their eyes on each other.

"What was that?"

Eamon peered into the distance. "I don't know. But it's coming from over there, and it's definitely getting louder."

He pointed to a thicket of trees about a thousand feet away. They stared, then sure enough, a few seconds later a man came around those trees and barreled toward them.

Eamon turned to Sherry, but something happened to her eyes.

"What the fuck?" she yelled.

He turned and saw the horror for himself. Behind the galloping man came the hellfire of aliens. Reptars — electric insects moving like lions, blue light licking their black skin as they skittered through the snow.

The man didn't make it.

He was maybe three hundred feet from Eamon and Sherry when what looked like an electric leash landed around his neck. It tightened, and he choked.

The man was yanked down hard into the snow then dragged violently away.

Eamon held Sherry as she trembled. Pressed his palm gently against her mouth to keep the boiling scream inside it. Pushed his body against her, holding her tight with his free arm, his hand flat against her belly.

It wasn't easy to know if the aliens had eyes. They might have a thousand. But one of them had its head turned toward them, pausing as the other continued to tromp through the snow, back the other way, as if Eamon and Sherry were just another couple of trees in the forest.

After the longest six seconds of his life, and surely Sherry's, the second alien turned back around and bolted ahead.

A violent blur, then he was keeping pace with the first one, the man thrashing and gasping behind them, eyes still bulging, hands out, reaching for the two humans as though either could help him.

The aliens were gone, and Eamon and Sherry were alone. Maybe more than ever. Because what had they seen, and how did it change things?

It was a while before either of them spoke. Hard to break the quiet and admit things were different forever again.

"What was that?" Sherry finally asked.

"I don't know."

"Why do you think they took him?"

"I don't know."

"What do you think it means?"

"I don't know." And then he laughed, because that's what you had to do after three *I don't knows* in a row.

"What if they're rounding us up now?"

Eamon didn't want to admit it, but even the air smelled different. Either it was his imagination, or something was burning. Maybe they were rounding everyone up, including the humans.

"No." He shook his head, working to convince himself as much as Shelly. "They saw us and left us alone."

"Maybe they only had one of those leash things."

"Enough power to move millions of their kind across who knows how many galaxies, but too forgetful to bring a second leash? That's like the aliens in Signs being allergic to water."

"Something is different, and …"

Sherry trailed off, but it wasn't like she lost her thought so much as the thought itself was too painful to finish.

"What is it?"

"I just realized … this is the first time I've actually been scared of the aliens."

Eamon just looked at her.

Sherry explained. "I was so miserable with my mother, I guess I was grateful for the invasion. At least after you all found me. Then even though what happened to Poppy was awful, the four of us ended up somewhere safe, and sure it's been terrifying here and there, plus all the challenges with William. But I was never scared of the aliens."

"That's because you never had a reptar about to rip you apart."

"I don't think that's it." Sherry wiped a tear. "I think it's that they've only attacked people in opposing groups so far. In all the stories from during the invasion until now, it's been when people are fighting. But that guy was all alone in the forest. Just like us. That makes me feel like none of us are safe."

She swallowed and looked around the forest as if suddenly paranoid.

"Come on. Let's get back to the cabin." Eamon held his hand out, and she took it.

They walked in silence.

Where they would usually want to chew on the reality on their way home, steeping in quiet now felt better than lingering around the unfortunate truth.

"Do you feel that?" Sherry asked, back at the Cottage, but not yet inside.

Eamon nodded. Of course he did. How could he not. The heavy scent of nothing that permeated his nostrils with something he couldn't explain, despite his being able to see the same sort of dawning all over Sherry.

She broke into a run then tore into the cabin.

Eamon made it inside a second behind her. He only saw the back of her head, but he could imagine the dread. The alarm and the outrage. Flight or flight at war in her legs.

Jefferson looked worse than he did after the fall, his body even more broken. It looked like he'd tried to fight, then paid a heavy tariff for the effort. Whoever had murdered their friends was kinder to Jolie, maybe because she didn't put up a fight. She would have looked peaceful by comparison, her body on the other side of the living room floor, lying more like a doll than a scarecrow sprawled across it. Her body looked almost at peace. Only thing keeping it from seeming like Jolie wasn't just taking a nap was that gash running ear to ear along her neck, and the river of blood running out of the hole and soaking the floor between lovers.

Eamon's paralysis broke. He charged through the house shouting his son's name, starting in the bedroom before checking every room and ending his search outside. Then he held his palm out to Sherry as he stepped out the back door and onto the porch. "Stay back!"

"What is it?"

"I'm not sure yet."

But Eamon knew. He just had no idea what it meant, or if anyone else was waiting to finish the job.

One of the clown kids, stabbed to death, his body sprawled in the blood-soaked snow.

He turned back to Sherry, then stepped aside to let her see.

She gasped and grabbed his arm, forcing herself to stand upright. "So Jefferson got one of them …"

And Eamon finished, "But it wasn't enough to keep them from taking our child."

Chapter Six

Angel was in her room, nursing Sophia.

Sunlight felt great through the window, warm as the solace itself.

The last eight months had been hard. Nothing was worse than losing Craig, though it all amounted to a lot of trauma and torture and shock. Stonefall was a Godsend. She started to feel better the second she arrived. It came in degrees, but she was edging nearer to normal, or at least as close as she could get with aliens in the sky.

And on the ground.

She shuddered, remembering Felony holding her tight to keep her from screaming as she did the same to Sophia. Their daughter would never know her father, but now, against all odds, Angel had been reunited with her own dad, giving Sophia the grandfather she never expected, or had for herself, and still wouldn't have if the aliens hadn't eliminated everyone inside the prison except him and his two chosen. Serendipity or purpose … one or the other put him in charge. Either way, Gleeson Crowe had been chosen.

She wondered about it a lot, despite trying not to. The "relationship" her father thought he had with the invaders made Angel uncomfortable.

It wasn't finding him in Stonefall that rattled her to the core. For some reason she couldn't explain, that part didn't surprise her at all. It was everything else, mostly the religion. Angel was a strong woman who didn't need the crutch that everyone in Stonefall seemed to. She didn't have a problem with religion. It was weird. Not at all for her. But also, whatever. To each his own. Here it felt creepy. Same for all that talk about her father's visions and the miracle baby he kept going on and on — and on — about. The one she kept telling herself he couldn't possibly mean.

Most of all, she *hated* being called Mother Angel, something her father started. His word seemed to stick like a lollipop on carpet, so it was the first thing she refused him. He didn't like it, so she was scared to say no to anything else.

Her room was small but still more than she ever thought she would have again. She lived with her father, but he had the largest residence inside Stonefall. The biggest house, not on either side of the street, but all the way at the end.

She might have more space living on her own, but her father promised staying with him was the safest place in the world, and given what things were like on the other side of those towering walls, Angel found that easy to believe.

There was a knock on her door. A beat, then her father's voice, softer than she was used to hearing it. "Angel, honey, are you in there?"

"Come in," she called quietly, not wanting to rouse a baby just seconds from sleeping.

The door opened, then he entered with a smile. He

gestured down at Angel rocking in the chair, giving his granddaughter life. "It's a beautiful sight."

"Thank you for the place and the peace to do it." Angel smiled.

He smiled back, deep with pride and pleasure. "I'm honored God brought you here to me."

She shifted in her seat, hoping her discomfort wasn't obvious. Her smile tugged down at the edges, reluctant to grow. "I'm so grateful to be here."

He sat on the edge of her bed, in between the crib and the rocker, and asked Angel the same thing he asked her every day. "Are you happy here in Stonefall?

Today he looked different. More expectant, perhaps. As though there was something specific he wanted her to say. Or maybe he merely wanted Angel to be honest.

But that was too hard. She didn't know her father well, and from the little she remembered, looking into his eyes and telling him what she thought wasn't something she could do. It had never been possible, and living in this little room in her father's tiny town amid an alien invasion — or maybe occupation — wasn't going to change that.

She gave him another smile, even harder than the last. "Of course I'm happy here."

Sophia stopped nursing, pulled away from Angel's breast, then looked around the room. Her gaze fixed on her grandfather, and she started to giggle.

"You can tell me. Whatever it is on your mind. I want to hear it."

He opened his arms for Sophia. Angel covered herself up then passed his granddaughter over. Cradling her, tipping his body back and forth on the bed, he looked up, his eyes expectant, still waiting for Angel to answer.

She gave him a nervous little laugh. "There's nothing I want to say."

His smile somehow seemed wise, and it looked strange on his hanging face. "But there is."

And so Angel finally admitted it. "I feel … overwhelmed."

"Overwhelmed," he repeated, as if tasting the word. "In what way?"

"It's the atmosphere … I'm just not used to it."

"Of course. This is all so new. It will feel like home in no time."

"It's been two months." Angel smiled. Hell, she was in this deep already. "And it's also you."

"Me?" He looked up from Sophia, surprised and — Angel was stunned to see — vulnerable. "What do you mean?"

She didn't want to make him angry, but there was no other way to say it. "With your conversion. I mean, I'm happy for you, it's just that this is all so new."

"My faith in God makes you uncomfortable?"

The way he said it … that was exactly what Angel was talking about but didn't know how to say without sounding crazy or hurting his feelings.

"I'm just not sure I fit in here."

"Why wouldn't you fit in here?" His face scrunched, as though Angel was giving him a foreign concept to chew on, something he'd never even remotely considered.

"I'm not religious, Dad. And all the women here are. I stick out."

"You only have to stick out if you want to. There are plenty of ways to participate in the community."

"But I'm not comfortable," Angel insisted.

"You will be," he said, without any doubt.

Because he wasn't listening, or maybe she wasn't explaining.

She shook her head. "I'm not so sure."

And now her father seemed troubled. He stood, gently set Sophia back into her arms, then started to pace, stopping only to mumble under his breath to himself like she sometimes saw him do, but this time with his back to her.

He finally turned around to face her. "He who speaks truth tells what is right, but a false witness, deceit."

"What does that mean?"

But instead of answering, he spit another verse. "For my mouth will utter truth; and wickedness is an abomination on my lips." A beat then he added, "Speak your truth, child. I cannot help you otherwise."

And so she blurted, "Women here are marginalized!"

That clearly wasn't what he expected Angel to say. His posture warped with his expression. "Explain yourself."

His giant form loomed over her as she slowly rocked in her chair, his hands clasped and hanging low, making Angel feel like the little girl she hadn't been in a very long time.

She looked up and into his eyes and told him the truth. "The language everyone uses here, it doesn't feel right. The ancient passages everyone is always passing about, there's something wrong with them. *You shall not covet your neighbor's house, his wife, slaves, oxen or donkey.* So in other words, women are property, just like the slaves and the animals. How is that relevant to now? Today?"

"You're being a bit literal."

"Isn't everyone here?"

"The Bible gives us a guidepost to follow. It isn't—"

"Exactly!" That might have been the first time Angel had ever dared to interrupt him. "And look at how it's being used. The people in Stonefall aren't exactly modernizing the text, Dad. In last night's sermon, *you* said, 'For Adam was formed first, then Eve, and Adam was not deceived, but the woman was deceived and became a transgressor.' So unless I'm getting this wrong, you're saying women are supposed to be silent because they were created second and sinned first?"

Angel stopped there. She had plenty more to say, but her point had been made. No reason to get ugly with examples, like how the book of Judges says a Levite forced his concubine out the door to get gang raped, then after she died he chopped her corpse into a dozen pieces. Or how according to the Bible, an unmarried woman can be compelled to marry her rapist, so long as the monster could afford the standard price.

She didn't want to fight. He was trying, and that was more than she had ever seen from her father before. He had changed so much from the man she barely knew. He was once violent, alcoholic, and selfish. Now he was none of those things.

Except for maybe the first one. Angel heard stories, though she had yet to see it herself. He no longer looked like a bloated alcoholic. He looked healthier, happier than she ever remembered.

He looked at her for a long time, studying her face while sitting with her words. He finally responded with a shake of his head. "I'm disappointed your mother raised you without God."

"Are you kidding?" Angel's anger surprised her, rising like a cobra from inside a basket to strike him. "You have no room to criticize Mom! At least she was there for me, and she was a good mother."

Then, even though she didn't want to fight, there was no way to stop the last part from coming out. Angel had already gone this far, and the final thought couldn't be stuffed back into its bottle.

"You couldn't even stay out of jail long enough to—"

She stopped. Choked. Couldn't get another word out.

Angel was suddenly afraid for her life, thanks to that look in her father's eyes.

His rage was frothing, turning to fury. Or worse. And she was suddenly a frightened little girl, staring up at a demonic father who couldn't keep the temper inside him.

He looked like he was going to hit her, and Angel was sure enough to flinch as she shielded Sophia's body.

But then something changed. His attention had drifted to something else, and suddenly he was back to mumbling.

It went on for a while, his skin like taffy as his face contorted into a series of wild expressions. He kept murmuring under his breath. The only thing Angel could hear was something she might have even imagined.

You're right, Brother Roy.

Then he was back, with the ire gone from his eyes and a new calm apparent in his body.

"Who were you talking to?" Angel asked.

"No one." Then he came over to her, kneeled, took her hands in his, and looked right into her eyes. "You're right. I *was* an awful father. I failed you in every way, and I'm sorry. But I want to make things right."

He started to cry, and Angel could not only see that he meant it, she could feel it like sun through the window. He had never said anything like that, never owned up to anything let alone something to cast him in words like *failed* and *awful.*

He wrapped his arms around her, and together they cried with Sophia in between them.

When they finally parted, he looked into her eyes, and Angel looked back without blinking.

"I understand how you feel about religion. I was the same way. But please, keep an open mind. He has shown himself in miracles, and soon you will see. Keep an open mind and an open heart, and the child God has promised us will be delivered."

The braying walkie on his waist felt like the period at the end of his sentence. He brought it to his mouth, never looking away from Angel. "What is it?"

It crackled, then a man's voice came through the speaker. "Children are a gift from the Lord; they are a reward from him."

"I'll be right there." Then he stood and lowered the comm, holding his hand out for Angel. "Come with me."

"Where are we going?" Angel's heart beat faster, her knees quivered in anticipation, her baby a balm against her body.

"To see a miracle," he said.

Chapter Seven

Gleeson wanted to give Kirk a slap on the back, but that seemed too informal a gesture. Almost blasphemous, considering. Maybe he would have anyway, if he was still drinking. If Roy would let him, without giving Gleeson such a hard time. Instead he pulled the man into a deep hug, holding him tightly until Kirk eventually, and awkwardly, held him back.

"May the Lord now show you kindness and faithfulness, and I, too, will show you the same favor because you have done this."

Kirk bowed, then confirmed what he implied on the walkie. "We have the child."

Gleeson beamed, enjoying Angel's curiosity. They shared a nice moment, just now. Crucified something old to resurrect something new. And when they were finished, almost to the second, God called to celebrate. The Lord wanted Gleeson to show his daughter a miracle, prove His existence and might.

"Is he safe with Brother Marc?"

That was the plan. Marc's wife owned a nursery before

the invasion. The child was to go directly to his quarters for inspection upon arrival.

Kirk nodded. "He is."

"And where are the child's parents?"

"No idea." Kirk shook his head, looking bothered. "I wish we did. But we found the baby alone."

Roy came marching up between them, clearly agitated. He tipped his head toward Kirk. "You believe that? *They found the baby alone?*"

Gleeson ignored him. Roy had beef with Kirk, ever since the night of Noel of The Forsaken's public execution.

Maybe it was the implication from Roy, but the hairs bristled on Gleeson's neck. "Alone? What do you know?"

Angel straightened, holding Sophia closer to her chest.

"We didn't need a lot to go on, but Percy did have a list of lots owned that could possibly match what you saw in your visions. And we ran into some people who'd seen a couple with a kid, so we went to investigate. I knew it was right the second we got there; the whole place felt like Holy Land. Like it does here, Father. But we were too late …"

"Too late for what?" Gleeson asked. "The child was alone?"

He could feel Angel getting increasingly nervous beside him.

Kirk nodded. "The cabin had been attacked. His parents had already fled."

Angel gasped, and in a disbelieving voice asked, "They left their baby behind?"

"See," Roy said, "she don't believe it, either."

"What sort of attack?" Gleeson asked.

"A group of child soldiers, wearing clown makeup."

Gleeson shook his head. The world had much to atone for.

Roy wouldn't stop pacing. "Something ain't right. An

ox knows its owner, and a donkey its master's manger. Can't you smell it, brother?

Gleeson didn't have time to deal with this. Not now, with Kirk and Angel waiting, and with wonders to revel in.

He and Roy hadn't exactly been seeing eye to eye since the Noel thing. Maybe they were overdue for an argument. He was pissed that Gleeson hadn't invited him to the sermon, *deliberately left him,* out so he kept insisting. And look what happened when he wasn't there.

"I'm telling you," Roy continued, talking nonsense. "Even the stork knows her seasons; the turtledove and the swift and the thrush observe the time of their migration. *This is a mistake.*"

"Are you okay, Dad?" Angel asked from somewhere faraway.

"He's fine," Kirk said.

"We'll discuss this later." Gleeson turned his back on Roy and returned his attention to Kirk. "Any other survivors?"

Kirk shook his head, then answered in a way that made Gleeson miss Percy, so matter of fact without any compassion. "Only the child."

Gleeson sighed, sorrow nesting with glee, and clapped. "Well, then. Let us pay Brother Marc a visit."

Kirk led the way so Gleeson could walk in step with Angel, his grandchild still in her arms. "I'm glad we were able to talk, Angel."

"Me, too."

She seemed closer to him, yet also somehow further away. Perhaps even scared. The weight of this miracle might be too much. If it was anything close to what Gleeson had been feeling, the light might be too bright for them all.

They knocked on the door, but Brother Marc wasn't

home. Instead, his wife Sarah answered. She opened the door with kind eyes and a wide smile, a long finger pressed to her dry lips, then led the foursome inside and closed the door behind them.

"Welcome, Father," she whispered.

Gleeson bowed, then watched as Kirk and Angel followed his lead.

"This way." Sarah led the three of them down a stubby hallway and into a closet -ized room. Inside there was a handsome crib, out of place in such drab surroundings, in what was otherwise barely more than a barn and manger.

Gleeson looked down at the child and immediately gasped. The child looked almost gray, save for the glowing scars on his cheek.

While he had seen the boy in his visions, he had not seen the thing that made him most unique — the scars. Why hadn't he seen them?

"What's wrong with him?" Gleeson asked.

He moved to gather the child in his arms, but Sarah put a hand out to stop him. "Let him rest. Please, Father."

"What's wrong with him?" he repeated.

"He is sick but seems to be getting better rather than worse."

"How can you know that? How long has he been here?"

"Only a half-hour or so, but—" Sarah didn't trail off, she *stopped*.

"But what?" Gleeson pressed after several seconds of silence.

When she finally opened her mouth again, her voice sounded like she was making a confession. "He *said* something."

"What did he say?" Gleeson asked.

"*I'm okay*," Sarah recited in awe.

That news was supposed to surprise him like it had her, but he'd seen the child speaking in his dreams. Kirk should've looked shocked, but he didn't. Gleeson could hear Roy saying, *See brother, I told you, there's something not right there,* but at least he had the courtesy to stay out of the tiny excuse for a nursery.

Kirk's lack of surprise was a disappointment. Almost irreverent. Roy sure would've thought so.

Angel's reaction was something else.

She inched closer to the crib, as if approaching a rattling snake, then peeked close enough to see the child inside it. When she saw the boy, she instantly started to cry. Like water at the lip of a pot finally boiling over.

"What is it?" Gleeson turned from the miracle to his daughter. "Are you okay?"

"No …" Angel shook her head, choking, trying to catch her breath. "I …"

The baby started to stir.

She jumped back, afraid.

Sarah put a hand on her arm. "What is it, child?"

"I'm not a child!" She pulled away, clutched her baby tighter. Dared to peek again.

The child started to cry. Screamed his little head off. Like someone pouring lava atop him.

Sarah scooped the baby out of the crib and offered him comfort. But the child refused, screaming and thrashing his limbs.

She handed him over to Gleeson, already waiting with wide open arms.

But the baby didn't like that, either. Maybe it was slightly more preferable than Sarah holding him, but not much. The child seemed to heat up as Gleeson turned toward Kirk, then cool as he quickly turned away. Hopefully Roy wouldn't gloat about that.

Angel was still upset, tears welling in her eyes but too proud to fall. She handed Sophia to Sarah then opened her arms. Gleeson filled them with the miracle, stepping back to watch the baby instantly begin to calm. He stopped screaming, and although his body still shook, he was clearly starting to settle.

Angel rocked him, her tears now finally falling to land on the child. She turned to Sarah. "What's wrong with him?"

"I think he's suffering from whatever trauma happened before he came here. And, of course, he's sick. But until a few moments ago, I felt he was getting better ... I ..." Sarah stuttered, her guilt for the situation like hives on her body.

"It's okay," Gleeson assured her, putting his hands on her shoulders. "You've done your best."

Angel looked up at her father. Kirk was still watching them all, and Roy was back, appearing behind Sarah, standing on the opposite side of the still-open door, in a room too claustrophobic to close it.

"What was all that about?" Gleeson looked from Angel to the baby.

"You heard her," Angel said. "He has PTSD or something."

"No," Gleeson said. "I mean with you, just before that?"

"Oh." Then Angel took her time, a full minute or so spent rocking the child, probably knowing it gave her an excuse. "I know this baby and knew his parents."

Sarah sucked in her breath. Kirk finally seemed surprised about something.

"How?" Gleeson asked. "From before the horseman?"

Angel looked at him, obviously bothered by his phrasing. But then she snapped out of it. "From just before I came here. I was with a friend of theirs when Craig ..."

She didn't finish, or have to.

"Who are they?" Gleeson asked.

"Real nice couple. Took us in. He saved Sophia's life when she was sick. He ... healed her with his hands."

Gleeson ran a hand across his forehead, mopping sweat from his brow. "You knew? Before you came here, you already knew about God's Light and never told me?"

"I wasn't thinking of the baby as God's Light, Dad."

"But you knew the child was a healer!" Gleeson was working to control his temper. "Did you think it was a coincidence?"

Roy observed the scene without comment.

"I didn't know what to think! There are aliens in the sky. Everything's different. Maybe babies can heal people now, and mine either can't or hasn't gotten the memo. And it's not like you mentioned the most obvious thing about him — the glowing scars!"

"I hadn't seen the scars in my visions," he confessed, shaking his head, a crazed fury clawing for escape. "Why didn't you tell me? You could have led me there. You've been watching us stumble around for months."

"Because even if it was the same baby, the parents were nice people ... and I didn't know what you would do to get your 'miracle baby.'"

"You thought I would harm this child's parents?" Gleeson's anger turned hot.

"No." She shook her head. "I don't know."

Gleeson drew his breath, about to rage, but Roy raised a hand to stop him. "Don't do it, brother. This isn't her fault. She is righteous. Courageous in the face of your anger. She is not the enemy in this room."

Ignoring Roy, he turned to Angel. "But I told you God

had shown me the child. Why not serve as His Light, leading my way?"

"That's God's job," she said.

"Brother," Roy said, his hand now on Gleeson. "Corinthians 16:13. *Be on your guard; stand firm in the faith; be courageous; be strong.* That's what she's doing, brother. You want her to see the Light? It's your job to show her."

"You're right," Gleeson finally said. "I asked God for a miracle, and he has delivered. We could not know where the child was until it was time. Had we gone to visit before now, the babe would not have been ready to receive us. He would not have needed us as he does now. We are there for him in his time of need, to save him from starvation and give him as a gift unto the world. Thank you, Brother Kirk, for being there. And thank you, Angel, for sharing your story."

"Can I take care of him?" Angel asked.

"Of course," Gleeson said, without looking at Sarah or giving her any more thanks. "God would want it no other way."

The baby was no longer crying.

"Do you know his name?" Gleeson asked.

"It's William," she said. "Or Sweet William. Like the flower."

"Sweet William," Gleeson repeated, looking up at a low roof rather than the heavens. "Welcome to Stonefall."

Chapter Eight

THE WORLD WAS STILL SHAKING, and Sherry wasn't sure she'd ever recover.

But she couldn't worry about that now. Despite her crumbling, she had to keep it together.

William was Eamon's son, but Sherry had been nursing the baby since birth. And for a while, before Eamon finally emerged from his shell, William was all she had in the world.

She lost a baby, just before the invasion. Now she'd lost another. The weight of that truth was collapsing her lungs and making it harder to breathe.

"Why would they do this?"

"Plenty of reasons," Eamon said. "Food and supplies would be the most obvious answer, but there's also revenge and insanity. We already knew they were looking for us. This is what happened after they finally did."

Sherry didn't know if she should feel relieved or resentful. Maybe they could've saved Jolie and Jefferson, maybe they could have fought back and kept William safe, and maybe the sweetest couple she ever knew wouldn't be dead right now. But all of that felt like an unspoken lie.

If Sherry and Eamon had been at the cabin, they would've been butchered like everyone else.

"Why would they take William instead of … you know?" Sherry asked.

"They know he's special. That's how Jefferson said he found this place."

"Jefferson is different."

"We always knew this was a risk, staying here," Eamon said, giving her a reminder she didn't need.

"It was a risk anywhere."

Eamon changed the subject. "Maybe that woman isn't their mom. Or a mom at all. What if she's raising orphan bandits? Gathering kids wherever she finds them. Like what's his name from Dickens. Finnegan."

"It's Fagin. From Oliver Twist."

"I'm pretty sure it's Finnegan."

"It's Fagin, Eamon. Are we really arguing about this?"

He sighed. "I can't even tell if they're the same kids or the same number of them each time. The makeup is confusing, and they're all different sizes. Better at hiding than we are. Maybe there are more of them than we think."

"What about Angel?" Sherry asked, ignoring everything he said.

"What about her?"

"Do you think she told someone about William? And they came back like we always worried they would?"

"It's the Family Circus, Sherry. One of them is a clown-cicle outside."

"I know, but do you think that she's the one who told them? Or that whoever did got it from her?"

"Do I think Angel told Circus Mama where to find us?

No, I don't. I can't imagine that … or why you would even think it. They were looking for us already, so it's not like—"

"I don't know," she said, cutting him off. "It's just … something feels wrong."

"Of course something feels wrong." Eamon pulled away to throw his hands in the air. "We got home to murdered friends and a stolen baby."

"I know, I know … I'm just scared."

"We're going to get him back," Eamon said. "I promise."

"How can you promise that?" Sherry was crying, her tears more angry than sad.

"Because the only way I'm going to break a promise like that is if I'm dead, and I'm not planning on dying any time soon."

"Those are only words," Sherry said. "What are you going to *do*?"

"Jefferson showed me a bunker not too far from here. It's the perfect hiding spot. It's small, but still big enough to keep you safe until I can get back."

"No way, I'm coming with you."

"You need to stay safe, Sherry."

"What makes you think that bunker is safe? You know where it is, why can't someone else? Or many someones?"

"Because Jefferson showed me, and—"

"Well, good thing the place is invisible to everyone else!" Sherry was breathing fire into the snow. "I'm going with you to get our child back. And I'm not asking. Soon as we bury our friends, we're out of here together."

"Okay. Of course." He took her hands. "But we don't have time to bury any bodies. The ground is frozen."

"Then let's go get our baby now."

Chapter Nine

Eamon was ready for battle.

Fortunately, Jefferson taught him to make homemade armor by working on Eamon's together. They had started on Sherry's, but the old man's slaughter killed his participation in the project. Eamon finished as best he could, matching the work on his chest plate when working on Sherry's. The armor was assembled from ceramic tiles he and Jefferson ripped up from an abandoned cabin floor about five miles from the Cottage, medium weight denim they got from some expensive looking selvedge jeans in a bottom drawer of the same cottage, and construction adhesive from Jefferson's place in The Oaks.

Eamon was wrapped in padding. Sherry wanted him in all of it, but he insisted she take at least some. She argued that armor for her was unnecessary, so long as she stayed a safe distance behind like she promised, giving Eamon cover by way of bow and arrow. The padding was a limited resource, and Eamon would be dishing blows up close. Same for his dodging.

He finally relented, enough that his chest and limbs

were protected, with his mobility only slightly encumbered. And thanks to the hardhats — another posthumous gift from Jefferson — so were their heads.

Sherry had two knives, her bow, a quiver full of arrows, and months of practice behind her.

She wanted him to carry a baseball bat or a crowbar, maybe use Jefferson's spear. But Eamon refused until Sherry finally relented. This was an argument she wasn't going to win. He strapped a sheath to each of his thighs, and promised to draw the blades if he had to. But anything in Eamon's hands would only slow him down, at least when the fight was getting started. Eamon hated to use his fists, but he was raised to do little else.

"How do you know where to go?" Sherry asked.

They were loading a pair of bats and a crowbar into Olive, just in case. Eamon was surprised that the Family Circus left the vehicle. Even if they didn't want it for themselves or didn't know how to start it without the key, he would've expected them to burn it for spite. But instead of a smoking shell, they had a slightly uncomfortable ride to take them the seven or so miles from the cabin to where Eamon was relatively sure their enemies were hiding.

"We saw them a while ago while out on a run. Me and Jefferson, I mean."

"Why didn't you tell me?

"What was I supposed to say? 'Hey, you know the weird ass people who are after us? Jefferson showed me where they live. And now they're wearing makeup like clowns.'"

"That's exactly what you could have said.

"What would be the point?" Eamon asked.

"You being honest with me."

"I wasn't trying to be dishonest, I just didn't see a need to worry you. Jefferson didn't want to attack. He said it was better to steer clear, but he wanted to make sure I knew where our enemy was. Aren't you glad he did?"

"Of course I am. I just don't like being excluded."

"Well, there's no one around to exclude you from anymore."

It was the wrong thing to say. Now the silence was a pall.

About twenty long minutes later, Eamon pulled off to the side of the road then kept heading down a narrow path with dwindling trees.

"Are we here?" Sherry looked around. "It doesn't look like there's anything around."

"There isn't. We'll walk from here. It's still about a half-mile away, but we should approach slowly and without a vehicle. This is where Jefferson parked when he showed me."

"Oh."

They walked the road in silence, rounding the bend where Eamon saw the billboard advertising cheap rooms at the Montana Moss, then another ten minutes or so of walking until they arrived at a clearing where Eamon pointed to an old motel in the distance. An ugly old building. Squat and in the middle of nowhere. Shotgun construction. A dozen rooms on two sides, and Eamon couldn't imagine the place had ever been full outside the start of hunting season even once.

"Where are they staying? I mean, which rooms?"

"I don't know," Eamon said. "Probably all of them."

"You're expecting to knock? Starting on the left? You take one side and I'll take the other?"

"No, of course not." Eamon gave her a look. Sherry wasn't taking him seriously. "There's a long hallway down the middle. And doors are inside because it's winter. As long as we make it past the guard, everyone inside will be confined to a corridor."

Eamon pointed to the lone guard standing at the motel entrance. Sixteen or seventeen at most, though it was hard to tell with the makeup. She might've been younger than that.

"And you think they're all going to come out of their rooms and politely wait for you to punch them?"

"No, but this is what I do. In close quarters, I'm the Tasmanian Devil."

"And I'm just supposed to stand there behind you?"

"Shoot whatever is moving. As long as it's not me."

Sherry put a hand on Eamon's arm.

"What is it?" he asked.

"Are we going to kill the guard? I mean … do you want me to shoot her with an arrow?"

"No." Eamon shook his head. "There might be cameras. What if there's a generator or something? If they know their guard has gone down before we get there, we won't have a chance."

Eamon stopped talking and started slowly and stealthily approaching the motel.

The guard saw him maybe two seconds before Eamon had her in a chokehold, dragging her into the shadows and holding her until a limp body spilled to the floor.

He looked around, reasonably certain there weren't any cameras, and motioned for Sherry to join him

Then he entered the Montana Moss with raises fists, his teenage bride armed with her bow and arrow behind him.

Chapter Ten

EAMON ENTERED THE HALLWAY SWINGING, but there wasn't anyone there.

He kicked in the first door, and sure enough there was a clown on the other side.

She looked past the splintered wood and saw Eamon standing in the hall, fists clenched and floating under his chin. Her makeup was half on, and Eamon had a second to think she might have been pretty if not for the rainbow of horror. She picked up a bat — maybe there was one in every room — and charged him.

Eamon made space with his feet by stepping away then pivoting from the girl as she raced toward him. His timing was perfect, crossing the threshold a second before she arrived, then ducking to the right, waiting for her to spill through the open doorway, then hopping back through and clocking her on the back of the head.

Her bat hit the carpet a second before she did.

Eamon grabbed it, choked up, drove it down into her chest to make sure she wouldn't be standing back up for a while, then left the bat on her body, because as he said, *no weapons.*

Doors opened in a row down the hall. All of them on every side in an uneven display, as though the kid clowns were executing a routine they hadn't had time to practice. Some doors poured more than one teenager into the hallway. About half were in full makeup. In the flickering lamplight, Eamon could see some of the makeup was neither ready for battle nor scrubbed from their faces. Somehow, smeared and peeling was worse.

But Eamon was ready. They could come at him all at once, or one at a time. It didn't matter to him. If his opponents approached him one at a time, he could force their upper bodies back. The narrow hallway was perfect for that, even if it didn't give him the room required to swing a bat. That meant they couldn't, either. And as long as there was room for jabs and uppercuts, Eamon was at least two fists up on the rest of them.

The first two charged, as though that might be enough. A boy and a girl, both on the bigger side.

Eamon hit the boy. One to the head, a second to his body, then the third on the side of his skull.

The girl's eyes widened in terror as she watching him pummel her brother in arms. They somehow opened wider in the second before Eamon's fist landed between them.

The farthest clown got an arrow to the shoulder. She flew back and landed hard on the carpet. Eamon imagined Sherry's smile behind him.

Mother Circus was still nowhere in sight, but another three of her clowns ran toward Eamon.

He distracted with one hand and punched with the other, rearranging his pattern to keep his enemies off guard, throwing flurries and shoeshines as they charged him.

Another six. There were definitely more than Eamon expected, and all were now attacking.

Two more arrows found their marks. Eamon was surprised by how fast Sherry was knocking from the quiver.

He was near enough to his four opponents that he could easily smother their punches, leaning on the closest one and trapping him against the wall before using his stomach as a bullseye.

Eamon used faster, smaller throws on the next clown, an adolescent with pubic looking peach fuzz all over his face, leaving him with just enough room for an uppercut and a gut punch for his friends.

Mama Circus finally showed her repugnant face, grotesque in the shadows. Even free from makeup, the woman was ghastly. Her skin had been stretched by bitterness and worse. Eamon saw in her someone who found the invasion a means for opportunity and probably escape. A beacon for death drawing others to her evil and casting them in her image.

For that, she needed to die.

In the meantime, they still had the final six or so to deal with, hard to tell with Eamon now halfway down the hall, the remainder attacking at once, and more coming all the time. He didn't dare turn around, placing all of his faith in Sherry managing any danger behind him.

He slowly made his way toward Mama Circus, enjoying her escalating fear whenever he made it another few inches forward. Eamon wasn't leaving deathblows, though he also didn't mind if any of these kids were lying dead on the carpet where he left them. He was hitting hard enough to put the entire crew down and make sure they knew to leave his family alone. If he was here without Sherry, he might want to finish them all off with a knife.

But for now, ending Mama Circus would be enough.

Sherry dropped another two while Eamon knocked out four. The kids were all inexperienced. Nothing without their weapons, which only a few even had when they poured out of their rooms, and none knew how to effectively use them in such a narrow hallway.

One kid stood between Eamon and Mama Circus. He turned back, ordered Sherry to hold her fire, then faced his enemies with raised hands and a smile. "Come here, kid, and I won't kill you."

The kid obediently came. He was tall and lanky. Barely wearing makeup. He had a few inches on Eamon, but maybe half his weight. All knees and elbows. An Adam's apple the size of actual fruit, bobbing up and down in his throat like mercury in a cartoon thermometer.

The kid probably wouldn't have come if he'd seen the knife. Eamon's fists were scary enough. Blood dripped onto the floor from knuckles he'd grated on the faces of his comrades.

Eamon drew in a blink and had his blade kissing the boy's throat before Mama Circus could finish her gasping.

"Please! Don't kill him," the woman begged with the first note of humanity Eamon had heard in her voice. Then she followed with something absurd. "He's only a child."

"They're all only children," Eamon growled, "and look what you're using them to do."

"You mean, stay alive? What are we supposed to do? We have to eat! You're the one coming in here and attacking us in our home!"

"Let me shoot her!" Sherry yelled.

Eamon kept his gaze fixed on the crazed woman, his

heels rooted to the floor, and his knife pressed against the hostage's neck. He ignored her and spoke to Mama Circus instead. "You eat by taking from others. We've survived without having to steal."

Eamon's voice found a darker, more disquieting tone. Ominous like thunder to herald a storm. "You came into our house and took our child. Where is he?"

Mama Circus looked surprised. Genuinely. She spent a moment head wagging and hand waving, stuttering while the boy tried not to squirm in Eamon's grip.

"I don't know what you're talking about," she finally said, and it was like even doing that had taken everything out of her. In a surprisingly brittle voice, she added, "*I swear.*"

Eamon didn't want to believe her because that left him without any son and a mystery to solve, but he was having a hard time doubting the woman or what looked like true bewilderment in her eyes.

"She's lying!" Sherry yelled.

Eamon took a risk and ignored her, focusing on Mama Circus. "Our cabin was raided. Our friends were murdered and our child was stolen. What do you know about that?"

"Nothing. I swear!" The woman went from clutching at her throat like as though wanted to claw it, to tugging at her hair like she was trying to rip it all out. "I don't know anything about it. None of us does."

"Bullshit!" Another declaration from Sherry.

"One of yours was there," Eamon continued.

"How do you know he was one of mine?"

Eamon wasn't going to answer that, so he stared and waited.

"Louis went missing two days ago. He didn't make it back from a scouting mission. That must have been who you found. But someone set us up because I didn't do shit!"

Mama Circus was yelling. Frantic, upset, losing control.

Eamon couldn't help but believe her. Looking at the woman, she was clearly unbalanced, but he had grown up with Jack Quinn as a father and knew how to tell when someone is lying. Her body language practically gave her an alibi, but her "tiny tells," as his father called them, supported her story. The flashes of true emotion few liars could hide, no matter their skill. The musculature that was too complex to control.

Those muscles won't be activated in the absence of true emotion because it isn't humanly possible. You see a tiny tell that says something you don't wanna hear? That's when you know what you gotta do.

The face betrayed a deceiver's true emotion, but right now that meant Eamon had to believe her.

Clowns were stirring on the ground, and unless Sherry started shooting them as they stood, things were about to get dangerous again. This time without surprise on their side.

"Tell me what you know," Eamon said to Mama Circus.

The woman refused to take the chance he was kind enough to give her. Instead, she charged.

Eamon didn't want to kill the kid, so he hurled him to the ground as Mama Circus came toward him, drawing a knife as she pounced. But it was barely a blade, a few inches long and good for not much more than spreading jam onto bread. His was longer, sharper, and wielded by a master. The metal slipped into her stomach like a swimmer gliding through water.

The woman stopped. Choked. Looked down at the knife then up at Eamon in surprise.

He had no idea what to say, but then he pulled out the knife and found a few words.

"What did you expect?" Eamon asked the woman as she fell to the floor, holding her stomach, blood gurgling out of the jagged aperture through her splayed fingers.

"What about him?" Sherry asked. "Do I shoot 'em?"

But Eamon knew she didn't mean it. That was only a cue.

So he looked into the kid's terrified expression but spoke to them all. "If we ever see any of you again, you're all dead. Every one of you. You hunt what you can and steal from no one. Do you understand?"

Murmurs of assent rippled down the hallway.

Eamon returned the knife to its sheath, calmly walked toward the exit, took Sherry's hand once she finally lowered it from her bow, then slowly stepped backward until they were outside of the Montana Moss and quickly making their way back to the Jeep.

"What now?" Sherry asked.

"Now, we find our son."

Chapter Eleven

Melinda was going out of her mind.

After working her entire lifetime, since she was a small child, a lighter load wasn't something she was used to, expected, or especially comfortable with. It had been something to dream about, back when such things were normal, and maybe even constructive.

As a child, she dreamed of growing up and getting out of the house, finding someone who would love her without always yelling and calling her names. But even then, Melinda assumed she would have her share of the work.

As an adult, she could dream of retirement. Nothing fancy, but Florida might be nice. She and Percy could get away from the winters that bit into her skin and kept chewing til spring. They could probably never afford that, but even a small cabin with a big fireplace and a smaller number of daily to-dos would've been enough for Melinda.

Those old dreams were dead, and even her new ones were gasping for breath. Here without Percy and so little to do. She kept talking to Ophelia, but found their conversations either too boring or entirely one-sided.

It had been two months since Percy's murder, and Melinda had never felt more alone. Not in her entire life. More than anything, she felt desperate for an ally. But in all that time with Ophelia, she now knew the girl would never be her willing accomplice, and that worse than indifferent, might even be dangerous.

She was sleeping with one of the snakes in Stonefall's grass, after all.

It didn't matter that Melinda had wanted to leave with Percy. Even after two months, she couldn't share the truth with Ophelia, worried it would end up whispered in her lover's ear. That arrangement made Melinda deeply uncomfortable, given their age difference and his being a monster.

Just one more thing they couldn't discuss.

She was trapped, but security inside Stonefall, and right on the other side of the walls, was tighter than ever. Same for in her own home where Ophelia was always around. Melinda couldn't even scream. Even if she were to get past the gate and beyond the guards, the moment she left, Gleeson would see her as a traitor. And she knew what would happen then.

Even if she was wrong, and he let her go, Melinda would be in the unknown without Percy. Left to fend for herself in the dead of winter. Freezing or starving or worse. Stories about The Forsaken increased her concerns. They didn't come more frequently, but they also weren't slowing, and it was terrifying to know there were people willing to brave the bitter wind long enough to hang an unfortunate soul upside down then gouge their eyes out before leaving.

There were too many monsters. In the sky and on the ground. For now, Melinda was stuck.

But maybe she didn't have to be. Maybe she had been living in fear without any reason. Maybe inching forward would be better than staying in place. The silence was too deafening to think about anything else. They used to talk before she was worried about every sentence and whether it might one day be used as evidence against her.

"Do you ever worry?" Melinda finally asked, breaking the silence.

Ophelia looked up from her knitting. "About what?"

"People getting inside?"

Melinda was asking about the tightened security, digging to see what Ophelia's too-old boyfriend might have told her. But she couldn't just come out and ask that. Instead, she had to inquire in a way that made it seem like she was worried about people getting in rather than out.

"Not at all. Kirk has a lot of guards stationed at the gate. Both sides."

Of course he does.

"But what if someone comes in with tanks or something? Do you think we have a way to escape? Like, a secret exit somewhere in the wall?"

Ophelia shrugged, eyes on her knitting. "I doubt it, but I don't think anyone is worried about a tank." She looked up again. "Are you worried about a tank?"

"No." Melinda shook her head.

"Then what are you worried about?"

"The Forsaken, the aliens, all of the starving bandits outside, everyone dying to get in here."

Eyes back on her knitting, Ophelia said, "Kirk is in charge of security, and he's the bravest man I've ever met."

"Bravery has nothing to do with it. An army shows up at the gates with enough firepower, even Thor won't be able to help us."

Ophelia shook her head. "If they show up with guns, then the aliens will probably come, too. Then she looked at Melinda like the woman's worries were ridiculous, her small smile sad and steeped in pity. "I promise, you don't have anything to worry about."

That nudged Melinda over the edge. "Don't you think he's a little old for you?"

"Kirk?"

No. Santa Claus.

"Yes, of course. Isn't he almost thirty?"

"Thirty-three, actually," Ophelia said, smiling like his pedophilia was something to brag about. Then, as though reading Melinda's mind, she added, "It's not like it's creepy or anything. I'm a full-grown woman."

"You're seventeen"

"Right," a defensive edge now lacing her voice, "a full-grown woman."

"You were sixteen when the two of you met."

Ophelia dropped her knitting. "What are you trying to say?"

The discussion — or argument if that's what it needed to be — was long overdue.

"It doesn't matter if you think you're soul mates or are certain this is destiny because of all the sweet things that man is whispering in your ear, but you two are different people in vastly different places in your life. Thirty-three isn't the same as seventeen, no matter what you think. Your emotional-self hasn't finished developing, Ophelia, and it probably won't for years."

"My emotional-self?" Now she was angry. "You've gotta be kidding me, Melinda. You're talking like the world is the same as it was a year ago. What does it matter, the difference in our ages?"

"It's a bigger deal than you think." She should have more than that, but caught off guard by Ophelia's sudden intensity, her argument crashed into a wall.

"Age doesn't matter, Melinda. It's the level of maturity.

You can't just assume that a seventeen-year-old or a twenty-five-year-old, or a sixteen-year-old for that matter isn't ready for an adult relationship! Some young people act like grownups, and a lot of grownups act like kids. You need to look at a person's values and perspectives before paying attention to some arbitrary date on a calendar. Liking someone older doesn't make me crazy, it makes me human. And him wanting someone younger doesn't make him weird. You have to do what makes you happy, especially now."

"But don't you think it's …" Melinda had to be careful. "A little … predatory? I mean, Kirk has all the power, and you're, for lack of a better term, the most eligible bachelorette. Doesn't that—"

"So I should feel bad for being wanted?" She stood, looking even more upset. "Kirk said this wouldn't have even made a difference a couple of hundred years ago. People wouldn't have cared. Girls are physically mature in their early teens. If they weren't married off, they became a hardship for their families. Made sense then, and with the world turning into what it is, don't you think it makes sense again now?"

"You said that a person's values and perspectives were more important than some arbitrary date on a calendar, right?"

"Right." Ophelia answered slowly, as though stepping around a trap.

"Well, doesn't his past concern you at all?"

"What do you mean?"

"He is, or at least *was*, a racist. Doesn't it concern you that a man like him hates someone like me?"

"Oh," Ophelia actually laughed. "He doesn't hate you. Kirk isn't like that anymore."

Like hell he isn't.

"How can you know that?"

"We talked about it. He told me God showed him the error of his ways after he was saved. He's grateful for Gleeson making him be friends with Percy because it showed him there wasn't much of a difference between them, other than a few ways they both grew up. Not even all that far from one another, as it turns out."

"You really think he changed? All the way, and just like that?"

"Well, sure. God changes us all if we let Him, and I think most of us in here started letting Him the second we knew there were aliens coming. Isn't that true for you?"

Ophelia looked at her, either expectant or accusatory, Melinda wasn't sure.

"Of course," she finally said.

"Kirk is a good man. Has been ever since he found God. He's changed. He's a soldier for Stonefall now. He would die to protect me, or any of us. He tells me so every day." Pride fattened her cheeks and brightened her eyes. "It's Kirk and all the other Brothers in Stonefall standing between us and the evil outside."

Melinda didn't even know where to begin and wished she'd never started. Their overdue conversation was another trap, waiting for her to waltz right inside it. Ophelia had been gulping the Kool-Aid, and there was nothing she could do to make her spit it out. Her words now were evidence later.

Again she was lost, alone with her pain, freedom from work like shackles at her wrist.

She needed something to pour herself into and keep her mind off of Percy.

The room was silent, but Ophelia wasn't knitting. She still watched Melinda. "I can talk to him."

"I'm sorry?" Melinda said, though she heard Ophelia fine.

"Kirk, I mean. If you're worried, I bet he can make you feel better. He always helps me." The tension was suddenly thick, despite Ophelia's smile. The poor girl probably didn't really understand it and wanted it to go away.

"That's okay."

"I really don't mind." Another smile.

"Please don't say anything, Ophelia. I'm not really worried much. I just wanted to talk, and you've already made me feel better. I didn't mean any of that stuff about the age difference between you guys," Melinda lied, "I was just thinking about my niece, and how she got into some bad stuff with an older man."

"Oh. You never told me about her before."

That's because she doesn't exist.

"I didn't want to make my worries your problem." Melinda laughed. "But I guess I did anyway. Sorry."

"It's fine. I'm glad we talked."

But Melinda wasn't sure Ophelia meant it.

The room returned to knitting, staring, and silence. There it stayed until a heavy knock sounded on the door — Kirk coming for Ophelia, so she could accompany him to Gleeson's nightly service.

"Hello, Brother Kirk," Melinda greeted him at the door with a bow of her head, pretending she didn't hate him.

"Hello, Melinda," Kirk said, surely playing the same game. "Will you be joining Ophelia and me for tonight's service?"

"Oh, I don't want to intrude. I'm happy to take my place in the back."

"We have a blessing tonight. You might want a front row seat."

Kirk's smile filled her with chills.

"What kind of blessing?" She didn't want to hear.

"The miracle child that Percy died trying to find is finally here."

"Praise the Lord," Melinda said, because screaming would be a mistake.

Chapter Twelve

"And He said, 'If you listen to the Lord your God and do what is right in his eyes, if you pay attention to his commands and keep all his decrees, I will not bring on you any of the diseases I brought on the Egyptians, for I am the Lord, who heals you.'"

Gleeson raised his hands and looked out at the crowd. Every eye was on him. He stretched the moment to bask in its majesty, holding his hands high, knowing he might live a very long life and still never get another chance to announce a miracle like this. This was his second, and most men lived their entire lives without ever getting the glory of one.

"Are we safe here in Stonefall?"

A chorus of *yeses* rolled through the flock.

"While the thieves and murderers run rampant through the wilds of Old Montana, has the Good Lord spared us from all that is outside?"

"*YES!*"

"He has taken care of us. Made sure we have everything required to survive this first winter, so we may plant in the spring and reap Eden among us. For our Lord is not finished with His miracles. And again, He has blessed us this day."

A hallelujah sprouted from the flock, followed by another four, then the fifth like an echo after several empty seconds.

"The unfortunate souls on the others side of the wall may see this last year as the end, but there inside Stonefall we know it's only beginning. God said, 'And if I go and prepare a place for you, I will come back and take you to be with me that you also may be where I am.' That time is now, and this is our place on Earth, before we ascend to join Him in Heaven."

Gleeson stared at the crowd, inspecting his Flock, pleased with everything but the lone pebble in his shoe.

Kirk and Ophelia were exactly where Gleeson wanted them to be, but Melinda was sitting alone. He was hoping she would be with them, and Kirk gave his word that she would be. Either Kirk had failed him, or Melinda was growing disillusioned like he feared.

She was important, perhaps more than Kirk or anyone other than Gleeson realized. She needed care, not abandonment. Melinda had lost her husband, a good man who God saved twice through Gleeson.

By failing Percy, he had also failed Melinda. He wanted to make that right and ensure she didn't continue to drift. But that would have to come later. Gleeson had a miracle to announce, and his Flock was eagerly waiting.

Arms still raised, he asked, "Have I ever broken a promise?"

"*No, Father!*"

"And did I promise a miracle?"

"*Yes, Father!*"

"Are you ready to see that miracle now?"

"Yes, Father!"

Gleeson lowered his hands, smiling as he paced, doing everything just like he and Roy had rehearsed in the mirror. The miracle was inside Stonefall, with Angel looking after him as God intended. The child was still traumatized and sick, and though quickly recovering, he was not yet ready for the Flock or their reverence.

But he couldn't just announce a miracle with nothing to see.

"The Lord has promised unto me, and I have delivered unto you. The Child of Light is now with us in Stonefall. He has been riddled with sickness, a victim of Satan himself, but the Child is strong and convalescing fast. Soon, we all shall bask in his glory."

Cheers erupted.

Gleeson was glowing.

Kirk was stoic. A good man hogging none of the attention, even though he brought the miracle home. Instead, he was squeezing Ophelia's hand, sharing his victory with someone he loved.

But Melinda's eyes were dead and disbelieving. Again, Gleeson felt an aching responsibility for taking his eyes off of her husband and allowing Percy to die.

"God promised and we waited. Now He has delivered, and that wait is nearly over. Soon, we will all experience His miracles firsthand."

Gleeson waited for the crowd to stop cheering, then stepped away from the front to speak with his Flock, one at a time after each person waited in line, blessing them all, thanking the Brothers and women for their service, promising the children they would be living better than their parents had in no time — they were lucky enough to grow up in the time of Christ's return, and the world had been waiting thousands of years for this particular winter.

The fire roared and the Flock was filled with sweating faces. It was time for their feast. Time to celebrate and honor the marvel among them, the miracle that would bring them closer to God.

"You did a good job up there, brother." Roy clapped Gleeson on the back once they were alone.

"Thank you," Gleeson said, already turning to walk away.

Things were tense between them, ever since the Father of Stonefall lost his temper in front of the Flock. Kirk bringing the child into their sanctuary made them even worse. Gleeson didn't understand the beef, nor did he want to.

"I'll drop it, okay?" Roy grabbed his arm and held it. A stick compared to Gleeson, but still he managed to turn the big man toward him. "We can agree to disagree on this one."

"Fine," Gleeson said, then started walking.

Roy followed a step behind.

Gleeson entered the dining hall and, just as he feared, saw Melinda eating alone.

"May I sit?" He pointed at the empty table.

She looked up at Gleeson with a smile that looked no more real than the paper flowers gracing her table. "Of course. No one else is sitting there."

Gleeson took his seat but had yet to make himself a plate.

"You're not eating?"

He shook his head. "Maybe later. I find food does little for me these days. Oddly, I find myself preferring the wanting of hunger."

A look of surprised understanding crossed her face. "I actually get that."

"What did you think of tonight's sermon?"

"I'm curious to see this baby," Melinda answered. "Where did he come from?"

"God, of course."

"Of course. But how did he come to be here with us in Stonefall."

"Brother Kirk brought him home."

"And where did Brother Kirk happen to find him?"

Gleeson smiled, wanting Melinda to understand he found no fault in her hesitance, or in her reluctance to believe. He saw it as something to be corrected rather than punished. The poor thing had nothing to fear.

"It is difficult to have faith in miracles after facing such a tragedy."

Melinda looked away, probably not wanting to cry. Yet the tears might soothe her if she allowed them to come. Perhaps he could help her with that.

"Percy was a good man, and I loved him like a brother." Gleeson sighed. Then gently tipped Melinda's chin toward him. "I can tell you do not believe me. You cannot understand how I could have loved him like a brother when to your mind I barely knew him at all. Is that right, Melinda?"

She nodded, even though it looked like she was afraid to do so.

"You have nothing to fear," Gleeson assured her. "We're on the same side. And you're right, I did not know Percy long, nor perhaps all that well. Who knows how close the man I knew was to the one who slept in your bed. I'm sure there were differences. But I saw into your husband's heart, Melinda. I saved his life twice, and both times I felt God echoing His Grace inside me. I'm sure he told you that."

"Yes. Many times."

"Do you believe me when I say his death will not go unpunished?"

"Yes. Of course."

"Is there anything I can do to help you? To make you more a part of this community?"

"I miss working," Melinda said. "Is there anything you can do to help with that?"

"Oh? I thought you would enjoy having time to yourself. To reflect. I was trying to help."

"I've reflected plenty." Then softer, "I've always found that if you want to get over something, the worst thing is to stay home thinking about it. Best to get out and stay busy."

"Well then, we shall find you some appropriate work. But your talents were being wasted before."

"What do you mean by that?"

"A lot of the younger women here look up to you."

"Oh, I doubt that," Melinda said.

Gleeson smiled. "But they do. You are strong, and they know it. You would be the perfect person to lead our Women's Group."

"Lucinda's already doing it."

"True," Gleeson agreed. "But she is also seventy-four and not doing so well. She would be happy to step down, especially if there was someone so obviously right for the job to take her place.

"That's very kind," Melinda said, looking down at her mostly empty plate.

"So … is that a yes?"

She looked at him for a long while, and all the while Gleeson kept looking back, trying to ignore Roy, wanting to ask what the hell he was thinking, staring at him like he was.

"Yes, Father," she finally said. "And thank you."

Chapter Thirteen

Rosa was trying to cheer her brother up, but it just wasn't working.

She was listening to everything he said and responding whenever appropriate. And not just looking back and pretending to hear him, but actually *actively* listening without distractions. Such conversations were easier these days. There were no phones to check every few minutes, but basic listening skills had dulled enough that for the first few months after Astral Day, people were suffering from the dampened attention spans that had become epidemic in the modern world, before it was gone forever.

Rosa made eye-contact, without staring of course, and tried to comfort her brother whenever she could. Touch was a language in and of itself — something Rebecca had taught her — but Mikey didn't want anyone to touch him, though she assumed the rules were different for Katrina, the obvious cause of his current distress.

He finished bitching, so Rosa repeated herself yet again, despite her hollow words. "I'm really sorry she's so sick. It's—"

"But not sorry enough to let me get what we needed from Garvey."

"Can we please stop having this argument? I've told you a thousand times, it's not Garvey I'm worried about. It's Braxton. He'll kill you, Mikey. And he'll laugh while he's doing it."

"I told you a billion times, it's *Miguel.* And how do you know that?"

"I've heard stories."

"Exactly, Rosa. *Stories.* What do you think people are saying about us? About our armor wearing bears? We probably look like the bad guys."

"I doubt that. We've definitely never done anything to deserve the reputation. Unlike Braxton."

Mikey already had his mouth open to respond, but someone knocked on his door. "Who is it?"

"It's me," Rebecca called. "Can I come in?"

"Of course," Mikey answered, though the door was already swinging.

Looking at Rosa, she said, "I thought I'd find you here,"

Rosa was still bothered about their last run and had sort of been avoiding Rebecca ever since. But she couldn't keep it going much longer. Rebecca would want to talk, and unless Rosa wanted to throw her arms in the air and yell *hell with it!,* they would have to hash it out eventually.

She kept her voice neutral. "Well, here I am."

"Do you have a minute to talk?"

"Sure." Rosa gestured toward an empty seat beside her.

"In private?"

"Is that necessary?"

Rebecca sighed, clearly irritated at Rosa for making her

dance. "Fine, I guess not. But I need you to suit up. We're riding out to the Slums."

Mikey was at attention immediately.

"Why are we doing that?" Rosa asked, now wishing she'd given Rebecca her moment.

"To get our medicine from Garvey."

"I want to go!" Mikey said.

Rebecca ignored him. "I've already rounded up Solomon. I need you ready in ten minutes."

"Who else is going?"

"Just us. You, me, and Solomon."

"Is that safe?" Rosa asked, surprised by the decision.

"Safer than it would be if we went there with more."

"And why is that?"

"Because we're messengers. A mute guide and two women are hardly a threat."

"But one of those women is a leader here, and Garvey knows it. Doesn't that make it more of a threat?"

Rebecca shook her head. "Not at all. Garvey can vouch for us, tell Braxton we're not violent."

"Sounds like a lot of assumptions. How do you even know he'll be there, or Braxton for that matter? And what makes you think he'll hand over the medicine even if he is?"

"Pain killers are more valuable to men like them than medicine."

"We're trading our pain killers?" Rosa asked.

"You're trading our pain killers?" Mikey echoed.

"Come on, Rosa. We're wasting time. You're needed." Rebecca turned around and headed for the door. She stopped at the threshold and looked back at Rosa. "Ten minutes."

"Your girlfriend sounds pissed," Mikey said, once the door closed behind her. "What's up with you two?"

Rosa ignored the question. "Are you hang out here after I leave or find something to do?"

"I'm supposed to meet up with Paul," Mikey said.

She nodded.

After wishing her well, he left.

Rosa usually liked to leave The Reserve whenever possible, mostly to feel like she wasn't a prisoner of what the world had become. But right now she didn't want to go anywhere. She still felt a bit raw when it came to Rebecca, and in a way she wasn't comfortable with and didn't understand. It wasn't anything she even wanted to talk about, at least not yet, but it was sitting between them, and Rosa couldn't exactly ignore it.

Whenever they went out lately, Rebecca managed to do something that left Rosa feeling unseated. The last time was their worst excursion so far — turning her back on those people, and after they'd already refused them at The Reserve gates. It felt especially appalling because of what happened to them at the gates of Stonefall. Rebecca may as well have killed them — and just because there wasn't a doctor among them? Ridiculous. There was plenty of work to do, and they had plenty of controlled land. They didn't need to be nearly as conservative with their resources and space as Rebecca kept insisting.

Rosa might buy the argument if it was being made about the winter, but whenever she mentioned it in any context, Rebecca clearly meant this was the way things needed to be for good.

Rosa strapped on her armor and weapons, reminding herself of all the reasons why this was a good thing before going to meet Rebecca. People in the Reserve were sick, including Katrina. Maybe this would help to heal things between'n Rosa and Mikey, once she was no longer suffering from pneumonia.

It shouldn't have been a big deal. Before the invasion, coming down with the flu or pneumonia, the two afflictions hitting most of their sick, would have required a simple visit to the local doctor. Pneumonia was hard on the body, but fairly common, and thanks to modern medicine, not all that hard for a healthy patient to recover from. But it might as well be the old days now.

The key to stopping pneumonia in its tracks was a prompt diagnosis followed by immediate treatment. A simple chest X-ray was enough for a diagnosis, and with appropriate antibiotics, treatment could start. But they didn't have easy access to either of those things. And fluids, like rest, just wasn't enough.

Rebecca smiled as Rosa approached her, trying to be pleasant.

Rosa returned her smile, gave the same one to Solomon, climbed onto her horse beside Rebecca, then trotted beside her. Solomon stayed on his feet several yards ahead.

This wasn't like tracking her brother and Paul. They were headed straight for the Slums, with Solomon leading the way, far enough ahead already to leave Rebecca in the peace and quiet she apparently wanted.

"What's wrong?"

Rosa didn't want to look at Rebecca, but she turned and met her gaze, anyway. "I don't like this."

And in her schoolteacher's voice that Rosa mostly loved but sometimes loathed, she said, "And what is it you don't like?"

"Any of it. This is crazy. We're walking into a hostile situation. Garvey left for a reason, and I don't exactly think he misses us. What makes you think he won't kill us the second we enter the Slums?"

"Braxton's men could have hit us at any time, but they

haven't. What makes you think they'll attack us once we're there?"

"There's a big difference between launching an assault and slitting our throats when we're right there in front of him."

"Braxton is smart, not crazy. I think he sees The Reserve as an ally or a possible trade partner. At worst, he'll allow us to build up so he can take what he wants later. But right now, his efforts are focused outside of Yellowstone. He's establishing his reputation, wants to make people terrified of him."

"If he wants to make people afraid of *him*, then why is he using that stupid name?"

"Because a man can be killed, but The Forsaken cannot. He's minimized himself as a target and turned his fear mongering into a cause. What he's done in a short period of time is impressive."

"Impressive?" Rosa repeated.

"In purely practical terms, yes," Rebecca said, though her voice had fallen to almost a whisper.

"So, like how the concentration camps were really efficient at killing people."

"You know what I mean."

Rosa shook her head. "I'm not sure I do."

Rebecca let it sit for a while, then with more humility in her voice said, "Point is, Braxton is going for easy victims. He doesn't actually want to fight. He wants to win — not lose men or sacrifice power."

"So we wait for him to get stronger and eventually wipe us out?"

"We'll be getting stronger, too. The risk of attacking us will always be too great, and as long as The Reserve stays strong, we can always make a deal. Cold wars have lasted throughout all of history."

"What do you mean, 'we can always make a deal'?"

"I'll know when I hear it." Rebecca shrugged. "But we can always negotiate."

"Why would you want to negotiate with a man like that?"

"You would rather we die?" Rebecca was pleasant, curious rather than confrontational.

Rosa was aghast. "Of course not. But the Reserve can't be friends with a monster. With the worst of humanity."

"It's a new world, Rosa. And the oldest ways still work. There have always been uneasy alliances between nations. How is this any different? If we want the Reserve to grow stronger and become something much greater than it is so life can continue no matter what happens, for at least as long as the aliens allow it, then we can assume Braxton will want the same thing."

"You're talking about making a deal with the devil."

"Exactly," Rebecca said. "Because it's either that or no deal. And the second one leaves us all dead."

Chapter Fourteen

The Slums were gorgeous.

Rosa knew the story. Same as everyone in The Reserve.

Its real name was The Majestic. A group of Montana entrepreneurs purchased the land a decade prior to Astral Day. They were bathing in money individually but had more than God as a group. So they bought three hundred fifty thousand acres with easy access to roads, then built themselves something majestic enough to impress Montana herself.

A place for them to meet a few times a year and mastermind their entrepreneurial asses off. The ninety percent of the time they weren't using the place, they could make it available for rent on any one of the glamping apps the filthy rich used to book impossible locations with embarrassing price tags.

Posh tents with luxury linens and two-thousand thread count sheets. Chandeliers hanging overhead. Locally-sourced decor. Pristine trails and panoramas to die for. Wood burning stoves, piping hot water, and showers big enough to host an orgy.

When the world went to shit, Braxton Kincaid decided he wanted to live like a king. There was one place in Montana where he could do exactly that. So he made himself feel right at home in the ten-thousand square foot house, leaving the luxury tents for all his lieutenants — the name he gave everyone he trusted but didn't want living in the big house with him.

Rosa was surprised to see fresh construction in addition to all the tents. Rebecca was right — the man had ambition.

She couldn't restrain her rattling nerves. They were headed right for the big house. Solomon had pulled back, so the three of them could make their approach together. Various members of Braxton's army of corruption were eying the intruders from outside their tents.

A hundred feet shy of the first tent, Rosa gave them fifty-fifty odds of leaving the place alive. Halfway between the first tent and the big house, she reduced them to one in four. By the time they were just feet from the porch and Braxton was staring down at them with a sneer, arms across his chest and a long sword strapped to his back, Rosa was sure she'd be dead before the hour was over. Solomon might make his escape, and Rebecca probably had some trade in mind for her life, but Rosa didn't stand a chance.

Campfire talk inside The Reserve had been filled with rumors, and terrified retellings on the road were common. Braxton perfectly fit the description. Six and a quarter feet tall, with massive shoulders. His right arm a sleeve of tattoos, which no one ever should have been able to see in the dead of winter. But Braxton was bare chested, his Adonis physique on full display, proving bitter cold meant nothing to him.

To Rosa's surprise, and probably Rebecca's, Garvey was right beside him.

Braxton tipped his head toward the trio, then turned to Garvey. "You know 'em?"

Garvey nodded.

Rebecca stepped to the front of their trio. "I'm Rebecca, and these are my friends, Rosa and Solomon. Maybe they can be your friends, too. We've come to make a trade."

Braxton shook his head. "I don't make trades."

Rebecca continued, undeterred. "As I'm sure you already know, we're from The Reserve, where Garvey lived until he stole some of our medicine and supplies then brought them all here to you."

"Meaning they're mine now," Braxton said.

"Of course. All of us figured what's gone is gone, and we had no intention of retaliation or any planned attempt at recovery. But a sickness broke out at The Reserve. It's bad. We've already lost a couple of people, and more will die if we don't do something about it."

"Makes sense you'd want the medicine." A flat statement. Braxton kept standing there with his arms crossed. And still, Garvey said nothing.

"That's right." Rebecca stated the obvious.

Braxton shrugged. "If sickness broke out in your place, stands to reason it might break out in mine. Do you agree?"

Rebecca nodded.

"So doesn't it make sense for me to keep my medicine?

"I think—"

But Braxton didn't let her finish. His face changed and he uncrossed his arms. Tromped down the stairs in front of the house, stood two steps from the bottom so he was still towering over them, then said, "How do I know you didn't bring the sickness here?" Then, with paranoia growing like a summer weed in his voice, said, "Was this your plan? Make us all sick, weaken our defenses, and launch an attack?"

Rosa stepped forward, not timid or tentative in any way. She was determined and decisive, dead-set and unwavering, even if she was shaking inside. Solomon stood a few feet off to the side, his body tensed and ready to strike.

"You know we have the numbers and the bears. If you don't, then Garvey can tell you." Rosa nodded at Garvey, still standing at the top of the stairs. "We could wipe this place out if we wanted. We've made a *choice* to be good neighbors, and we're here to offer you the same opportunity. If we don't make it back home, we *will* be missed. You do anything to us now, later, or at any point in the future, and you will be inviting The Reserve to unleash hell upon your people."

Braxton laughed, then turned to Rebecca. "She's got a mouth on her."

"She does," Rebecca agreed. "Are you interested in making a deal, or not?"

"Probably not. But let's see what you've got."

Rebecca pulled out a bag of painkillers. It wasn't anywhere near The Reserve's full stash, but it was a lot, and still more than Rosa thought they should have brought. Garvey started twitching, eyeing the sack like Gollum ogling Precious.

"Codeine, Vicodin, OxyContin, and more. You want them, they're yours. And we have more for our next visit."

Braxton held out his hand, waiting for Rebecca to fill it with drugs.

She dismounted, then displaying an impressive level of bravery, handed her bag to the human beast.

He peered into the bag and inspected several bottles.

With a nod of satisfaction, he cinched it closed, tossed it to Garvey — who was practically foaming at the mouth — then turned back to Rebecca. "There will not be any trade today, or ever."

"Then give us our pills back," Rosa said.

Braxton grinned. "Turns out, these painkillers here are the *exact* price of the toll for setting foot on my land. A fair trade for letting the three of you leave here alive."

"There's no reason we can't establish trade between our outposts," Rebecca said.

"Oh, I can think of plenty of reasons," Braxton laughed, "starting with my troops being more able than yours."

She tried again. "You'll lose a lot of lives."

"But mine won't be one of them. You want a fight, we can have one. But I suggest you turn around. Let Silent Bob take the two of you home, maybe express a little gratitude for being lucky enough to leave with your lives."

And Rebecca had wanted to make a deal with this man. She believed he could be reasonable. Rosa knew such expectations were ridiculous. A benevolent dictator was about as easy to buy as the virtuous pirate or the gold hearted whore.

There was nothing else to do but turn around. By the time Braxton finished his threat, they were surrounded by a few dozen men and women, all armed with the sort of weapons that would turn death into a lingering torment and leave them longing for the immediacy of a bullet's release.

They rode away from the Slums, dejected. Solomon wore a river of emotion, more than Rosa had ever seen. Layers of defeat and distress in his eyes. Rebecca was disappointed as well, but her mood was different, and a little unsettling.

The silence stretched and became almost holy. No one wanted to break it. They rode for miles without a sound. Rosa could only guess at what her friend and lover were thinking.

Solomon was probably conjuring a strategy, drawing detailed maps in his mind that he'd commit to paper and share with the rest of them later. Rebecca was surely conceiving their retaliation. She had been sure this would work. But now their painkillers were gone, and even if they left with their lives, her pride was on Braxton's front porch.

But Rosa was most worried about Mikey. She pictured the look on his face, the bright expression when he heard they were making a trip for medicine, and that his Katrina might have a chance after all. They were returning empty handed, and his hope was endangered.

Mikey would do anything, no matter the risk, to get it — and his Katrina — back.

Chapter Fifteen

"Everything will be okay in the end," Eamon promised. "If it isn't okay, then it isn't the end."

Sherry squeezed his hand.

John Lennon said it first, or at least something like it. But Eamon had been saying the same thing to Sherry for the last few mornings, holding her hand, the two of them standing over a sad set of makeshift graves. Jefferson and Jolie, buried in snow, shallow but the best they could do for now. The kid was on the other side of the Cottage, far from their place of reverence.

The routine was the same every morning. They started each day only after paying their respects, then went into the wild, looking for the baby that had been stolen from them.

Other than getting William back, the only thing Eamon wanted in the world was to make Sherry feel better. Their loss hit him hard, but it had pounded her into the ground. Nothing worked. Not the rubbing or the crying or even eating sugar from a bag. Sherry was well past sad. She was heartbroken and woebegone. Completely inconsolable.

Yesterday, the third since coming home to the horror, she finally had a breakdown and sobbed, face down in an empty bathtub for hours. Around dusk, she finally got out, comatose, then went straight to bed, buried under the covers.

Eamon didn't know what to do, but his best was apparently nothing. He could only be there when she needed him and stay aware enough to disappear when she didn't.

Yet even in silence they knew their routine. She let go of his hand when they were done paying their respects then followed him to Olive.

Eamon started driving, but like usual they had nowhere to go. There wasn't a list of locations where their baby might be found. They had to get out there, keep turning rocks, asking questions whenever they saw anyone out on the road.

But no one knew anything, and neither of them really expected anyone to.

He wanted to ignore the worst of the rumors, but a few kept circling like sharks in the sea. They scratched at his brain. Long nails in soft meat, making Eamon imagine things he did not want to.

Tales of The Forsaken sent visible chills through them both. They'd even seen three of the crosses for themselves. No one seemed to agree on who they were or what they were trying to do. They had heard a few stories about people kidnapping children for barter and sex. Others about cannibals. Ruthless raids that left everyone dead, their remains stumbled upon by the narrators of such vicious stories, all of them haunted.

The rumors about Stonefall were less frightening, but also worse in a way, because while The Forsaken didn't have a spot on the map for him and Sherry to go, Stonefall did. If William was there, then they would have to try getting inside a place that declared *ENTRY ONLY BY INVI-TATION. TRESPASSING PUNISHABLE BY DEATH* on a dozen signs a mile around their perimeter.

But it could also be the aliens, and that was the scariest prospect of all. Maybe they recognized William as special and wanted his son for themselves. If that were true, he would never see Sweet William again. The dim glimmer he was still able to hold like a nugget of coal losing its glow — hope his son was on Earth, waiting to be found — would die if Eamon were to discover he'd been spirited into the sky.

Sherry didn't want to discuss any of it, so Eamon kept everything inside. It festered there, rotting his insides. Most of the time he wanted to scream, occasionally he wanted to cry, but he always longed to talk. To say what needed to be said so it wasn't sitting like a reek in between them. But Sherry was a walking nerve, raw enough for a feather's touch to send her leaping out of her skin. He couldn't help worrying. Maybe she was withdrawing too far. And he was letting her go and soon would lose her, same as William.

Eamon was barely hanging on himself.

Sherry looked over, probably sensing his worry, and set her hand on his knee. After an inert few minutes, she moved it back and forth. Eamon took it as an invitation. After four hours of driving and for the first time not seeing a soul on the road, with the bitter wind slapping them hard in the open cabin, they headed home early.

Eamon finally spoke.

"I think—"

"We should go to Stonefall," Sherry finished.

They were burning time and fuel with nothing to show for it. Their supplies were thinning, and with all of their attention fixed on William, they weren't worried about restocking.

Eamon could feel her fear, a mirror and magnet beside him. It had been the unspoken truth, the place they would eventually have to go, but neither of them wanted to say it loud. Acknowledging that truth opened a door to the dread. Even if their son was in Stonefall, the odds of them getting out without dying essentially didn't exist.

And yet they would go forward, anyway. Stand at those gates, demand entry, and maybe draw their final breaths before they were slain right there in the snow.

"Now?" Eamon asked.

"Might as well," Sherry said.

Three miles from the Cottage, Eamon turned Olive around. Made it another half mile before he ran over something sharp in the road. The Jeep could only go so fast, and they kept their speeds low thanks to the brutal wind and frozen road, but Eamon was still going fast enough to fishtail.

Olive screamed against the icy road while Eamon surprised himself — and apparently Sherry, judging by her expression — by handling the wheel like a stuntman, turning it just so, righting the car enough to keep them from crashing into a tree. It veered hard, then dipped down into a ditch, instead.

"You okay?" Eamon asked.

Sherry put rubbed her fingers against her forehead, then looked at them, covered in blood. A nasty gash, but she was otherwise fine. Eamon's heart was pounding out of his chest, but he wasn't even scraped.

Sherry nodded, jarred but alive. "That was amazing, what you did. We'd probably be dead if I was driving."

"Lot of good it did us. Now we're on foot."

But at least they were finally talking, holding hands as they walked the three and a half miles back to the Cottage, going as fast as they could to stay warm, still bundled up against the icy wind, but without any of Olive's heat to keep them from freezing.

After an hour or so of comforting small talk, Sherry finally said spoke her mind. "Do you think he'll be there?"

"We'll know by day after tomorrow. Mañana we get a new car."

"How are we gonna do that?"

"I don't know," he admitted, not wanting to worry. Working cars with keys or fobs were hard to find. Gas was even harder. Their 3D-printed Jeep was a miracle, one of many that Jefferson had either given or left them with. But now it was gone, and Eamon had no idea what they would do. Still, the faith that they would do *something* was like another layer of warmth on his shoulders.

"I wish Felony never left us. None of this would have happened."

"You don't know that," Eamon said.

"Even if it did, the three of us could probably get the Jeep out of that ditch. Especially since he's like both of us or more, all by himself."

"I'll try not to feel like less than a man."

"You know it's true." Then Sherry laughed, showing him she didn't mean anything by it.

The rest of their walk was quiet, though the silence was softer than before. And when they got back to the cabin, at least one of their prayers had been answered.

Sherry gasped, then ran to greet him. "Felony!"

Eamon stood several steps back, unsure of what to do. He was thrilled to see Felony, and yes, it was a prayer answered, but for him, a nightmare had also returned.

"And who is this?" Sherry asked, nodding at the man standing outside their cabin next to Felony.

"That's my brother," Eamon said.

Chapter Sixteen

Eamon was drunk.

But Sherry was drunker, and both his brother and Felony were well on their way.

Not only had Felony finally returned with Liam as promised, they came with a van, its every square inch stuffed with supplies. Not all of them practical, but that didn't matter. A decade of Christmases was living in the back. Tons of food. Nuts, dried fruit, and cured meats. Cases of liquor, a few cashmere throws just for the comfort of it. Felony even brought Sherry a caboodle of makeup, because *Even at the end of the world, a girl should feel pretty.*

And, impossibly, Eamon was enjoying his brother's company. It was like the old days. The ones that didn't exist, from before Eamon truly understood the depths of his family's poison and how they dripped it into the water supply of everyone around them.

"Do you remember the Dugout?" Liam asked.

The word filled him with memory. Or more than that, nostalgia. Deep and aching. Sepia-tinted remembrance for a time Eamon probably recalled a little wrong, since it was such a glowingly happy impression, and the rest of his recollections were shaded in colors unpleasant at best and vile at worst.

"Barely?" Eamon answered, though it felt like a question.

"It was a hideaway back at Dad's old office. He would have these big meetings, and a bunch of people would be there. Mom always kept us home, didn't want us anywhere near the place. But after she died, Dad didn't want to have to worry about what we were getting into, so he would just bring us down to the office.

The memory grew clearer.

"What you were getting into," Eamon said.

"You always hated it." Liam laughed. "Had problems with the family since before you could burp. Dad would yell at me to keep you quiet, so I made us a fort. A bunch of wooden crates, along with two chairs and a big umbrella. But we always had snacks, drinks, and music."

"I remember the umbrella," Eamon said, feeling the smile on his face. "It was red, but it had … bumblebees? No …"

"Ladybugs," Liam said.

"Right … Ladybugs. And did you used to sing to me?"

Liam looked embarrassed. Eamon couldn't remember the last time he'd seen that. "Yeah, I did."

"You sang to him?" Sherry seemed shocked, and she barely knew the guy. She took another long swallow of vodka, her words already slurred. "What did you sing?"

"'Hey Ya!'" Liam admitted, now starting to blush.

Sherry laughed.

Felony said, "What? It's a good song."

Eamon was submerged in the memory. "I remember that," he whispered, almost reverent. Then, like a tax upon the emotion he added, "I'm glad you're back."

It felt great to remember they had been close. Those times were ancient, but maybe they could revisit them now that the boys were orphaned from the evil that spawned them. Perhaps they could be allies in the way they never could have been when Jack Quinn was sitting at the head of their family's table.

"So, when are we gonna hear all about your adventures … and where all this stuff came from?" Despite taking her time to get the words out, and working not to slur, her *stuff* still came out like *schtuff*.

Eamon and Sherry had already caught the guys up on everything that had happened with Jefferson and Jolie while he was gone — their arrival then their murder in the raid that robbed them of their baby.

The men were vigilant in their promises for vengeance, and having been raised in their shadow, Eamon could almost believe it. They promised they would get William back. He watched Sherry clinging to every word, a finger per syllable to juggle them all if she had to.

Felony shrugged like it was no big deal. "Things are different in the cities."

"Way different," Liam added.

"There's still a lot of chaos, but also news. Easier to hear what's happening elsewhere in the world when everyone's talking about it."

"Not that you can tell what's a rumor or a lie," Liam said.

"Do you know anything for a fact?" Sherry asked.

"Oh, sure," Felony nodded, trading a glance with Liam. "We saw plenty ourselves."

"Aliens?" Eamon asked in a hush.

"Of course," Liam said, then left it at that.

"So how about all those supplies?" Sherry asked again, since the boys had been vague so far.

"You know Billings," Felony shrugged, not answering. "The west end's nice, and sort of stayed that way, but the north and south went to shit as expected. Someone burned down the AMC Classic. They went into every one of the individual theaters and started a fire. And film is apparently an accelerant. The place is a pile of ashes."

"The supplies," Eamon said. "Where did they come from?"

"We were in the west end because the north had gone to shit, so the two of us figured—"

"Wait," Eamon interrupted. "We still don't know how you two ended up together."

Felony looked at Liam. Apparently, this was his story to tell.

Liam looked down before his gaze was back up and on his brother. He had something painful to say, despite it feeling like a splinter getting pulled from Eamon's soul.

"Dad's dead."

Eamon looked down, like anyone would expect him to, bolted his stare to the table for long enough for his respects to appear suitably paid, then raised his head to hear the rest.

"I know you didn't get along, but he was our father."

"How did it happen?"

"All at once and not much of a surprise. I was there, but there still wasn't anything I could do about it. There was a riot. Small given it was Billings, and surprisingly well-mannered, except for the places it wasn't. Climax was one of those places. Just about anyone who knows about the Quinns knows where we operate. Aliens in the sky? Time to hit the big boys hard. Make sure they stay down for the occupation. Who knows what they were thinking, but they weren't off their mark. We knew it was coming and were still unprepared. It was like a hundred people all got the same idea at once. Or a few groups of a dozen each. Maybe an army of assholes, who knows."

Liam stopped. Took a drink. Wiped his mouth and went on with the story.

"We were overrun. Everyone taking shots at us. They went for the vault. Some asshole with a face tattoo. *A face tattoo, Eamy!* He asked Dad for the code, told him he'd put two bullets in his dick then a third in his face if he didn't give it up. So Dad starts laughing, baiting the guy until he asks him what in the fuck is so funny?"

Another drink, longer than that last one.

"And Dad says, 'I'm just remembering the time I gave your mother a Portuguese Breakfast.' Then there was this terrible moment. Seemed to last forever. There were sixteen or seventeen people in the room all around us. And bodies everywhere. All our guys were dead. Dad is waiting for the face tattoo to ask him what it is, with the asshole obviously not wanting to. Eventually, the guy takes a big step forward so the barrel of his gun is a sneeze away from Dad's forehead and says, 'What's a Portuguese Breakfast?'"

He stops. No liquor this time. Just a long pause that felt like the picking of a scab.

"So Dad looks up and he smiles. Then he explains what it is while Tattoo is just staring at him, then finishes by saying, 'And your mom ate every bite.'" Liam paused, swallowed, and finished. "Then the guy delivered on his promise. Two in Dad's dick and a third in his face, though he waited maybe five minutes before he finished with the last one. I can still hear him screaming. I was right there on my knees beside him the entire time."

Sherry wasn't making a sound, but tears were in neat lines on both of her cheeks.

Felony had obviously heard the story before, but he looked devastated all the same.

"How did you get out of there alive?" Eamon asked.

"I gave them the code, then I told the guy about the safe in our panic room. He didn't believe me, thought I was bullshitting to stay alive, but he was willing to let me take him there with the barrel of his Baretta pressing into the back of my head. Once I showed him, he believed me about the second safe. We had a standoff outside it because he didn't want to let me in by myself, but he didn't want to go in with me and have me trap him inside."

Liam turned to Sherry, explaining. "The panic room has a safe inside it, but it's activated with facial recognition. None of them could get inside the safe, even if they were inside the room. Only me, and I had to be alive. We were like that for a while, staring each other down, but he couldn't kill me if he wanted what was inside. And the longer we stood there, the more he wanted it."

"What did you tell him was inside?" Eamon asked.

"I wouldn't. And it was really pissing him off."

"Can I ask a question?" Sherry slurred, raising her hand.

Liam raised his eyebrows.

"Why didn't he just, you know, break a finger or something."

"Because I told him that the scanner would run a diagnostic, and that if I was under duress in any way it wouldn't open."

"Is that true?" Eamon asked.

"No!" Felony answered for him, laughing.

"I don't even think he believed me, but he also wasn't willing to take his chances. I argued that they had all the control. As long as they promised to let me live afterward, I'd give them whatever was in the safe. He finally relented and let me inside. I opened the safe while he stood at the entrance aiming a gun at the back of my head. Then he stepped aside, waited for me to pass, and slipped out behind me. I gave him a satchel stuffed with an absurd amount of valuable jewelry, including all of Dad's diamonds from that thing in Cheyenne."

Sherry was perched forward, dying to hear what came next. Felony looked eager for the punchline. Eamon could guess what was coming, because he'd seen what was in the safe, and knew his brother better than anyone else in his life.

"He looked in the satchel and liked what he saw. A lot. Started showing it to his friends. Seemed plenty happy with me. Might have even let me go. Gun to head, I think he probably would have. But despite that being the situation, I couldn't take the chance. So I took one of the grenades we kept in the safe for just such an occasion — I'd hidden it while grabbing the satchel — and pulled the pin. I counted in my head, and when it was time, I tossed the grenade then slipped back into the panic room just as the timer went off and the door fell from its housing into the floor. The place went boom a few seconds later. I waited for a while, then left the panic room with enough of a haul to trade my way out."

Liam was always loud and brash and full of himself. But today, for the first time in a long while, it worked for Eamon.

"Wow." Sherry had been sipping her vodka through the story. Her glass was empty, her eyes were fluttering shut. "So how did the two of you end up finding each other?"

"I paid three diamonds for the biggest van I could find. Then I drove to each of our safe houses, seeing if any of our guys needed help and picking up supplies and whatever else I could find in the locations."

"I found him on Miriam Road," Felony said. "The van

was half-full already. We decided to finish stocking it in the city before coming to you. That was a few weeks ago. It was hard getting out of Billings and back here."

"Can you tell us that part of the story tomorrow?" Sherry asked, practically falling out of her chair.

Eamon scooped her into his arms and carried her into their bedroom.

He tucked Sherry in and kissed her cheek. She was already snoring.

Felony and Liam stopped talking when Eamon entered the room.

Liam looked over and said, "We're going to get your son back."

And Eamon said, "I'm counting on it."

Chapter Seventeen

"*Please! Don't kill him!*" *Mama Circus begs. "He's only a child."*

And Eamon roars, "They're all only children, and look what you're using them to do."

Sherry is pleading for him to let her shoot the woman, but Eamon ignores her, instead demanding that Mama Circus tells them where she's hiding their son.

She gives Sherry a hideous cackle instead, laughter leaking from her cracked face. It takes her forever to stop, then deadpan and sober she says, "We've got your baby, and you're never getting him back!"

Then they're out of that ugly narrow hallway, and there are no bodies around them. They're somewhere warmer, where the heat is almost suffocating. A big, commercial kitchen of some sort.

"What's that smell?" Sherry asks, and she can see by the look on Eamon's face that he smells it, too.

Mama Circus laughs even harder and skips over to a bank of ovens like a schoolgirl about to play hopscotch then opens the center oven with a flourish.

"You'll see," she says, still laughing. "Go ahead, and take a look inside!"

She does, but her world starts to melt at the edges the second she sees it — her Sweet William cooking, his skin already charred and popping.

Sherry screams into the woman's evil chortling as the universe liquifies around her.

Then that world disappears and Sherry is suddenly somewhere else.

She's grateful to be gone, away from that place where there's only leaden guilt to weigh her down. With all those fallen bodies, innocents imprisoned by a madwoman's whims.

The air is suddenly warm, despite the freezing air, and now she's surrounded by people and the seeds of tradition, germinating thanks to the preacher pacing the stage. The citizens — or Flock, as he calls them — are rapt. Watching, listening, waiting to see what he might say.

People are eating and drinking, sleeping with soft pillows to cushion their skulls, night terrors nowhere to be found. Full bellies and hearts, minds freed from the slavery of incessant unease.

Sherry hears something ... the unmistakable heartbeat of her child, a rhythm she's felt against her chest every day until her son was stolen away.

She follows the sound. It's getting louder, from the ticking of a clock to the banging of a bass drum.

When Sherry opens the door, she sees her. It takes her a moment to recognize this woman she knows.

But then Angel looks up. She sees Sherry and smiles.

Sweet William looks up at her, too.

His eyes are bright like the stars.

And he says, "Hi, Mommy!"

Sherry was thrown violently back into the world.

She opened her eyes, totally sober, then rolled over to rouse her man awake.

"What is it?" Eamon was groggy, but still up enough to hear and understand.

"I know where he is," Sherry said. "I saw William with Angel."

Chapter Eighteen

THE STAGE HAD BECOME Gleeson's favorite place in the world.

Every sermon was special, but some seemed to sit on him like a fur coat, warming him despite the Montana winter. This was one of those — two big announcements in one. The last three months had finally ironed out the tribulations of Stonefall's first half-year. What happened with Percy outside and with those captured members of The Forsaken a few days before that seemed to change everything for the better inside.

He could feel it in the air, and so could everyone else. People would stand in line to tell him. Not just the Brothers heading their families, but the women and children who were smiling, knowing they were safe from those visitors looking down on them from the sky because Stonefall was righteous and true. It had been spared.

Everyone knew their place. Tonight there would be two significant changes, and when the sun rose again in the morning, Stonefall would be that much stronger. Even the situation with Roy was improving. He sat off to the side, watching the sermon in silence.

"We have come a long way since we first fortified our walls." Gleeson said, transitioning from the end of his sermon to the first of his announcements. "We were all lost, and Stonefall's women needed guidance and hope. Someone with the life behind her to see the promise of tomorrow. We needed a Women's Group, and so The Good Lord gave us Lucinda. Now her work with the Women's Circle has come to an end."

He found Lucinda in the crowd and smiled. The Flock, for the most part, followed his gaze.

"When Joshua had grown old, having lived many years, the Lord told him, 'You are old and have lived many years, but much of the land still remains to be possessed.' Gray hair is a crown of glory. It is gained in a righteous life. Lucinda has given to Stonefall, and now Stonefall shall give back to Lucinda."

Gleeson noticed how old and haggard the woman actually looked. Yes, this was needed. And perhaps overdue.

"Lucinda has been an inspiration to the hardworking women of Stonefall, and now she is passing that duty to another from our Flock. Melinda, would you please stand?"

Melinda stood and half-smiled, shy under the light of all that attention. Stonefall admired her, and now they would hold her in even higher esteem. The Flock looked happy, especially Ophelia, beaming as though Melinda were really her mother. But Gleeson couldn't help but notice Kirk sitting beside her, and the look on his face showed he wasn't pleased.

He remembered the man Kirk had been before God filled the sky with His gleaming silver promise. Back when he'd been friends with Walter and a servant of the Aryan Nation. He was supposedly healed from his sinful thoughts, but taking into account the way Roy was watching him looking at Kirk, Gleeson was really starting to wonder.

The attention died down and Melinda reclaimed her seat.

Gleeson gave the Flock his widest smile so far.

This was it, the moment he'd been waiting for since the child arrived at his doorstep.

Since his vision three months before that.

Since the sky first brightened over the prison.

And maybe since the moment of his birth.

"You all know Mother Angel," Gleeson said, looking past the crowd to his daughter standing in the back, this time with the child in her arms. "And you know of God's promise to bring us a babe that has been blessed with His Light. The Lord Himself has chosen you both to be here with us. Please, Mother Angel, will you bring Sweet William up here to the stage?"

The crowd turned as one, reverent while watching her pass.

Angel stepped onto the stage, displayed the baby with the glowing scars, waited for the crowd to finish gasping, then just as they rehearsed, she set William on the ground so the Flock could watch him toddle about.

They were in awe. Stunned even.

No one had ever seen anything like the child. His head seemed too big and his body too square. His jaw was both long and wide. His shoulders were straighter than any baby's should be, and he walked as though he already had kneecaps, four years ahead of schedule. No one had ever seen a baby so ancient and knowing.

"You can all see the Lord flows through this child," Gleeson said.

Murmurs of assent rippled through the crowd. With great ceremony, Gleeson collapsed his giant frame down onto the ground, so even though the giant still towered over the baby, the expanse had dimmed between them.

"But he is very young, and we must be careful not to push him. The sun's light is unlimited, but it can only shine for so long each day. The same is true with our Sweet William. He has been born unto us as a healer, but we must be particular about how and when he uses God's gifts."

Gleeson turned to the baby. "Would you like to tell them why?"

And William said to the Flock, "I don't like when it hurts."

The gasp was so heavy that for a moment Gleeson thought it might douse the fire. Perhaps the Lord made it flicker. Roy definitely noticed. There were many murmurs, but more than a few of the Flock were deeply weeping.

"Melinda," Gleeson said, still sitting but now staring into the mass. She found his gaze and he smiled. "Would you please join us up here?"

Still clearly uncomfortable with the attention, Melinda made her way to the stage.

"You know everyone inside Stonefall, is that correct?"

"I do." Melinda nodded. "More or less."

"Can you tell who among us is in the greatest need of healing?"

Melinda looked surprised by the question. She started to answer but stopped, then seemed to consider as she looked out at the Flock, her gaze hovering on one pocket before drifting to the next, everyone following her eyes to see where they might land.

They finally settled on Ruth Waters, a woman who was too young for the crippling arthritis that in truth would have already had her living outside of Stonefall if Gleeson hadn't known that William was on his way to deliver the Lord's promise.

"Ruth," Melinda said in an uncertain voice. "Ruth Waters."

Gleeson smiled and invited her to join them on stage. William watched her walk from her seat to the front, while everyone else in the Flock held their eyes on the child.

"Would you like to tell us about your suffering?" Gleeson prompted.

The woman nodded, her head bobbing as though hope had left a spring in her neck. "I have arthritis."

"And why do you think you have arthritis?"

"I'm not sure," she shrugged. "I got diagnosed young, at twenty-three. It's always been a part of my life."

"How has it affected you?"

"Oh," a pained laugh. "It's awful. The aching's deep in my joints, so it radiates into the rest of my body. Sometimes it gets so bad in my thighs, I can't even sit, and it feels like my bones are grating against each other when I move."

"Where does it hurt?" Gleeson asked, his voice compassionate.

William was looking up at Ruth with curious eyes, studying her.

"Everywhere." The aching laugh was back, but now buoyant with hope. "My feet, ankles, wrists, and fingers, mostly, but like I said, it's everywhere. Sometimes the pain is throbbing, and sometimes it's sharper, like more of a shooting through my bones. It can be hot and burning, or dull and constant. I've felt it all."

"And is it possible that this is a spiritual condition?"

"I ... I don't know," Ruth said, uncertain.

"God created a world without sin or sickness. He fashioned a world without death. Made it perfect, until Man ruined it. The diseased and dying world we live in now is the result of that fall. So tell me, Ruth, do you have faith?"

"Yes ... of course I do."

"Have you been holding back on your Sins and Transgressions?"

Ruth didn't answer.

Melinda watched him. She almost looked scared, as though he would do anything to this poor woman beyond encouraging the child to heal her.

"Is it possible your sickness is a spiritual condition?" Gleeson repeated.

"I don't know ..." She shrugged, looking suddenly upset, probably feeling naked up there in front of the Flock. "Maybe?"

"Tell us what you've been holding back, Ruth, so that the Lord will allow William to heal you. So the bones in your body may finally stop aching."

"I have impure thoughts about Brother Matthew," she declared, looking out at the crowd. "I think about him and me while his wife is in the laundry."

"Anything else?" Gleeson asked.

"I stole some milk three weeks ago. And bread a few months before that."

"Is that all?"

"I ... I think so."

"Will you please show Ruth the Glory of the Lord's Forgiveness?" Gleeson asked of the child.

William held his hands out for Ruth, and without any words she knew what to do, pulling his little paws into her palms and closing her fingers around them. She drew his discharged purity into her body.

Almost glowing, her cheeks flushed and her mouth formed a perfect O of pleasure. She was breathing heavy, then heavier … was almost orgasmic as she reached a crest then descended down the other side.

William stumbled a few steps then fell onto his back, skin ashen and eyes lifeless.

Angel scooped him up into her arms.

Ruth flexed her nimble fingers in disbelief.

"How does that feel?" Gleeson asked.

Her awe was obvious, but through flowing tears she said, "I can't believe it. I haven't felt this good in forever!"

The Flock cheered. Roy nodded approval at Gleeson.

He smiled, more certain of God's power than ever. They were lucky to have His Grace.

And now Gleeson knew exactly what to do with it.

Chapter Nineteen

THE LIGHT MIGHT HAVE BEEN TOO bright if Gleeson didn't
see infinity as an invitation.

And so he approached it, wanting to be filled, knowing
the Lord was allowing him to see things here in the
heavens of this lucid dream He could not show him while
he was only a man, walking the Earth.

Here he was infinite, part of the heavens and everything that was so much greater than himself. It was as
though he was seeing the world's data all at once. Not just
thoughts and experiences from now, but from all time,
yawning both behind and in front of him, an endless
procession without beginning or end.

This was the infinite behind the veil. What only the
angels could see. And the chosen like him.

It wasn't just data. Gleeson could hear their prayers. *See*
them, even. A trillion pinpricks of light, though each could
be zoomed in upon. Lived inside, if he wanted.

So many languages, and even though Gleeson had
barely ever left Montana, and then mostly only to hit
northern Wyoming, he could understand it all. Many

tongues from all around the planet, past and present, then one he did not recognize. Though it was familiar, he'd never heard it before now. Because only in this dream with verity like a gospel had Gleeson been given a glimpse into the world of angels. The chance to hear them sing and talk and wonder aloud.

Their chatter was music, and to hear it for longer than a whisper of wind he would surely have to die.

But Gleeson was ready for that, if God were to call him.

He bathed in the light until being called to enter the dark.

Battles beyond his imagining, settling into conquest and seizure, a subjugation of humanity in hopes of who they could be, casting the planet into dispassionate judgement, the *will they or won't they* of spiritual ascension, then finally an extinction to wipe out the head of humanity, leaving it with but a few strands of hair.

The only way to establish an era of everlasting peace.

Hell unleashed so that Heaven may reign.

Yet amid all the battles and chaos, Gleeson could see some humans thriving despite their Judgment in the sky. Great cities built, where Heaven's Rule was like blood in the bodies of all who lived there.

Do you understand?

The angels were asking, so Gleeson said, "Yes."

Do you know what to do?

And he did.

These cities of God did not belong to him, but Stonefall did, and Gleeson would make his tiny hamlet worthy of the Good Lord Himself. He would act as His son, bringing the Light to His people.

Gleeson would make sure his city was worthy of passing Judgment when it rained. His flock would be brought before the gates and granted entry, where they could then look down on a thousand years of peace on Earth.

He delivered scripture to the angels.

The Lord Himself will descend from Heaven with a shout ... then those who are alive and remain shall be caught up together with them in the clouds to meet the Lord in the air.

Gleeson could see how it would end, just as it had ended before.

There was a great earthquake, such a mighty and great earthquake as had not occurred since men were on the Earth ... and great hail from Heaven fell upon men, each hailstone about the weight of a talent.

Gleeson was drawn toward a Light, brighter than any other. Walking then drifting without using his feet, finally floating across the expanse like a mote in God's eye.

He stopped at the baby.

But William was no longer only a baby.

Nor only a child, teen, full-grown adult, or withered old man.

He was all of them, each moment of every stage at once. As if Gleeson could see both seedling and tree. Oak and acorn. Cone and conifer.

In every version of William, his mouth moved like a conduit, speaking his data, inviting Gleeson to swim in his truth.

He longed to know more, to get closer to the child.

To hear everything he had to say.

He kept stepping closer, inching toward the Light. But it was too bright, and the screech of his details too loud. The angels were singing, and he would be invited to join them as soon as he finished his work on Earth.

Gleeson opened his eyes to the brilliant light of a new

day, more assured than ever that their miracle was a Godsend because for the first time, the angels had joined the Lord in His chorus.

He got out of bed and fell to his knees in mediation and prayer.

There he stayed for an hour, one with himself and the world, repeating a mantra Roy said would work in both the best and worst of times.

This is the day the Lord has made, I will rejoice and be glad in it.

This is the day the Lord has made, I will rejoice and be glad in it.

This is the day the Lord has made, I will rejoice and be glad in it

...

Over and over and over.

More than a hundred times before he rose from the floor then went to answer a knock at the door.

"It's Kirk," he said from outside the room.

Gleeson opened the door with a bow then swung it wide so the man could enter. "Brother Kirk. Good morning."

"Good morning, Father."

He stared down at Kirk, waiting for the Brother to talk. There had to be a reason he was knocking on the door to his quarters instead of waiting for Gleeson's rounds like always. "What is it?"

"Some of the people are getting restless."

"About what?"

"About the child. Everyone who is sick now wants the child to heal him."

"When you have a burn, do you not wish for an ointment upon it?"

"Of course," Kirk answered, as though he had

expected that exact response. "But I'm not sure they understand William is a limited resource."

"I explained it last night," Gleeson said with a wave of his hand.

"It isn't enough." Kirk shook his head. "Perhaps we should have kept his talent a secret."

"Can you believe this?" Roy asked, appearing between them.

"Miracles are not meant to live in the shadows, Brother Kirk. We can look upon a sunny horizon, even as we stand in the rain. Stonefall needed a reason to believe, and now we have one. The requests are expected. Everyone will have their turn in His Light, so long as they have fully surrendered to Sins and Transgressions."

"How do we make sure there isn't some sort of a riot?"

Another wave of his hand. "There will be no such furor in Stonefall. Melinda can handle the requests."

"You're putting her in charge of both the Women's Group and this? Do you really think that's such a good idea?"

"Why wouldn't it be?"

"Do you really trust her that much?" He looked as though he truly had no idea how he might answer.

Gleeson looked over at Roy, studying his expression before turning back to Kirk. "What are you trying to say?"

But Kirk just shook his head. "Never mind."

"He's playing you," Roy warned. "He's planting seeds of doubt, brother. Leading the witness."

Maybe so. But still Gleeson wanted to know what Kirk knew. Or thought he knew. "No *never mind* about it. What's on your mind?"

It was an order, not a question, and Kirk had better comply.

With a reluctance Roy would rightfully identify as

dishonest at worst and a show at best, Kirk said, "I heard a rumor, is all."

"Spit it out," Gleeson said, feeling a growl inside him, trying not to notice Roy taking a seat in the corner to watch the exchange. "What sort of rumor?"

"That Melinda and Percy were planning to leave."

"Why would Percy ever want to leave Stonefall? He had it good here. I don't believe it." Then, with barely a beat in between the two thoughts. "When was this?"

"Right before he was taken by The Forsaken."

"We all know rumors are more exciting than the truth," Gleeson said. "And easier to spread."

"I trust the source."

"And from where did this gossip originate?"

"Ophelia. She was living with them and heard Percy and Melinda talking. Just that morning before we all went out, in fact."

Roy was wrong. Kirk wasn't trying to play him, he was trying to protect him from the truth about Percy. He had seen it in the man's eyes and heard it in his voice. Percy *was* planning to leave.

"Why are you telling me about this now?" Gleeson demanded.

"I only found out after he was dead, and until now there never seemed to be a good enough reason to trouble you with it."

"The truth is never a trouble." Gleeson sighed and started rubbing his temples. "What's the reason now?"

"Ophelia thinks Melinda might be thinking about leaving, and maybe that's fine. It's not like we want anyone inside Stonefall who isn't truly grateful to be here. But you're giving her a lot of responsibility, and it could be upsetting to a lot or our people if she was to suddenly disappear after all that."

"You're right," Gleeson said. "Thank you for keeping me informed. I'll look into it immediately and see what I can find out."

"Very good, Father." A slight bow.

"Is that all?"

"One more thing. We have a lead on The Forsaken. I'm taking some men to investigate."

"Good. Let me know what you find out."

"Of course, Father."

Gleeson closed the door behind Kirk, then turned to Roy. "What about Melinda? Tell me what you're thinking. Is Percy's woman a threat?"

But Roy only stared back. For once his old friend had nothing to say.

Chapter Twenty

EAMON WAS STARTING to remember why he disliked his brother so much.

It didn't take long. The first day back was great. Eamon found himself happy to see Liam. He never doubted Felony's return. Those weren't just reassuring words to Sherry. Deep in his heart, somehow, Eamon knew. But Eamon's feelings about his brother was a surprise, and the honeymoon was a good one. Unfortunately, it was already over.

They were on their way to Stonefall, and unlike a few months ago, its location was no longer a mystery. The place was still an enigma — what happened behind those walls and what kind of man the Father of Stonefall actually was. Rumors ran far on both sides of the spectrum.

"So just to recap, we're heading to a bible camp that used to be a prison, run by some crazy guy who may or may not be nailing people upside down to crosses, and all on account of your teenage girlfriend having a dream about some woman she met a couple of months ago, maybe being with a baby that ain't even hers. That about right?"

"No," Eamon said, low so that Sherry couldn't hear him. She was a few paces ahead, walking with Felony. The plan was to pull Olive out of the ditch, then ride the rest of the way to Stonefall. But his brother was being confrontational, trying to get his goat, draw him into the old back and forth he still apparently thrived on, though the long months of Liam's absence in his life had taught Eamon exactly how much he could live without it.

"What did I get wrong?"

"Stonefall used to be a prison, but whoever The Forsaken are, I don't think they have anything to do with the town or the people there. And Sherry's had visions before. Same for Poppy, before she was gone. Turned out they were both right enough that we learned to listen. Felony included. You can ask him yourself if you want to."

"No need," Liam said. "I've seen what Felony will do for some well-toned ass. I just didn't know that shit was contagious, though considering you and Poppy, maybe you were the one who infected him."

It didn't deserve a response, and Eamon would have been happy to ignore him until after the Jeep was freed from the ditch, but Liam wasn't about to let it go.

"How old is she, anyway?" Then, when Eamon said nothing, "Never pegged you for the jailbait type."

"She's eighteen, asshole."

"When you met? Or yesterday?" Liam laughed. "Just so we're clear, I'm not judging. Great job. Seriously. She's a fine piece of ass, and younger is better than older when it comes to snatch. It's like any kind of meat — dries out the older it gets."

"I'm not listening to you," Eamon said, hoping Sherry wasn't, either.

"Sure, you are. Don't feel bad about your desires, baby brother. This shit is biological. A man's want for a younger woman is like an Eskimo longing the sun. Sure, there are some fat asses under twenty, and some MILFS who pray to the gods of pilates, but for the most part young girls are tighter, firmer, and more pleasing to look at."

"In case you haven't noticed, no one is doing pilates these days. And besides, beauty is in the eye of the beholder. You're talking about it as though there are universal truths. During the Renaissance, being heavy was a sign of wealth."

"Great. Obesity was hot a thousand years ago. You want a girl with her nipples closer to her bush than her chin, be my guest. Then maybe you can give your brother a turn with Sherry."

"Fuck you, Liam."

"You can act pissed at me all you want, but it's not like I'm pulling shit out of my ass or telling you a secret. After a certain age, women deteriorate."

"Seriously." Eamon stopped, angry enough to grab his brother's arm. "You need to stop it. She's not just my girlfriend. For all intents and purposes, she's the mother of my child and damned good at her job."

"That right?" Liam smirked, Eamon's hand still on his arm. "That why your son got stolen away? Because she was doing such a great job watching him?"

"I already told you, that wasn't her fault. She was with me when it happened."

"Oh, that's right. And whose idea was that?"

"It was both of ours. Sherry wanted to do more than her share. It wasn't enough, tending to William and taking care of the cabin. She wanted to hunt and help out on supply runs. So I took her out to show her what I know, and we *both decided* to leave—"

"Your son with an old man and his old woman?"

"Jefferson was more capable than any either of us."

"I'm sure that's true, but if I were you, man, I'd keep that to myself."

Eamon let go of Liam's arms and kept walking.

His brother was undeterred, still laughing like an asshole a couple steps behind him. He took two long strides to catch up. "You're taking all this personally. I'm just talking."

"You're trying to piss me off. Get me going like you always do."

"Just like the baby of the family. Always thinking the world revolves around him. Your mistake was putting your faith in that old man. I don't care if he was Yoda, you should never trust anyone other than family."

Eamon stopped walking again, and turned toward his brother. "What would you know about family? You've never been married or had a child to worry about. You've never had to make the tough choices."

Liam laughed again, but the tone this time was different. Condescending more than mocking. "Of course you would think that. Because *you* had the luxury."

"What's that supposed to mean?"

"Exactly what it sounds like. I didn't have time to bring a child into the world because I was too busy serving our family. The one we were both born into, but only one of us ever gave any shit about. Ever had any allegiance to, or showed any loyalty for. You always thought you were better than the rest of us, and it was long before you went off and married that hippie chick who brainwashed you, turning you against your family even more than you already were."

"That's not—"

"You were a sanctimonious little narc even when we were kids."

"Because I knew the difference between right and wrong?"

"No, Eamon. Because you were an asshole about it. You didn't distance yourself so much as give us dirty looks from afar, letting us know at every opportunity that you were—"

"In case you don't remember, I had to get the hell out of Dodge on Astral Day, because I was back to working for the family and—"

"Because you said you wanted another chance. And then you begged me to give it to you!"

He was yelling, and that was the last thing that Eamon wanted with Sherry well ahead but still in earshot if Liam was going to be that loud.

"Let's just drop it."

Liam followed Eamon's gaze, then turned with a sneer. Lowered his voice, though it was still too loud. "Don't want your girlfriend to hear, huh?"

"I mean it, Liam."

"I know you do. Look at you, with your heavy breathing and clenched fists. How much would you love to hit me right now?"

Eamon didn't answer.

"You've never had the balls to hit me before. Why is that, Eamon? Especially seeing as how it was always what you were best at. I can understand why you would want to act like a chicken while Dad was still alive, but he's dead, so what's stopping you? Why not lay me flat, if that's what you really want to do?"

Liam looked at him, still smirking, still baiting him.

Felony and Sherry had stopped walking. He had his hand on her shoulder, silently telling her to wait, it would all be okay. He should know, he'd seen it plenty.

"I don't want to hit you, Liam."

"Sure you do. You've wanted to knock my teeth out ever since I called that granola crunching MILF in waiting of yours a … what was it? … *Pussy that wasn't good enough to fuck your family for.*"

"I'm not going to hit you."

"And why not? You obviously want to."

"Because," Eamon said, meaning every word, and making it obvious by the way he leaned a few inches forward, so Liam was close enough to feel the heat of his growling breath. "If I punch you now, I'll kill you. Felony will try, but he won't be able to stop me. I'll hit you in the throat first, to keep you from breathing, then I'll turn your face into oatmeal while you're sucking air from your teeth. Bury you in the snow on our way to Stonefall and never think of you again."

Eamon was enjoying Liam's surprise. The way he kept blinking, and the way his breathing had changed. The way his brow was suddenly beaded in sweat.

"You ever say another word about Poppy or Sherry again, and I won't be so idle. You got it?"

Then something happened that had never happened before. Liam fell another step back and said, "Got it," with what almost sounded like a note of respect.

Eamon started walking again, and after a long look from Sherry in front of him, so did she. He wondered what she thought of the exchange. If he had scared her with his sudden savagery, or if that's what she would want in her protector. Was Sherry jealous, thinking maybe he was still in love with his wife and only with her because he had no other choice?

Liam didn't let the silence linger for long. "You're so ungrateful."

Eamon keep walking.

"You've never appreciated what was given to you. Not ever. We tried to teach you to grow up, to be a man. Dad, Felony, all of us. But you could never get over thinking your way was *the* way. And now what, Eamon? What are you gonna do now that the world's gone to shit? You're gonna have to get your hands bloody eventually, brother."

Sherry reeled around toward Liam, started marching right toward him and yelling once half way there. "Your ass must be jealous of all the shit that comes out of your mouth. You don't know the first thing about anything! Your brother was a beast, the way he went in looking for William. He's just too proud to tell you about the way he went into that old motel, so he gave you the gentleman's version. I don't know what your problem is, but I'm guessing it's hard to pronounce and we would all be better off if you would just shut the hell up!"

Then she turned back around and tromped back toward Felony, leaving the brothers alone.

Liam muttered, "Might want to keep your kid in line."

Sherry turned back around and yelled, "I'm not a kid, asshole! Now apologize!"

She didn't finish the threat, or need to. The blend of her anger with Eamon's was plenty.

Though his grin still had shit in it, Liam said, "Sorry for making a joke," then he walked ahead past Sherry and fell in step with Felony.

They walked in silence until Sherry took his hand and whispered, "Do we *have* to ride with him? Can't we just tell him to get lost?"

"He's a dick, but he's the only family I have in the world."

"*I'm* your family," Sherry said.

"You know what I mean. And hate him or not, he's

exactly the kind of person we want on our side while looking for William."

"Fine, Eamon. I hope he helps us find William. But be careful he doesn't turn our family into yours."

Chapter Twenty-One

Rosa hoped she wasn't getting sick.

She felt awful, and there was a definite tickle at the back of her throat. But it could have been psychosomatic. There were enough people coming down with pneumonia that the word *epidemic* — they steered clear of it for a while, but now it seemed unavoidable — had entered The Reserve's lexicon.

The potential trade with Braxton was a bust and left them off worse than they'd been before. If they couldn't get any antibiotics, most of the people in The Reserve currently suffering no longer would be, but for all the wrong reasons. Blood tests proved the pneumonia was bacterial rather than viral.

They were running out of options, and Rebecca was crazy enough to suggest a return visit to the Slums, waiting until Braxton made a run and left his underlings behind.

"We can convince Garvey if we can get him alone," Rebecca said.

"Sure," Rosa agreed, "but how are we going to know

when Braxton leaves without having someone stationed there?"

"So we have someone stationed. Solomon can watch, then come back and tell us as soon as he leaves."

"Got it. We leave Solomon in danger, then he can come back to The Reserve once we know Braxton has left the Slums, and he'll let us know that we have anywhere from a few minutes to a few days."

"I think we both know what we need to do," Rebecca said.

As much as she hated it, this time Rosa agreed with her girlfriend. "Everything about that place gives me the creeps. Always had, even when it was a prison."

"Did you ever see the place when it was a prison?"

"Of course not," Rosa said. "It was in the middle of nowhere. But I knew it was there, and of course we all had stories. Point is, it's even creepier now."

"But you've heard the rumors. Gleeson Crowe apparently has some miracle child."

Rosa scoffed. "Please tell me you're joking."

"Seriously, I heard that—"

"Please tell me you don't believe it. Gleeson will say anything to fortify his cause or get people to join him. What makes you so sure it's true and not just another lie?"

"I wouldn't say I'm sure. But I don't think Gleeson wants anyone to know about the child, at least not outside of Stonefall. The rumor feels like a leak."

"Probably because that's what he wants you to think." Rosa argued. "Gleeson could easily 'leak' a rumor he wanted us to believe."

"Sure, he could. But why?"

"He's always working his PR. This could be that." Rosa shrugged. "It doesn't matter, anyway. We're not going back to Stonefall for a 'miracle baby,' right? Don't you want to see if he'll make a trade for some medicine?"

"Yes, but there's more to it than that. This is an opportunity to improve The Reserve."

"How so?" Rosa asked.

"By looking around, observing, maybe taking notes. Gleeson Crowe has the strongest community in this part of Montana. Don't you think there's something to learn there?"

"Of course. All dictators can teach us something about maintaining order in a disorderly world."

Rebecca huffed, probably as sick of Rosa's sarcasm as Rosa was of her wayward compass. "If we're going to approach Gleeson and ask for help, don't you think we should be doing so with an open mind?"

"Right. Because his is so open."

Rosa let that one hang, her dander up. By all accounts, Gleeson was a monster. Rebecca would argue — and had — they couldn't take the word of outcasts from the community, since their opinions would of course be colored. But Rebecca was telling herself the story she wanted, or needed, to hear. The girls had firsthand experience with Gleeson and that was plenty.

They had approached him once, about three months after Astral Day. The Reserve was organized enough to have established an early trade route, and it was obvious Gleeson was building something impressive, and possibly lasting, from among the prison ruins. But he'd been dismissive of their being gay, calling it a "slight to the Good Lord." He wasn't openly hostile and didn't threaten or hurt them in any way, at least not physically, but the man had muttered something about the sexually immoral being like slave traders and promise breakers — a contradiction to God's teaching.

"That was a long time ago," Rebecca said.

"It wasn't even a year."

"Times have changed. Things are different. Days are weeks and months are years. There are goddamned aliens in the sky, Rosa. And on the ground. Are we really arguing about this? Do you seriously not think we should go?"

"No, I don't."

Rebecca looked over at her, shocked.

Rosa finished. "I think *I* should go. I'll find a way to convince him, but I want to go alone."

"Absolutely not. You're—"

"You can't just dismiss me out of hand, Rebecca. You're talking about loading up a caravan and heading out with some of our best people. Plus the bears."

"Well, of course."

"But that will seem confrontational. Like *Help us or else!* I don't think that's the way to handle this. We go together, then we're those two lesbians he kicked out of his place six months ago, coming back with what might seem to Gleeson like aggression. But if I go alone, I doubt he'll recognize me. No reason I can't be a girl of faith looking for help."

"You know the rules. No one leaves The Reserve by themselves."

"Right," Rosa said, "and those rules are there for a reason. But this situation is different. I'll be fine once I get to Stonefall."

"But what about before you get there? There are too many bandits, Braxton's men are on the road, and now we're getting reports of aliens hunting people."

"We both know that's probably not true."

"Even so, you need to take someone with you. Solomon, Baldwin, anyone."

"No," Rosa shook her head. "Anyone I take decreases

my odds of getting through the gate and making our plea to Gleeson while simultaneous weakening our defenses here. We need everyone present, in case Braxton decides to attack while he sees us as ailing and ready to fight."

"One person won't make a difference."

"Exactly."

"I mean for us," Rebecca said. "It could make all the difference for you."

"I'm willing to take my chances. You need to let me."

Rebecca sighed. Rosa rarely drew lines with her lover, but they were always deep when she did.

Rebecca was clearly upset by the time their argument settled and they were saying goodbye. Embracing her partner filled Rosa with chills — she couldn't pretend that despite her words of assurance, this might be the last time they ever saw each other.

Though she wanted to hurry and get out of The Reserve before losing too much time, that last thought upon leaving sent her to Mikey's. If this might be the end, she had to say goodbye to her brother.

But not even two minutes there, Rosa was thinking she probably should have ignored her first instinct, and slipped out of The Reserve without saying a word.

"I'm coming with you," Mikey said, insistent enough to remind Rosa of her exchange with Rebecca.

"You can't." Rosa shook her head. "I'm going alone."

"You're going alone?" Paul repeated, looking up from the corner where he was thumbing through an old Wilderness magazine.

"Are you taking a bear?" Mikey asked.

"Just me. I'm going to ask for help. Bringing a battle bear isn't just a sign of aggression. It could give Gleeson a reason to believe we're really not all that bad off."

"Maybe you could trade for one of the bears," Mikey suggested.

"That's not a bad idea. But there are too many variables. I'm not confident about what would happen around all those people if the bear got spooked. That could be bad for all of us. So, like I said, I'm going alone."

"And like I said, I'm coming with you."

"*We're* coming with you," Paul said.

"Neither of you is coming with me. You're both staying here. I told you the plan and why I needed to go alone."

"Right," Mikey nodded, "so you look pathetic. We can help with that."

"We're both kids," Paul cut in, seeing where this was headed. "You're his older sister and I'm his friend. Instead of warriors and battle bears, you've got a couple extra mouths to feed."

"You could get killed," Rosa argued, feeling her position slipping, like loose rocks rolling down a mountain trail.

Mikey shook his head. "No way. Why would Gleeson kill us? From everything we've heard, he exiles people who don't like his way of doing things, and he's obviously nuttier than a sack of almonds. But he doesn't just murder people for no reason."

"I'm more worried about the trip there," Rosa said.

"Then you should definitely take us." Paul was suddenly standing right beside Mikey. "We both know your brother is going to follow you the second you're outta here, and I'm going to follow him. This way we all go together."

"*Please,* Rosa. I need to help Katrina."

Rosa sighed, hating not having a choice. "Fine. But you will follow all of my rules, and you will not engage if we're attacked unless I give the order. Understood?"

Mikey nodded and his Paul followed.

"Okay," Rosa said. "Then let's get to Stonefall."

Chapter Twenty-Two

Sherry and Eamon were on their way to Stonefall, but neither was saying much. Not to each other or to anyone else. Sherry was pissed at Liam, Eamon, and Felony. In that order. She was upset with the entire situation, furious it was turning from something uncomfortable into something downright ugly.

Liam reminded Sherry of every monster who had ever wanted to hurt her — all the assholes she went to high school with. The group of jocks who verbally abused her before raping and ruining her. And as much as she hated to admit it, Eamon and Felony reminded her of all the people who allowed it to happen.

The only thing necessary for the triumph of evil was for good men to do nothing in its presence, and Sherry felt that truth like a second skin upon her now.

Liam was an excellent example what was wrong with the world and why an alien invasion might not have been such a terrible thing. Of why, even when people should be coming together as one more than ever before, Sherry knew deep in her heart that it could never, ever happen.

The lines between good and evil were porous, and the planet's unfortunate present made it easy for the wrong one to thrive.

After that first blowup, the remaining walk to their Jeep was a bit like a funeral procession. They were relieved to see the vehicle was still around when they got there, but there was no glee on their faces. They managed to get Olive out of the ravine, but did so in grueling silence, grunting through their labor, with Liam and Eamon pitching dirty looks at each other from one bumper to the other.

It took all of her effort not to start yelling. Every part of her wanted to turn around and scream all the things she'd been thinking throughout their hours of silence.

She settled for whispering. "How long do we have to stay with him?"

"I told you, I don't know. As long as we need to."

"He's an asshole."

"I know," Eamon agreed.

And so it went. Every few minutes Sherry would engage him again, though she never said anything new, and thus the conversation never went anywhere fresh.

Finally, just as Sherry was wondering if this was the new normal and there would be this distance between them forever, Eamon turned toward her in the back seat, took both of Sherry's hands, and whispered, "I understand how you feel, and I promise this isn't permanent, okay? We'll figure it out."

His words were full of effort, and the exertion was clear his face. Only then did Sherry stop to think about how hard it had to be on her man. He knew his brother was an asshole, he'd said as much from their first conversation, back when she met her new friends after they picked her up on that bridge, right about the time when Sherry had been willing to end her tender life.

They were about ten miles outside of Stonefall when Felony began to slow down.

"What's up?" Liam asked from the passenger seat in front of Sherry. "What do you think that is?"

They were all looking into the distance. Beyond the snow-covered ground, blinding white on both sides of the road. Past the gray skies and skeletal branches. Far ahead was a black fog of what might have been anything. Maybe a fire, or some sort of vehicle belching exhaust. Human or alien, predator or prey, flight or flight.

"Are you sure about this?" Sherry leaned forward and put a friendly hand on Felony's shoulder. "Maybe we should stop. Turn around. Or …"

The thought hung as Olive rolled toward the smoke now filling the cabin.

"That stinks," Sherry said. "What is it?"

Felony said, "Rubber."

And though it could not have been any less appropriate to the situation, Liam added, "Like your dildos, baby brother."

"I'll turn around." But Felony couldn't.

Two large SUVs, their make and model obscured by all of the grating and homemade armor around them, were blocking their way.

"You're doing great," encouraged a booming voice from a crackling speaker behind them. "Keep going like you're doing. Just like that."

Two minutes later they stopped beside an old Honda Pilot, its shell on fire with a family of four lying slain beside it.

"Motherfucker," Felony said.

"We got this," Liam assured him.

Sherry squeezed Eamon's hand, probably harder than she had ever squeezed anything before.

Again, the voice boomed from behind. "Go ahead and kill your engine. Then step out of the vehicle and make your introductions. Don't be shy. My name's Braxton Kincaid. If you've not heard of me, surely you've heard of The Forsaken."

They piled out in unison. Sherry's foot hit the snow just as the group's obvious leader took two steps forward, raking her with his eyes and making her feel like something hollow about to be filled in all the wrong ways.

Braxton was big and broad. A born athlete like Felony, or perhaps even bred for the apocalypse. Everyone was bundled up, on both sides, except him. He was bare-chested and wore tight denim and scarred leather armor, both bloodstained. Must've thought he was Conan, with that giant sword strapped to his back.

"So, aren't you going to introduce yourselves?"

Braxton was smiling, enjoying this. His eyes were still scraping Sherry. Same for the half-dozen dangerous men standing behind him. And probably all the people in the SUVs.

"I'm Felony," he said, taking the ball, pretending this was all a friendly game, friends passing on the road, a hilarious anecdote waiting to happen. He raised his hand and patted his chest. Then he pointed to Liam, Eamon, and Sherry in turn, introducing each of his friends as he went. No harm in honesty if this was the end of their lives.

Braxton said, "You want to tell us where you were headed?"

"Funny you should ask." Liam sounded an awful lot like Felony had recently described the asshole's father. "We were on our way to a custom shop a few miles from here. We heard they were having a big post-apocalyptic blowout. Mad Max costumes are on sale. We figured it was time to start looking the part instead of dressing for warmth. But it looks like you guys already got there. I hope you left something for us."

Braxton laughed. Then, suddenly, two of the six men behind him had their crossbows drawn, both aimed at Liam's forehead. Sherry didn't turn to see for herself, but she imagined the men behind her were aiming quiet weapons as well.

"You'll have to excuse my friend. He gets a little mouthy." Felony smiled, then like a magic trick produced a pair of pistols from nowhere, one glistening in each of his palms, reflecting sunlight throwing beams against the snow. "Well, well, will you look at that ... I'm not sure how I managed to start packing *two* guns when you didn't even see me get that first one in my hand, but here we are and now there you go. I pull the trigger, it's boomtown for all of us."

Braxton laughed again, almost appreciatively.

"Well, this is nice. Most of the folks we end up pulling over around here just bend over and take it. That family there ..." he eyed the bodies, "... you should've heard them begging. But look at you, with all your piss and balsamic."

Cool as a snow cone in winter, Felony said, "Why don't we all give our trigger fingers a rest and have ourselves a conversation."

"Sure. You first."

Sherry could feel Eamon thinking beside her, assessing the situation, waiting to make his move. And if it wasn't totally nuts, she would swear she could *see* his thoughts.

Eamon said, "So, what's the toll?"

Braxton turned toward Eamon. "I'm sorry?"

"You're obviously the troll in the situation, and we're trip-trapping across your bridge. So what's the toll for crossing?"

"You think there's a price you can pay that's gonna let you onto the other side of my bridge?"

And Eamon said, "I do."

"Lower your weapons, men." He wiped his mouth, stepped forward, and looked Eamon right in his eyes. "I'll take your deal if I like it. But if I don't, we get to torture you to death, and I don't want to hear any complaining before the torture actually starts. Are we cool?"

Eamon stole a glance at the slaughtered family and the husk of the still burning Pilot. "Sounds like a plan."

"So, what do you have for us?"

Eamon glanced at their Jeep. "You're looking at it."

"That thing?" Braxton shook his head. "Nah, seeing as I'll just take that after I kill you, I figure it's already mine."

Sherry was terrified. She had tried to keep the worst of her thoughts at bay, but now they were there, beating their fists on her door. Because Sherry *knew* what they would do to her. It had been done to her before, and this time promised to be so much worse. Her skin was burning with both the memory and the forecast. These men would throw her into the fire, only after they finished.

Eamon shrugged. "Good luck using it."

Braxton raised his eyebrows, waiting for Eamon to finish.

"You do want this little Jeep. Her name's Olive, and she's saved our life several times. I don't know exactly how it works, but I don't need to, because it always does. Or did, I suppose it's yours now. We got it from our friend Jefferson. It was his, before he was murdered. The whole thing was 3D printed, if you can believe that. It's crazy fuel efficient and nimble. You'll love it. Problem is, you're gonna spend a helluva long time trying to crack the five-digit code."

Eamon waited a moment. Braxton wasn't quite getting it. So he clarified. *"No keys."*

Braxton nodded. "So you give me the code, and if it starts you can go."

"How do we know you'll let us leave?" Felony asked.

"Fair question," Braxton said, seeming to consider. "I've never made a trade. But good on you for getting us there. How about we make it simple? You aim your pea shooters at us, then we drive away and leave you here."

"You could just circle around," Liam argued.

"Stay here by the fire for an hour."

From behind his side of the staring contest, Felony said, "You could be waiting."

"Well then I'd have to ask you about the practicality in that." Braxton looked around at his men. "Do you think we all want to wait an hour just to be petty? We have our fun, but all in the process of making our haul. That Pilot right there was busted and wasn't ever gonna start working again. Everything else they got we loaded into Becky already."

He nodded toward the slightly smaller of the two tank-sized SUVs.

"Named Becky since that was the first girl we found on the road. Maybe we'll call the next one Sherry." Braxton gave her a wink.

"Deal," Eamon said, with disgust in his voice.

Sherry fell in love with him all over again, for using his mind instead of his fists.

No words after that. No well-wishing or even a simple goodbye. They all climbed back into their two vehicles, drove around their homemade roadblock, and took off. They weren't even a hundred feet away when Liam proved his lack of gratitude.

"Great," he grumbled. "Now we have to walk ten miles in the snow."

Chapter Twenty-Three

Eamon's heart was pounding for a while after their exchange with the bandits.

He wasn't even sure where it had come from. At no time did he want to start swinging his fists. Something had changed enough to slow him down in all the right ways. Now he wanted to study the page before he felt ready to scribble. Almost like Sherry's needs were bleeding into him. Sun beating down on the roof of a house he could only warm to after stepping outside.

But now it was someone else's turn to save them. Felony's, specifically. Fortunately, he'd been down this way with Angel and knew where there was an old warehouse that might still be abandoned.

They were desperate for shelter, a place to feel safe and not worry about the elements or the men who haunted Montana. But Felony's spot-on sense of direction was failing them all.

"I don't know what to say, man." He kept scratching his head and his neck and his arms.

Eamon could feel Sherry getting increasingly nervous. And if he were to heed those thoughts he couldn't possibly really be hearing, she wanted him to speak her mind.

"What are we going to do if we can't find this place?"

Eamon had asked Felony, but Liam answered.

"Hopefully we don't die, seeing as you lost us our wheels and shelter."

"Maybe we should find a place to stop," Felony suggested. "Start a fire. Just because we've never had to sleep outdoors in winter, don't mean we can't."

"We're not sleeping outside," Liam said. "How much farther could it be?"

"About a mile ago, I thought less than a mile," Felony admitted, sounding less certain than ever.

He asked for another ten minutes of walking and Liam begrudgingly gave it to him, telling him he was a quitter for not seeing it through and reminding him every sixty seconds or so that he was an asshole who couldn't find his way out of a Walmart. Eamon felt bad for his friend, and an odd comfort in knowing his brother was an equal opportunity dickhead, getting in Felony's face like he was.

When his ten minutes were up, Felony threw his hands in the air, admitted defeat, then built them a fire while Eamon and Liam worked in hostile silence to fashion a temporary shelter. Sherry kept guard against Braxton and his men or any of the other human diseases that might find them vulnerable in the snow.

"I guess I don't have to worry about the aliens," she joked. "They show up, we're all dead."

Felony didn't laugh at her nervous twitter like he normally would have, his searching eyes seeking an ideal location for their shelter. He was explaining out loud, talking about snow-depth and tree type while Eamon listened and Liam pretended to.

"You need to find evergreens with low-hanging boughs," Felony told them. "Then you can dig in and make the shelter."

They burrowed into the tree until Felony joined them, with a reminder that they needed to be careful. They could get stuck if the snow cascaded down and filled the hole. It was slow, methodical work, digging until they got to ground level, then converting the pit's floor with boughs to insulate the shelter.

Sherry helped to pack out the walls once they finished, stabilizing the shelter from snow. Once they were all inside, they covered the hole they came through with more boughs to keep their heat in and the snow out.

It was tight and terrible, but better than spending a night in the elements.

But Liam ruined even that. All bravado, no heart.

"We should circle back in the morning. Forget the stupid religious compound or prison or whatever. See if we can find Rocky Horror and fuck his shit up."

"That's a terrible idea," Felony said, so no one else had to.

"No, it isn't. Now's the time. It's the last thing they'll be expecting."

"Even so, what would we gain? And how would we even find them? We don't have a vehicle or any clue where they are." Eamon knew it was a mistake the moment the words left his mouth.

Liam wore a big, stupid grin, glad his baby brother had gobbled the bait. "We can get our Jeep back for starters. But it might be a good idea to go ahead and take all the weapons off their persons after we kill them."

"We're not doing that." Felony stated the obvious, not bothering to add they couldn't, even if they wanted to.

But Liam kept going. "You can't appease people like

that. Only thing Braxton will understand is a boot to the teeth, and I oughtta know because I've dealt with men like that my entire life."

"You mean like Dad?"

"You don't know dick about shit," Liam snarled. "Dad was the man he needed to be for us, and you should have appreciated that more than you did."

"Men like Dad brought misery into a lot of lives, Liam. Sorry I had a hard time celebrating it."

"You've always been such a sanctimonious pile of shit, you know that?"

"Of course I do. You spent my entire life telling me." Icy air plumed out of Eamon's mouth. He imagined the roaring fire, still burning on the other side of their shelter, half-ashamed to picture himself shoving his brother into the flames, and half-humiliated not having the balls to actually do it.

"Maybe I would've stopped after the first thousand times, if you heard even one of them."

"I heard," Eamon said. "I didn't agree."

"You never had a problem benefiting from our family when it suited you. When you needed money or when you needed to run from the law, or during any of the other times growing up when you got to act like a prince but cry like a pauper." Liam turned to Sherry. "He didn't have you fooled, did he? You didn't think Eamon was some kind of knight in shining armor, did you?"

She looked between the brothers, clearly frightened by the prospect of whatever might happen next. But she didn't give a shit about Liam's accusations. Sherry knew who he was, for better or worse, and in some ways more than Liam.

"Don't talk to her." Eamon glared at his brother, daring him to push it an inch.

Felony had one hand out, ready to grab Sherry, who looked ready to leap in between them, the other extended toward the Quinns. "Let's cool it, okay guys?" But there wasn't much hope in his voice.

The only sound was an unsettling silence, and the lightest whistle of air, not unlike the angry breeze passing between gunslingers on opposite sides of the street.

Liam finally turned to Sherry. "My baby brother has trouble seeing things through. Next time he has trouble finishing with you, come and find me. I'll take good enough care of you for both of us."

Eamon's fist found Liam's jaw. Even though his brother had to be expecting the swing, it was still one hell of a strike, causing Liam to lose his footing, stumble three steps back, and plant his ass in the snow.

Then Eamon was on top of him, one hand at his brother's throat and the other fist pounding his face.

Liam grunted, then shoved his open palms against Eamon's chest, loosening his grip enough to wiggle out from underneath him.

He rolled away, grabbed Eamon's shirttail, and yanked him hard to the ground.

Sherry moved to intervene, but Felony dragged her back.

Eamon could barely see them, twisted down onto the ground like he was, but he heard Felony tell her, "Let them work it out. This is how they do."

But the brothers were already separating.

Liam's face was bleeding in several places, and it would be three times the size by morning.

It could have ended there, but fuck Liam. "You know why you always defend Dad, don't you?" He didn't wait for an answer. Instead Eamon took two steps forward until he was back in his brother's face. "It's because you were always nothing without him. And now that he's dead, you're even less than that."

Liam was going to kill him, die trying, or walk away. In that second, Eamon was fine with any of them.

He opted for the third. "Fine, Eamon. See how long you both survive without my kind helping you."

He started to leave, but impossibly, Sherry reached out to stop him. "You can't go out there. You'll *die*."

"I'd rather die in the cold then live in here with him." Liam finally turned from his brother and turned to Felony. "You coming?"

Felony gave Eamon and Sherry a face full of apology, then shook his head and followed Liam out into the cold, leaving them in the shelter alone.

She could have said anything once they were gone, but Sherry took his hands and said, "Thank you." Then she gave him a kiss on his lips once they parted. "What do you think we should do now?"

There was a rustling at their shelter entrance, then Felony slipped back inside.

"I made him wait so I could draw you a map. Here you go." Felony handed a piece of paper to Eamon. "That should get you to Stonefall. Despite my apparently losing a warehouse, those directions are good."

"We trust you," Sherry said, then she gave him a long hug.

"Everything will be okay." He hugged her back, whispering so Eamon could hear, but Liam who was surely listening on the other side of the shelter most likely could not. "He's gonna get himself killed if I don't go with him."

"I know," Sherry said, pulling away.

Eamon and Felony embraced, then he was gone.

They looked at the map. Below the scrawled directions to Stonefall was a message.

I'll talk to him. We'll join you as soon as we can. Take care of each other until then.

167

I'll talk to him. We'll join you as soon as we can. Take care of each other until then.

Chapter Twenty-Four

MELINDA KNOCKED on Gleeson's door and waited for him to answer.

Every time she expected someone else to open his door, seeing as he was the Father of Stonefall, but it was always just him. Angel and her baby lived with him and William, but other than that, Gleeson seemed to enjoy being alone. Maybe that was so he could sink into those voices in his head. She'd seen it plenty, the way he sometimes spoke to his shoulder. So had all of Stonefall, though few of its citizens would be willing to admit it.

Gleeson opened the door, smiled at Melinda, then invited her inside. "Thank you for coming."

"Of course, Father." Like she had another choice.

He led her over to the small sofa and loveseat, then sat in the loveseat like always. "Have you considered my request?"

"I have." Melinda picked up the steaming tea that was already waiting then blew on the top before taking a sip.

Gleeson wanted her to suggest someone from Stonefall with an especially tragic story, someone in obvious need.

The star of his show, Melinda couldn't stop herself from thinking.

"And?"

"And I do have someone to suggest. Bailey Jensen."

"I know Bailey," Gleeson said, looking surprised. "She is not the sort of choice I expected."

"Why is that?" Melinda asked, even though she knew.

"She seems able-bodied. Does she have some sort of ailment we cannot see?" He leaned forward, and to his credit appeared as though he was trying not to be rude. "Is it something *female?*"

"Yes, her ailment isn't easy to see, though I have spotted it. And no," Melinda shook her head with a friendly smile. "It isn't female. It's her mental health, Father. Bailey suffers from depression."

"Oh …" Gleeson looked to his left, into the corner. A slight nod, then he added an, "I see" that was already implied.

Melinda waited a moment before adding anything else because she could clearly see him digesting. Sure enough, a half-minute was gone before he figured out what he wanted to say.

"She always seems so happy."

"Only when you see her. She's bipolar, Father. Left untreated, we run the risk of that moving into mania."

"What does that mean?" Gleeson asked, surprising Melinda with obvious respect.

"It's chemical. There's nothing she can do to control it, and we don't have the medicine she needs here in Stonefall. I don't know how we can get it. Bipolar brains don't operate like other brains … The Lord's made them different. Medication and treatment both work, but …"

"Does Bailey *believe?*"

"Bailey Jensen is a good person," Melinda answered.

"But has she accepted the Lord into her heart? Not just said the words, but felt the Light?"

Melinda shook her head. "I can't presume to know what is in another person's heart."

"Of course not. But you know what you feel and think. That's what I am asking you. *Do you think Bailey Jensen has accepted God into her heart?* This is not an idle question, Melinda. It is important we save the righteous first. Perhaps even essential to our survival."

"But why? No disrespect, Father, but shouldn't we be saving the sickest people first? To strengthen our community so it can grow? Isn't that what you asked me to do?"

Melinda didn't like the taste in her mouth, the way her skin was starting to prickle, or the scent in the air, pregnant with danger. The ground was thin ice and eggshells. Like always, she couldn't help but feel every question was designed to test her loyalty or intelligence.

"Yes. That is exactly what I asked you to do. And we must strengthen our community so we can grow, one individual at a time. Thank you for reminding me of my words. But I don't mind telling you," Gleeson leaned forward as if to tell her a secret, "the interpretations of the Bible surrounding the Second Coming and the Tribulations are wrong."

"Oh?" Melinda didn't know how she could possibly respond, this man presuming to know God's truth, even after millennia of better men transcribing it.

"I have had other visions, and I will share with you now what I will soon be revealing to all of Stonefall. *God is here now, and He is Judging us.*"

Gleeson gave her a moment to let that sink in, then finished telling her why Bailey Jensen wasn't good enough for his help.

"Those who are good will usher in a thousand years of

peace. Some will be granted long lives, and others who have perished will be resurrected. Like Percy, perhaps. Imagine enjoying a thousand years of peace with your Percy while the rest of humanity stands in line for Judgment."

Another moment trapped between the margins. Did she take Gleeson at his word, that he wanted to hear what she had to say and respected her opinion, same as he reminded her every time he requested she come by? Or did she follow her fears and hedge her arguments, knowing the hammer would eventually fall?

She thought about what Percy would have wanted her to do and realized that at least here in this moment, she couldn't do anything else. Not after this monster had raised his name from the grave just to help him get his way.

"But if they're already righteous, then won't God save them anyway? Shouldn't we focus on bringing the sinners around and showing them the error of their ways?"

Melinda's heart was pounding out of her chest. Two simple questions and she may have failed the test, setting herself up for exile or worse.

Yet, Gleeson didn't look upset. With a smile he said, "I believe it's our duty to create new cities devoted to God. Heavens on Earth where men, women, and children of righteous faith will live as one with the angels."

"That is a beautiful vision, Father. But do you see any room for mercy and forgiveness in this new world of ours?"

"Of course. The Lord is merciful."

"But are we forgiving enough in Stonefall?"

The question caught Gleeson off guard. Melinda might have gone too far.

"Why are asking?"

"There are some among your Flock who worry about

Kirk and some of the others exiling people for mere disagreements."

He leaned back again and gave the corner another inspection. The expression on his face seemed to say *Fair point.*

"Do people fear me?" Gleeson finally asked.

Melinda hesitated, but only for a second before giving him an honest nod.

But then he said, "Do *you* fear me?"

And Melinda had no idea how to answer that. Did the Father of Stonefall want to be feared or loved? Thinking about the time he lost it on stage, pacing back and forth with blood dripping from the tip of his rebar, bashing in a child's head in front of his father while most of his supposed Flock foamed at the mouth.

It had been a horrible show, and if not for that garish presentation, they might not ever have *needed* to leave.

Melinda remembered the rebar coming down onto Andrew's head, the blood, his friends and family aghast, Percy wanting to race onto the stage. She had to pull him back then, just as she had to pull herself back now.

Of course she feared him. Only The Foresaken terrified her more. But she could never tell the Father of the Stonefall such a thing to his face.

So instead she said, "No, I do not fear you, Father."

"Should anyone fear me?"

"The wicked, of course."

"And you have never feared me? It is okay to say yes, Melinda. I am asking for your truth, after all." Like everything else he said, it sounded like a test.

"I have never been afraid of you, no. But I do confess to being nervous." Then before he could ask and perhaps peer a bit too deeply into her heart, she said, "Like the time when you had to … make an example of those people on stage."

She swallowed, couldn't help it, had to add, "… and that child."

"Of course." Compassion found his face. Gleeson reached across the open space between them and took Melinda's hands. "You had every reason to feel shaken. That was a terrible night. But you must understand, that wasn't a child. It was an enemy waiting to kill us. That had to be done for the safety of us all, and even if I was loathe to do it, the task fell to me as the Father of Stonefall."

Her memory wasn't a liar, and there was nothing this monster had loathed about his swinging rebar that night.

"I understand. Percy always said you were a good man. He never doubted it. Not for a moment, and especially that night. He had never felt more devout. Said you didn't delight in killing anyone, especially someone so young, but it was your job to protect us all."

Melinda wiped at an intentional tear.

"Maybe if we had caught their kind earlier, Percy would still be with us."

"But someone will say, 'You have faith and I have works.' Show me your faith apart from your works, and I will show you my faith by my works."

"I'm sorry?"

"Sometimes the only thing to do is that which must be done. Thank you, Melinda, for having this talk with me. I gave you my trust and asked you to find me the worthiest people. I believe that Bailey Jensen is in need of saving. Please make sure she is ready to join us onstage during tonight's sermon."

Gleeson stood, motioned to Melinda it was time to leave, then led her toward the door.

She spent the rest of the day with Bailey, making no

promises as to what might happen during the sermon because Melinda wasn't even sure of what she believed herself. But she did want to prepare the girl as much as she could for the thing that none of them understood.

Then it was finally time for the sermon, and her body was humming. Not so much consumed by flames as smothered by smoldering coals that had nothing to do with the fire keeping them warm through the show.

She held Bailey's hand as they waited through his scripture, Gleeson every so often meeting their gazes and giving them a smile, obviously pleased about what was coming. But Melinda had spent all day talking to Bailey and knew in her heart more than ever that Gleeson or Kirk or any of the higher ranking Brothers would have cast her out of Stonefall after one honest conversation.

At twenty-four, Bailey had already been with ninety-four partners, most of them paid. That's when she stopped, figuring there were at least a few she probably couldn't remember or forgot to count, and if she hit a hundred before her twenty-fifth birthday, she'd have to kill herself.

Bailey grew up with more privilege than most, with her dad owning a contracting company and winning a load of contracts. But her parents got divorced her first year at Montana State and sent her world into a tailspin. A stupid reason, maybe, but Bailey was bipolar and didn't take it well. Crack helped for about five minutes. Then she was paying for her habit with tricks. Bailey made good money before she started looking like a literal crack whore. She decided on early retirement and would've earned her one-year chip if the meeting hadn't been on Astral Day.

Gleeson's sermon was almost over, and Melinda still hadn't seen Kirk. His absence made her nervous, but then, so did everything else about the man. Angel was standing on the other side of the stage area, holding the child. It seemed slightly larger than the last time Melinda had seen the baby, or creature, or whatever it was. Perhaps it was an innocent child like everyone seemed to believe. But she couldn't help thinking it might be a demon, since a devil like Gleeson wanted to hold it so close.

"Melinda!" Gleeson snapped her out of her reverie. "Who among the Stonefall faithful is most in need of healing?"

"Bailey Jensen," she said, raising Bailey's hand in hers and squeezing it yet again at the top.

Gleeson turned to Angel, inviting her and the baby forward.

Melinda approached the stage with Bailey, ignoring both the shivers through her body and the way the child was eyeing her, looking *through* her, almost radiating some sort of …

Something changed.

It was Bailey's turn, but the baby reached for Melinda. She stared at her hand as though she had no control of its movement, watching it drift closer to William, until they were touching and it was like a circuit was closed between them.

I just want you to know I will always love you.

Percy spoke inside her mind.

She was shaken. Stunned. Outside of herself.

Relax. Everything will be okay.

Either Melinda was losing her mind, or right now she was fielding two miracles at once.

Chapter Twenty-Five

Rosa had always loved Montana winters. But even cold as it was outside their vehicle, this one was Hell on Earth.

She usually looked forward to seeing wild bison roaming the snow-capped mountains, traipsing through countless acres of unspoiled frontier, a winter wonderland like even the best of Hollywood couldn't ever hope to capture, taking in the steaming hot springs that cleared her sinuses and her soul.

Rosa preferred it in the south, Yellowstone over Glacier Country, and this time of year she was used to seeing the best of it. Some of the rangers moonlit at SnoWay, a coaching company that let part-time adventurers explore the majesty of Yellowstone in the winter without facing exposure to the bitter elements or having to strap snow-shoes to their feet. A bit like a tour bus, but with heavy tufty wheels that could handle the cold weather terrain.

Rosa was one such ranger, taking tourists to see Old Faithful, Steamboat Geyser, and Gibbon Falls. This year, she missed it. The clomping of their horses in the snow felt like an unlikely reminder and oddly lonely.

"You're not saying much."

Rosa looked at Mikey. "Aren't you the one who's always telling me to shut the hell up and that I talk too much?"

"He's just bored," Paul explained. "We were playing spot the animal, but he doesn't know any of them."

"No," Rosa agreed, smiling at Paul. "He doesn't."

Mikey rolled his eyes. "Oh, I'm dumb because I don't know the difference between a marmot and a hoary marmot."

"No," Paul said, "You're dumb for a lot of reasons. That just makes you inattentive."

"What's on your mind," Rosa asked.

"I don't have anything on my mind."

"Okay." She wasn't going to argue. If he wanted to talk, great, they could talk. Otherwise, Rosa was going to keep right on walking, wishing she could be soaking in hot springs or chowing down on barbecue bison. Anything would be better than the freeze-dried chili mac and beef, which didn't taste like even one of the three.

He wasn't silent long. "How bad do you think it's going to get? I mean the pneumonia and everything else?"

"I'm not sure how to answer that, Mikey. It's a lung infection, and that can be severe or mild depending on a lot of factors. But you know as well as I do, we're dealing with a lot of variables completely out of our control. Are you asking about the Reserve, or about Katrina specifically?"

"It's Miguel, Rosa."

"Fine. Miguel, is this about Katrina?"

"Of course it is."

Rosa sighed and even felt bad for the kid. She'd never seen a puppy so in love. "Katrina's alveoli have filled with fluid. There might be pus in her lungs, but right now we have no way of knowing. That can make it almost impossible for her to breathe enough oxygen into her bloodstream. Fortunately, she's strong. She's not too young or too old, and if this had been a year ago, she probably never would have caught it. Even if she had, it would have been a trip to the doctor to put it behind her. Problem is, because she's young and seemingly healthy, she had walking pneumonia for a while. We didn't know, and now it might be in both of her lungs."

It was all information he already knew, but Rosa figured it must be doing him some sort of good to be talking about it. He was looking at her intently, hanging on every word, maybe hoping one of them might offer some glimmer of possibility he'd never considered before.

"And medicine might take care of it? The right antibiotics?" Two questions that were more like affirmations.

Paul looked over at his best friend in sympathy.

Rosa said, "Yes. That's what we would hope."

"But the chances are good … if we get the medicine from Stonefall?"

Rosa nodded and gave him a *yes*, though she hated how much he made it feel like a promise.

"What happens if they won't give us anything? If we get there and this Gleeson guy just turns us away, like he did to you and Rebecca the last time?"

"That was a different situation. And what else do you want me to do? We're going there, and right now that's our best chance."

"I know. It's just, I'm wondering if we can't get any medicine, how likely is that more people will die? Could it wipe us all out?"

"No, it won't wipe us out, no matter how bad it gets. Pneumonia isn't that kind of sickness. Right now, the infected are quarantined, and we've also isolated those connected to them separately, so—"

"But Katrina could die, right?"

Rosa was hesitant to answer, but it wasn't like she could ignore the question. "Yes, she could die, but even if we get back to The Reserve without any medicine, she's strong. She'll make it through this. You have to believe me."

Rosa was working to believe it herself.

"Even if it doesn't kill her, or any of us, what about the next sickness? What about the next winter, or the one after that? We need a doctor and more meds. We'll die without both."

"Of course, man," Paul said, trying to reassure his friend. "That's why we're on our way to Stonefall now."

"But we all know that's a long shot," Mikey continued to argue. "What happens when we're turned away?"

"*If* we're turned away," Rosa corrected.

Mikey didn't amend his statement. Just kept waiting on her answer instead.

"We'll figure it out. We always do."

But that wasn't good enough for her brother.

"I mean, what are you going to do, Rosa? What are *you* willing to do to get what we need?"

"We'll cross that bridge when we get there."

"Well done is better than well said," Mikey scoffed. "And that wasn't even well said."

Rosa had been patient, holding it together despite her brother being a little dick and blaming shit on her that wasn't even remotely her fault. "You know what, Mikey?"

"Um, guys ..." Paul said, then when Rosa didn't respond immediately he started tugging on her sleeve and pointing ahead, off to the side of their vehicle near a bend in the road and an upcoming bridge.

Rosa spied it too, and immediately slowed. "Fuck."

"What is it?" Mikey asked, even though he could see the same thing as both of them.

"I have no idea." Rosa rode her horse to the bridge, stopped where it started, then dismounted.

The boys followed.

No one bothered her while she surveyed the situation, and after looking long enough to have some idea of what she was seeing, Rosa turned back to the boys and nodded to two SUVs on the bridge below, about a half mile away.

"I don't see Braxton, but that's definitely The Forsaken. And it looks like they're on their way to Stonefall, too."

"So what do we do?" Mikey asked. "Now that we're at a literal bridge to cross?"

And Rosa said, "We follow their trail as best we can."

Chapter Twenty-Six

"That shit wasn't cool," Felony said.

Liam ignored him, no surprise. It would be that way for a while. The rest of tonight, tomorrow, maybe the day after. However long the little dick-headed prince felt like pouting about it.

"We won't get far. It took all four of us to build that shelter. What do you suggest we do now?"

"Find a place," Liam said. "Where's that warehouse? We should've stuck with trying to find it in the first place, instead of sleeping under a tree in the goddamned snow."

"I told you. I lost my way, I don't know where the warehouse is."

"We'll find it." After a beat, he added, "And I'm sorry, okay? I just can't be around my brother right now."

That was about as close as Liam ever came to an apology, and a lot more than Felony expected, especially as bitter and cold as it was, with them tromping through the snow and an icy wind biting into their faces.

Felony didn't believe in miracles, regardless of the nonsense they were hearing from Stonefall. But maybe he should be more openminded. Because at the edge of a blizzard, moments after Felony gave them no better than fifty-fifty odds of making it through the night without at the very least losing a few fingers or toes, there it was like a beacon before them.

As before, the building was empty, though this time it looked like someone had recently been there then moved out fast. The many rows of shelves were still full of little if anything that could help them. The space was the premium this real estate had to offer, and that was saying a lot. Even without any heat running, it felt thirty degrees warmer inside, with plenty of room to stretch out. Hell, you could host a battle royale in the place.

But there were some supplies still lying around the floor, including a two-thirds full rather large bottle of vodka.

Felony looked at the bottle then back at Liam. "Think anyone's coming for that?"

Liam bent down, grabbed the vodka, and started to unscrew the lid. "We'll say sorry if they do."

They laid their packs and their weapons on the floor, sat, then started to drink.

Chapter Twenty-Seven

"WE'RE NOT BETTER OFF," Eamon insisted.

"Well, I think we are." Sherry crossed her arms, seemingly desperate for the two of them to agree, but still not willing to fold.

"Even if I agreed about Liam, Felony's gone too."

"We made it for months without him."

"Sure, with Jefferson and Jolie. I'd be dead for sure. You, too, probably."

"We'll be fine," Sherry said. "I know it."

"You can't just *know it.* You—"

"I've known things."

Eamon sighed. Even if Sherry had the sharpest instincts of anyone he'd ever met, except maybe Poppy, they were alone in the freezing cold, in a shitty shelter, on a stretch of highway that had been tormented by bandits and worse for months, ten long miles from a place where they might get slaughtered at the gates, if the worst of the rumors were true.

"You have. But I'm just talking about the reality here. My brother's an asshole, but—

"Oh, he's more than that."

"He's capable. You heard how he got out of that scrape in Billings. Anyone else would've been dead like my Dad. He walked out of there leaving bodies behind him.

"Good for Liam."

"I understand how you feel," And he really, truly did. "But there's another side to him. I saw it that first night and so did you. Remember? We went to bed laughing, and you said, 'I didn't know I could actually like someone who's so obviously an asshole inside and out.'"

"Wait. Are you serious?" Sherry took a moment to look at him hard. Only after he blinked did she finish her thought. "You're saying I still thought he was an asshole, even after he was at his very best, on the very first night, when I wasn't used to his shit, which got so old in record time that it's already ancient?"

"You don't have to convince me that my brother is a dick. I know him well, and I'm with you, a hundred percent. But at least for now, we need to stay safe and find William. Even not taking into account that Liam is family, having him with us increases our odds of success in the thing we're trying to do."

"Well, I don't agree." Sherry sounded matter of fact rather than pissed. She reached out and took his hands. "Let's talk about something else, okay? Like, do you think we can make it to Stonefall tomorrow, if we start as soon as it's light?"

"I'm not even sure we should try."

"What? You're saying we should give up?"

"No, of course not. But our food and supplies were in the Jeep. We have the weapons we negotiated, but that's a crossbow, two knives, and a bow between us. Everything else, including the guns, are with Felony and my brother. Ten miles might be too long to make it in a day. I don't think we'll clear more than a mile an hour, and that's with steady walking and no breaks. Days are short, and the snow is deep. We don't know what's going to find us on the road. Or—"

"That's just a list of obstacles, Eamon. I'm not hearing you suggest any of the ways we could get around them. What are we supposed to do, go back to the Cottage? That's a lot farther than Stonefall!"

"I don't think we should go back. At least not unless we find a car or something. But we can take a day to regroup. Instead of heading into Stonefall, we can track Felony and Liam."

The last part came out almost mumbled because she'd hate it.

"No, Eamon. We can make it to Stonefall without them. Why waste a day going sideways when Felony already said he'd work on Liam and meet us there? If you want to hook back up with your asshole brother, *fine*. But—"

Sherry didn't have to ask Eamon if he heard that, because of course he did.

They stared at each other, neither of them daring to speak. Their fingers threaded together, hearts probably pounding in time.

That noise outside was a reminder of exactly how vulnerable they were. Their shelter could be surrounded, and there wouldn't be anything they could do except wait for an attack.

And now the sounds were in stereo. A heavy clomping, followed by a deafening *BOOM!* Over and over in a way that Eamon found himself thinking of *verse-chorus-verse.*

He leaned into Sherry and whispered, "I'm going to check it out."

"No," she whisper shouted back. "You can't leave me. *Please.*"

"I have to."

"You can't. It's too dark. You won't be able to see anything, anyway."

"I'll be careful, but I have to know what's out there. You know what could happen if we're surrounded."

After a long, long pause, Eamon felt Sherry's tears on his cheek as she whispered, *"Please don't leave me."*

So, he didn't. But the paralysis was a struggle. The labor of inaction almost too much. It burned in his body, made his muscles itch and his hair stand on end. Noises kept getting closer. Every fresh decibel heightened the threat.

Until Eamon could no longer take it.

He pulled her into an embrace, heart to heart and cheek to cheek. *"I love you, Sherry. But everything inside me right now is telling me I have to go. I promise I'm not leaving you. I'm keeping you safe."*

Then without giving her a chance to respond, Eamon slipped out of their shelter and darted deeper into the woods.

He wasn't a hundred steps from the shelter when regret began to set in.

What had he been thinking? Sherry was right. It was pitch black outside, and his flashlight was in the Jeep.

Except ... in the distance, something was glowing. Eamon didn't know if he would ever be able to explain what he was feeling, but there was a shining in his mind to match the one in his eyes, and every step made it stronger.

He was almost compelled, pulled so his feet were moving toward the light of their own accord.

The closer he got, the more open he felt. His heart, his mind, his very soul was soaking up the world around him.

Eamon felt a deep truth and a bottomless gratitude. For the world had not been swallowed by darkness—the light had come to give their planet a chance.

Beautiful. Enthralling.

Mesmerizing.

Eamon followed his heart and his mind and his soul until he finally reached the light. There, he stopped dead in his tracks then fell to one knee, crouched behind a Douglas fir wide enough to hide him.

Aliens. A whole mess of them. Titans, the ones that looked almost human. Perfect bodies, rippling with muscles. Powder white, only slightly grayer than the snow.

They were piling rocks on either side of the highway. Eamon had no idea where they came from, and each of the solid rock sheets had to weigh at least a ton. They were being carried one at a time by a pair of aliens, one on each side, laying the rocks like bricks in a wall.

Eamon was transfixed. He couldn't stop watching. What were they building and what did it mean?

He swallowed a startled gasp, not of danger but of recognition. This was the clearing where William had been born, where his Poppy lost her life, and where Sherry became a mother.

Eamon turned back, rehearsing the story in his head. What was he going to tell Sherry?

There's nothing to worry about. Those loud crashes were just the aliens stacking rocks on either side of the highway. Like two walls, blocking nothing. No … I have no idea what it could mean … and yes, it's the same place we went after Astral Day, but—

Eamon froze as two things happened at once. He heard the snapping of branches and boots in the snow, along with the distant chatter of voices. Both under and over it, he felt something screaming inside his mind.

It wasn't a new experience, it was the hum he sometimes heard between Sherry and himself, but this was more like a dying battery had been plugged into the wall. And along with the telltale sounds of danger — men in the woods between Eamon and the shelter — he felt Sherry's fear like the fluttering of a hummingbird's wings.

He wove through the forest, fast as he dared, his heart beating harder with every meter gained. He counted the flashlights and imagined her fear, wanted to stop the waves of terror rolling through his mind.

He needed to help, but Eamon had only his crossbow and the knife. Plus his fists, of course, and they could do plenty up close, but he would need to get near enough to use them, then pray it would be enough against the dozen men he could see, and however many were still buried in shadows surrounding the shelter.

Eamon drew his crossbow and aimed.

Chapter Twenty-Eight

AT SOME POINT the noises changed.

Became something else, more dangerous.

When Eamon left, Sherry wanted to scream. It was almost too much. Deafening silence, followed but a brutal-sounding scraping and a terrible crash. That same song kept playing on repeat, and after a while Sherry finally decided to surrender. When she did, it was beautiful. Even loud, the sounds were a lullaby.

A warmth spread through her body. Like light, but inside. And with her eyes closed, she could see Eamon. Sherry had no idea if what she was seeing behind her shuttered lids was true, but it was cast in the most brilliant colors she could ever imagine. Better than reality. She was peering through Eamon's eyes, peeking from behind a big tree and watching those giant white aliens pull giant rocks from two matching mountains to build what looked like a pair of twin towers on either side of the highway.

There was something so familiar about the place. So welcoming. A sanctuary for rebirth, or a repository of knowledge. Maybe both.

She tried to keep her mind on the light, but darkness seeped through the cracks. There was no fire, and that made it hard not to think about freezing to death. She knew it was unlikely, but worry was a festering wound. Sherry wanted to keep picturing those beautiful towers and Eamon swaddled in their glow, but instead she saw herself surrounded by teenage boys, circling her, turning into men.

Braxton, that man with the bare chest and leather. The way he looked at her, and the way his eyes gave the rest of his men permission. She swallowed, tried to get back to the light, sweating even in the freeze as she shook her head, working to expel the strobing images of them taking turns, using her, *hurting her* and—

There's nothing to worry about. Those loud crashes were just the aliens stacking rocks on either side of the highway. Like two walls, blocking nothing. No … I have no idea what it could mean … and yes, it's the same place we went after Astral Day, but—

Eamon's intrusion into her mind — or Sherry simply losing it — was interrupted by sounds that had nothing to do with moving rocks and were a little too far from the highway, coming from outside the shelter.

He'll be back any minute … he'll be back any minute … he'll be back any minute …

Over and over, a mantra in her mind, and because she needed it with all of that black and white swallowing the world, Sherry added some color.

He'll be back any minute, and then we'll be safe.

We'll get to Stonefall, where help will be waiting.

A reunion with Sweet William followed by the rest of our lives together.

It will just be the three of us, and that's exactly how it should be.

Sherry imagined them as a happy family together. A simple vision. They could live a good life in that Cottage. Who cared if there were aliens in the sky — she had seen into their light and knew they meant her no harm. Same for Eamon. Neither of them had darkness in their souls. Even the reptars, looking and moving like a midnight of insects, wouldn't want to feast on an empty meal like Sherry or Eamon.

Not when they could chew through the decomposing souls of the men she felt like the threat of a blizzard a few feet outside.

The noises grew closer and louder.

Sherry kept silently repeating that mantra to herself, the only thing that could keep her from screaming.

Then, the sounds were right outside her shelter. Sherry heard a laugh she recognized, having felt a marrow-deep chill when it left those bloodthirsty bandits earlier that day.

The walls shook, then Braxton, now also in a long fur coat, entered her shelter.

Sherry finally screamed.

Chapter Twenty-Nine

Eamon felt Sherry's shriek like he'd shoved his finger into an outlet.

He wanted to yell himself, but he bit his lip instead.

Blood filled his mouth, faster than he would have expected. He swallowed what was there, licking the metallic taste from his lips.

He told himself to relax. Nothing could have happened to her yet. Mad Max just went inside. Eamon couldn't get a shot off. Even after he saw Braxton sauntering toward the shelter, flashlights illuminating his long fur coat, the man was walking too fast and surrounded by the bulk of bodies. Even Eamon's best shot would be wasted. There was no way to hit Braxton, and Eamon wasn't willing to settle for one of his lackeys.

But now, with the leader inside and Sherry screaming, Eamon wondered what the fuck he'd been thinking?

He needed to get closer, so he crept in the snow, quietly as he could, taking long seconds he couldn't afford in between every step, because standing still was much too expensive.

Braxton dragged Sherry out of the shelter. He'd been inside for maybe three minutes, and that was good. The screaming quieted after the first several seconds, and Eamon imagined he was using the quiet to threaten her before bringing her out for a show.

By the time she was standing vulnerable in front of the bandits, Eamon was crouched just three trees away.

Braxton turned to his men. "She says she has no idea where her friends are. It's just her in this shelter alone."

"You build that all by yourself, sweetie?" yelled one of the bandits.

Then someone else asked, "It big enough for two of us at a time?"

A chorus of laughter erupted, followed by a third voice. "Or maybe three."

More laughter.

"Why don't you tell me where your friends are?" Braxton sounded almost pleasant. Like it was a simple question, not laced with an obvious threat.

"I told you, I don't know. Two of them marched off a couple of hours ago. The other one stomped off after we got into a fight."

"Hmmm …" Braxton said, looking genuinely thoughtful. "I believe exactly half of that."

He moved ever so slightly to the side, but it was just enough. For the first time, Eamon's view of Sherry was unimpeded, and he could see the terror in her eyes that she was trying not to show.

Braxton continued. "You're asking me to believe you're so hard to get along with that you've driven three able-bodied men away from what has to be some of the pinkest pussy in this part of Montana?" Braxton shook his head. "I don't buy it. I *can't* buy it. Not after the way I saw you and that boy eying each other — the one who looked like the asshole's kid brother." A big smile. "That's right, sweetie. I see things. So, where's your boyfriend now? And is he still carrying that crossbow?"

After Sherry didn't answer, Braxton stepped toward her, speaking lower so Eamon strained to hear him. "Let's set some ground rules. We'll tell one another the truth, no matter what. Starting now. So, honey, you wanna tell me your name?"

In a trembling voice she said, "Sherry."

"Well, isn't that pretty. And how about your boyfriend, what's his name?"

Braxton was back to blocking Eamon's view, but he could imagine Sherry furiously shaking her head, refusing to answer.

It's okay. My name doesn't mean anything. You can tell him.

Sherry hiccuped, then in an uncertain voice said, "It's Eamon."

Braxton looked back at his men, clearly pleased. Then he turned back to Sherry. "Excellent job. Now, there are two ways you can spend the rest of your life. As a willing part of our family — and I promise it's a coveted spot. You can live a better life than just about anyone, if you're willing to live it with us. There are a few among The Forsaken who like it when their women are fighters, but most of us had girlfriends or wives before all of this and prefer to remember."

He took Sherry by her arm, pulling her away from the shelter and into a common space. The men fell back, giving Braxton an open circle, making it feel to Eamon like the man was about to auction her off.

At least now maybe he could get a shot off.

"I'm surprised to find you out here. And I can't help but see it as providence. We let you go once, no harm, no foul. But running into a sweet piece like this *twice in one day*

... and now you're all alone? Am I really supposed to ignore the signs?"

Eamon had Braxton in his sites. He could pull the trigger, send the bolt from his crossbow into the asshole's forehead and sever The Forsaken's head. But things would be worse for Sherry.

Braxton continued to prove it. "Like I said, it's up to you. We have a place nearby, and we're gonna take you there now, whether you like it or not. It's a helluva lot warmer than this, and we can keep you safe. It's up to you, Sherry — you can leave this shelter willingly and give us what we need when we get home, or we can take you forcibly either place then kill you when we're done."

He waited a beat, then finished like he was asking Sherry if she cared for cream in her coffee. "Do you have a preference?

Go. Stay safe. I'll follow you.

Eamon had no idea if Sherry could hear him, but he was believing in the idea that they were sharing thoughts more with every real or imagined exchange. But Sherry was smart enough to stay alive, because even if Eamon was only muttering inside his own mind, she was already following Braxton to his SUV.

They loaded her up, destroyed the shelter, and killed twenty minutes or so waiting for Eamon to show.

One of Braxton's men eventually yelled, "How long do you want us to stay?"

He answered by calling into the forest. "Our friend Eamon has made his home in the shadows, and so like a coward, he has surrendered his spoils to us."

Eamon looked at the four SUVs, double what they'd seen at the roadblock before, with Olive now making vehicle number five. He waited for everyone to get inside and for all of the engines to start. He had been staring at the final one in the line for a while, grateful for the grating on back. As soon as the front car started to roll forward, Eamon crept the rest of the way from his tree to the vehicle's rear.

He grabbed on and clung to the frozen metal for his life, knowing it was for Sherry's, as well.

Chapter Thirty

Felony waited for the vodka to warm them a bit before finally stating the obvious. "You know, we could've worked things out back at the shelter. That sort of shit was dumb enough back in Billings, but now it's just stupid."

Liam took a swig from the bottle then laughed. "Aren't dumb and stupid pretty much the same thing?"

"There are degrees. And what you did back there is an order of magnitude stupider than any dumb shit I saw you do back in the day, given the circumstances of who we need to be now."

"Then why are you here?"

"You know I'm loyal, man. But you put me on the spot. What was I supposed to do? I wasn't about to let you get your fool self killed."

"And I appreciate it," Liam said, then surprised Felony with his second apology of the night. "I'm sorry, really. My brother just royally pisses me off."

"You need to put that shit behind you. Your father is gone."

"Maybe," Liam said, with what sounded an awful lot like a *yes*. "You know I love him, right?"

It was an odd thing for Liam to say. Eamon and Sherry said it plenty. But Liam only used the word *love* when talking about alcohol, drugs, money, and women. And never the women themselves, so much as the nefarious things he wanted to do to them.

"I know," Felony said.

But then Liam started to tell him a story, as if he needed to prove it.

"Have I ever told you about the gingerbread house?"

He had, but Liam wasn't looking for Felony to answer, talking mostly to himself. But he kept going, with barely a pause for breath after asking his question.

"Our mom was really into making gingerbread houses every year when I was growing up, before Eamon was born. We made them every Christmas. Me, Dad, and Mom. She had made them with her mom when she was young. She kept them, you know. The icing gets hard, but she always bought good candy and the houses were well made. After she died, Dad decided to keep them. Put the whole damn collection in the sewing room with a mess of her other stuff he couldn't bear to throw away but never wanted to see or think about because it hurt too much. So, when Eamon was like six or seven, Dad went into the room one day found there was a shit ton of candy missing from the houses. Just a little here and there, one or two pieces taken at a time, but enough taken through the years that the damage was noticeable."

Liam paused, this time actually needing the breath.

"Dad never even asked. He assumed it must've been Eamon sneaking into Mom's old sewing room and stealing all that candy. It couldn't have been me since I was there when we made them. I knew how special they were, how important they had been to her and still were to him. I was already a teenager, or close to it, and I sure as hell knew better. Even though Eamon never made one of those houses with us, he would've never dared to do anything so disrespectful. The couple of times I tried getting him to take a piece of candy, he refused. I'm not even sure why I did it. Something else to get away with, I suppose."

Another breath, another swig of vodka.

"Anyway, Dad just started pounding on him. The three of us were in the living room and I couldn't believe it. Dad was so big and Eamon was so small, and our dad just kept whaling on him, over and over and over, screaming, asking Eamon why he'd done it." Liam choked. "It was so relentless."

Felony delivered the punchline he'd heard a few times before. "And Eamon never said a word about it. Not during the beating, not right after it, and not at any other time since. He kept it to himself."

"Because that's the kind of guy my brother's always been," Liam took the ball. "So you gotta understand, I know who he is. And even though some of what I'm doing is admittedly me being a shit, some of it really is me trying to save Eamon from himself."

Felony gave him a moment, letting the story settle before saying what had to be said.

"Come on, man, it's just you and me in here. The two of us and that bottle of vodka. You trying to convince me that stomping off and leaving everyone to fend for themselves at a time like this was really the best way to handle it?"

Liam didn't answer, stubborn like always.

"So sitting here in this warehouse, the four of us split up, you really think this was our best move?"

"He threw the first punch. You saw it."

"Yeah, after you said that thing about Sherry. I wanted to deck you, too."

"You know where the door is." Liam gave it a glance in case he didn't. "Hope you can find your way back. Seems like your compass is a little wobbly these days."

"See, that's exactly what I'm talking about." Felony shook his head. "How was that necessary?"

"We're just having a conversation."

"That what this is?"

Silence lingered for a while after that, marked by two swallows from Felony and another three from Liam. They stared at one other, each of them knowing the standoff couldn't last.

What could possibly be the point in dragging it out?

"You were being stubborn and you know it. You're also rationalizing bullying your brother, saying you're doing it for his own good when it's really all about you."

"I am doing it for his own good."

"Maybe. But that's a chip in the cookie. I think the truth is simpler than that. Something you don't want to admit, despite you spending most of your life working not to like it's a full-time job."

"That right, Freud? Tell me more about how I feel. About all the little things I won't admit to myself."

"Gladly." Then Felony said what he had never been able to say out loud to Liam before, though he'd thought it occasionally over the years, then plenty once he was patrolling the dark nights outside their Cottage. "I think there have been times when you wanted to leave the family, too. And I think your father always terrified you, no matter how much you loved him. I think you admire Eamon, and that there are more than a few ways you even wish you could be more like him. But it's easier to act like you hate him. It hurts less. It makes you—"

"It isn't just a philosophical difference, Felony. Eamon's weak, and if we're traveling with him, then that makes us equally feeble. This isn't an argument about which way is right. It's the fact that Eamon needs to toughen the fuck up. You're only defending him because —"

"I'm defending him because he's right, Liam. At least this time, he is. And I'm not gonna pretend like I don't think you know it. Your brother's an idealist, sure. A Boy Scout, yes. But that doesn't make him weak."

"What do you know about it? I'm the one who grew up with him."

"And I grew up with you. I'd argue that right now I know Eamon better than you do. I spent half of this last year with your brother, driving him out to that cabin after you ambushed him. I watched his wife get smashed underneath a rock, then die a dozen times himself. But then he dusted himself off and picked up his son. Went on with his life. He didn't turn to darkness or violence like your father. And he didn't go out binge drinking and shoving his dick into anything he could find like we both know you would've. He acted like a man. So, my best suggestion to you, Liam, is to cut him some motherfucking slack."

Liam's face relaxed into something that looked almost thoughtful. He opened his mouth, but then it closed like a trap door shutting. His eyes went wide, and he was suddenly on his feet, jumping past Felony and racing to the window.

"What is it?" Felony asked, suddenly on high alert.

"I don't know. Maybe this is their place."

Felony stood beside Liam, both of them looking out the window at headlights piercing the darkness.

Four trucks, and men piling out of them.

"Fuck," Liam said.

Felony was already on his way to the weapons.

Chapter Thirty-One

When the SUV stopped, Eamon dropped into the snow.

A fast glance around, then he dashed behind the nearest tree.

They were at a warehouse that looked a lot like the one Felony described, the one they'd all been looking for earlier, before they built the shelter and had their big blowout.

The bandits disembarked, then Braxton took the lead. He was nearly out of earshot, but still talking loud enough that Eamon heard him say, "You know what to do. Search the place and kill any men you find inside. Save the rest."

He waited until they were all inside, surprised they didn't even leave a guard at the door, before leaving his tree to look for a second entrance. Maybe the guard was unnecessary. There probably weren't many people like Eamon around, willing to tackle a small army of murderous bandits by himself, hoping to rescue the woman he loved.

But doubt began to grab and taunt him, ask him if he had any idea what the fuck he was doing. Because he would probably die here, trying and failing to save Sherry.

And then what would happen to his son? His mother was taken when he was born and someone was there to take her place. Would the same thing happen to Eamon?

He circled around to the back of the warehouse and found plenty of doors, the third one unlocked. He lowered the flat handled knob, his heart out of control, wondering if the scent of pine would be the last thing in his nostrils as he swung the door open to whatever danger was waiting.

But there were only shadows, and Eamon slipped into them like the wearing of a blanket.

By the time he climbed onto the top of a metal shelf, the front one among a row of many, where he could look down at the action from below, Sherry was being led into the middle of a circle, much like the one Braxton had walked her into outside the shelter.

Eamon adjusted his crossbow, aimed it at Braxton, trying to keep his finger from trembling against the trigger.

The warehouse was cold, but nowhere near freezing like it was outside, and apparently warm enough for Braxton to surrender his coat. Maybe it was his imagination, and it could have been a product of the flickering light, but Eamon thought the leather armor had a few spots of fresh blood that hadn't been on it earlier.

He offered his coat to Sherry.

She hesitantly took it. Even though she had layers, it was a massive shroud of fur on her much smaller frame, and big enough to swallow all of her coating.

His voice had lost some of its menace and threat. Almost seemed reasonable. Definitely warmer.

"I want you to understand, this is an opportunity. Can we agree to start there?"

Sherry nodded.

"By nature of our vocation, men outnumber our women. Those men have needs. You're valuable, especially if I can keep you from getting banged up. And that includes in here."

Braxton touched the top of his temple, then leered at Sherry's body.

"Some of the older or uglier women can be fucked in the head. That's fine. But you're a peach, and I'd prefer you free of bruises. Only you're in control of that. You play nice, I'll play nice back. Can we agree we'd both like to keep your body unblemished and your mind free from trauma?"

Sherry nodded again, looking one flinch away from a whimper.

"Normally, things will be different. Just like any other quality working girl, we'll give you your own space, and your own schedule. My men will have to make an appointment, and on the rare occasion we use your services in trade for things our tribe might need, then our men at home will make the sacrifice. More won't be added to your bed. One an hour is fair, give or take. We have many men back home, and they'll all need to wait their turn."

Braxton stroked Sherry's cheek, up and down a few times, maybe waiting until the first tear fell, which of course it eventually did.

"But tonight will be different. You've excited a lot of my guys, and it isn't fair of me to make them wait. I let you go once today, and some of the men weren't happy. Right boys?"

Rumbles and grumbles of assent, all of them sounding somehow craven and pleased.

"Don't worry. You won't have to take us all. Most of the men here are actually rather modest and prefer a closed door. Myself included. Besides, I'm a lot to handle and not in a hurry. Can we agree that staying safe and appreciated by us is better than getting defiled, both before and after you're dead, then getting left in this warehouse to rot?"

Eamon needed to pull the trigger, but that would only delay the inevitable. A bolt in Braxton's forehead could never kill a dozen men.

Sherry whimpered, but by the grace of God she wasn't sobbing. She nodded, knowing the odds.

He searched for her thoughts but found nothing. The door that had been open between them, or perhaps it was more like a window, had turned into a wall.

"I'd like to introduce you to one of my MVPs. Gerald, can you come forward?"

Gerald stepped forward. A wiry man with a long beard that looked like he hadn't ever shaved. His hairs were so long, they were falling out. It was hard to tell from the top of that shelf and up in the shadows, especially with most of the man covered in hair, but Gerald had youthful face and ancient posture, putting his age anywhere between thirty and sixty-five.

"Gerald here is the one who swore he saw something in the woods. 'Just a glint,' he said. Maybe your Eamon running into the forest with moonlight glinting off of his crossbow. He had to convince me to pull over. I told Gerald he was an idiot, taking us off course because of a little moonlight. But he insisted, and now here we are. Only fair that Gerald goes first. It helps that that he likes it in public. Isn't that right Gerald?"

Gerald smiled, yanking his belt from the loops of his pants as he stepped toward Sherry, leering.

Braxton stepped away, giving Gerald and Sherry plenty of room.

Sherry began to undress, her face resolute. Stripping down herself and allowing Gerald to touch her only as absolutely necessary was her only way of claiming control.

The fur coat went first, then her giant jacket, followed by the softer one underneath. She left her top layers on, then moved to the bottom, removing her slightly oversized jeans before her thermal underwear. Eamon couldn't imagine a less arousing strip show. She turned around, bent ninety degrees, and began to lower her panties.

Gerald was already stroking his cock.

Eamon couldn't take it. He pulled the trigger and let his bolt fly.

It sailed straight into Gerald's temple. The man cried out, still alive for a split second after the tip pierced his brain, then spilled onto the floor.

"Find where that came from!" Braxton bellowed, turning in a circle, searching the shadows, his eyes passing over Eamon as he quickly reloaded.

But his next bolt wasn't in the crossbow before another one whistled by Braxton and landed in the shoulder of a man standing a foot to his right.

Braxton looked around, spotted a row of cabinets, then ran over and ripped one of the doors from its hinges and used the thing as a shield before marching back into the fray.

Another of the bandits went down, one more bolt flying from nowhere.

Then Eamon saw them. Felony and Liam charging from the shadows, heading toward the four men now surrounding Sherry.

She was kicking and screaming, keeping the bandits at bay. One got too close and her foot landed hard in his balls. The timing was perfect. He started to fall just as the second bolt left Eamon's crossbow and hit him in the head, rather than the square of his back.

The next closest guy was on already on her, but there was no way Eamon could reload in time.

Felony threw a knife. It landed in that guy's throat and reduced her assailants to two.

But now Sherry was on her own. Because the other seven were onto Liam and Felony. Coming their way with Braxton at the head.

Sherry ran, shoving past the nearest guy and running toward the shelves.

But she didn't make it far. The man was faster and grabbed her after only four steps. She managed to slip away, but only by an inch, and when he grabbed her again she lurched forward, crashing into the shelf where Eamon was perched like a sniper.

Shelves fell like dominoes. Eamon tumbled, and slammed his shoulder hard onto the ground.

He rolled, knowing what was coming, but one of the shelves fell on top of him, anyway.

The bandit who had been chasing Sherry let her go for now, turning toward Eamon instead and grinning, knowing the sniper in the shadows was now about to die. A few feet away he stopped, looked down at his empty hands, then turned around and walked off in the other direction.

Only then did Sherry see him, trapped beneath the shelf.

There was an instant of surprise immediately eaten by the horror of their reality — she couldn't reach Eamon in time and Braxton was grabbing her by the arm, roughly like he hadn't before.

She screamed as he dragged her out of the warehouse.

Then the man was back, raising the machete over his head.

"Adios," he said.

Chapter Thirty-Two

Felony buried his knife in the bandit's skull.

His body fell like a basket of laundry, revealing a wide-eyed Eamon behind him. Liam was wrong about his brother in every way. There he was, seconds from death, and Eamon was staring it right in the eyes without flinching. And that was after he'd fired his crossbow into the Hatfields-and-McCoys-looking motherfucker about to rape Sherry.

That was more than either of them had done.

Felony hefted, lifting the shelf enough for Eamon to wiggle out from underneath it. Then he dropped it to the floor, offered his hand to Eamon, and helped his friend to stand.

They hugged, still no words spoken.

Eamon yelled, "We've gotta get Sherry. Braxton took her outside!"

He bolted toward the exit without waiting for an answer. Felony followed, looking for Liam and counting bodies on the floor as he ran. He didn't see Liam or any enemies. The battle had apparently moved into the snow.

All four of the assholes who had surrounded Sherry were dead, the last one had his head crushed by one of the falling shelves a few feet from where Felony had plunged his knife into the bandit like a reverse sword in the stone.

Another four bodies littered the warehouse floor. According to Felony's math, there should be five left, including the big guy outside. And Sherry and Liam, if the two of them weren't already dead.

Eamon was nearly at the door when it exploded open and two of the bandits were back inside, looking like a mirror image of each other. They weren't twins, or even brothers judging by the look of them. But both had long hair, fucked up teeth, angry eyes, and a menacing curl to their salt-and-pepper-bearded lips. They were each holding a bat in their right hand and a knife in their left.

Big mistake, assholes. Choose one and use it well. Holding both was the reason they'd die.

Eamon was closer, and showed no fear. He ran straight for the guy on the left, leaving the other for Felony.

The bandit swiped, a wide arc launching out from his body, but Eamon saw it coming a mile away like he always did, came back with a wallop that was more than most men could take.

By the time he was gazing at stars and trying to collect himself enough to retaliate, Felony was grabbing the second guy's wrist. He tried to swipe down with his right, holding that bat like an asshole, making it as easy for Felony to fell him as it'd been for Eamon to get the other guy.

They were both on the ground, but it wasn't enough for Felony. He took his knife, cut both of their throats, then slipped the blade into its sheath, commandeered their weapons, and turned to face Eamon with a bat in each hand, since he was the sort of motherfucker who could handle something like that.

Eamon glanced at the exit. "You ready."

Felony raised each of his bats and shook them.

But they were expected. Three feet from the door they heard Braxton booming from outside.

"Come out unarmed and with your hands in the air, or they're both dead."

"Fuck," they said together.

Chapter Thirty-Three

EAMON STEPPED OUTSIDE with Felony next to him, but neither was willing to exit unarmed.

Fuck Braxton and his two men. The four of them had just managed to fell ten of the supposed Forsaken without taking a single hit themselves. They could get through this, too. And if not, well, at least they died on their feet.

That's what Sherry was telling him with her eyes, and what Eamon imagined she'd be telling him in the thoughts he could no longer hear, if he ever really had.

Liam and Sherry were each being held by one of the two remaining thugs besides Braxton. He stood ever so slightly behind them, still holding a cabinet door as a shield. Eamon had a loaded crossbow and his knife. Felony had the same, plus a loaded gun. A doomsday device if they needed it, because there was no way either of them was leaving Earth without sending those bandits directly to Hell.

"You didn't follow my directions," Braxton said. "Drop your weapons, or your friends are dead."

"We're fine just like this." Eamon held his aim and took a step forward.

"I can't hurt you," Braxton said, raising both hands to show them he held only his shield. Even the sword on his back had gone missing, removed in the comfort of his warehouse and never retrieved throughout the melee. "Our projectile weapons are inside. No reason we can't all walk away from this."

"Bullshit." Eamon shook his head. "We leave now, you'll be back later. Just like the last time."

"Fair enough. But I could say the same for you. Either way, that's a problem for our future selves."

"We killed too many of your men," Felony said. "You'll head back to your Honeycomb Hideout, rally the troops, and come right back out here looking for us. We'll never feel safe."

"Let them go," Liam said, voice strained with a blade at his throat. "I'm the one who pissed you off. So, do—"

"Shut the fuck up!" ordered the man with a knife at his neck.

Liam didn't know how to do that. "Look, I know where there's a mess of supplies. We were headed there in the morning. You let them go, I'll take you there myself. Hell, I'll join you. That guy's my brother, and while I may not want to ride with him, I don't want to see him dead."

"I said shut up!" The blade kissed his skin harder, a little too passionately. A lick of blood dripped onto the metal.

"I'll fit right in. You know the Quinn Family? Jack Quinn? That was my father. My kid brother never fit in, but I ran the business. I'm an asset. I can help you. Just think about it. Let them go and I can—"

The knife went too deep. Liam finally stopped talking.

But the standoff had gone nowhere. They were all standing there freezing, waiting for someone to flinch.

Despite Liam's flapping mouth, Sherry looked terrified to move an inch, including her lips. Braxton stood like a king behind them. Felony and Eamon had their crossbows aimed. Seven bodies and some had to fall, but for now no one lowered their weapons or batted an eye.

"I imagine the toll's gone up," Eamon called out.

"I suppose it has," Braxton yelled back.

"I'm sure we can make an arrangement. I see our old Jeep is part of your convoy, and thanks to our little scuffle, you don't have enough men to get all five of your vehicles back to wherever you're going. But we can all be friends. Like my brother said, we're Quinns. And if you know what that means, we're assets, even if the family name no longer matters. We're smart, and we can fight. Anyone would be lucky to have us."

"Right now, my men have a knife to your brother's throat and another one to your girl's. You'll see me dead the second you can. So, no," Braxton said, looking cold for the first time, "I'm afraid that won't work."

Eamon crouched down and set his crossbow on the ground. "You don't want us, fine. We know where there are stores of dried meat and munitions. Just—"

"Meat and munitions?" Braxton repeated. "Do I look stupid? You think I don't know *exactly* what's still around these parts for the taking?"

"You didn't know about us," Eamon answered. "Or our cabin, the Jeep, or any of the other supplies we still—"

"There's only one thing we want. You leave us the girl, we'll leave you be."

Eamon shook his head. "No deal. And that's not negotiable."

Braxton shrugged in a display of indifference. "Cut his throat."

The bandit nodded, then flung his arm back like he was yanking the cord on a leaf blower.

Liam's neck opened like a zipper. Eamon would never hear his goodbye. He didn't even scream. His eyes went wide with the realization of what was about to happen, then there was a puddle of blood on the snow.

But his body didn't fall, the thug kept holding Liam like a shield, protection from the bolts that would be otherwise flying from Felony's crossbow.

Eamon screamed for his brother. Rage and regret, sorrow and suffering, the earliest glimmers of mourning.

He could feel Felony wanting to pull the trigger, but still frozen, not knowing what to do with Liam already dead and Sherry still breathing. He didn't pull the trigger, and neither did Eamon.

But someone did.

The bandit was hit in the head from behind. Eamon only saw the bolt in the back of his skull as he fell face forward into the snow. The man holding Sherry turned to see what had happened, relaxing his grip enough for her to finally slip away and come racing toward him.

Eamon looked at Sherry, then past her to a woman about his age with what looked like two teenage males, the three of them running as fast as they could — still relatively slow in all the snow — and coming to their aid, the woman holding a crossbow and the two teenagers holding what looked like homemade spears.

Sherry made it into his arms, but the asshole behind her was close.

Braxton bolted into the shadows. Felony screamed behind him, "The next time I see you, you're dead! Then I'm going to mop the fucking floor with your head!"

No time for the crossbow. Eamon sidestepped in front of her, dodged the bandit as he swung a long blade toward him, then came back with an uppercut he'd feel for a week. He heard at least two of the asshole's teeth leaving his gums and knocking against each other. The bandit winced, and Eamon plunged a knife into his gut.

Felony was going one on one with the final guy, and taking his time since the asshole didn't stand a chance, toying with him. The man had no weapons and nowhere to go. Felony would punch him or kick him or cut him, then back off, let the man bleed, then come in for another round.

Eamon let him play and went to hold his brother.

He pulled Liam against his chest and cried. Deep weeping like he would have never done for his father, and loud like he never had for Poppy. Heavy sobs born from the floor of his soul, vented through his throat into the freezing air.

And just like that, Liam had lost his last connection to the world before it went to hell. And he couldn't help but mourn the future that would never be.

Chapter Thirty-Four

"Will he be okay?"

"I'm sure he will be, but he just lost his brother." Rosa put a hand on Mikey's shoulder. "You're looking at what it would be like if I were to lose you. I'm terrified of that happening. Every day. I know you think I'm too hard on you, but that's why."

Mikey nodded, but said nothing. Eamon, the man who might be the leader of this foursome minus one, was still sobbing over his brother outside. They were in the warehouse, where the guy's apparent girlfriend suggested they go to give him time to grieve, and to hell with the weather.

Rosa was proud of Mikey and Paul. They charged into the fray without knowing their new friends had handled half of the bandits, fully expecting to give their lives if they needed to. This entire time she'd been assuming he was only interested in saving Katrina and everyone else was an afterthought, but Rosa had seen him the boys in action, and reclassified them both as rangers in training. Exactly the sort of quality men The Reserve would be needing.

"Again," Felony said, approaching from behind. "Thanks for that."

"Sorry we didn't strike sooner. We had to drop back a couple of times to make sure we weren't spotted."

"If you had tried to help me, we'd all be dead," Sherry said for the third time in a few minutes of conversation, as though desperately wanting for Rosa to know she'd made the right decision.

"What are the Slums?" Felony asked.

"It's where these assholes all live," Paul answered. "There are a bunch more of them there. Braxton will want blood after this."

"He's right," Rosa nodded.

"Is it as awful as it sounds … the Slums, I mean?" Sherry wanted to know.

"No," Rosa said. "Not at all."

"It's a fucking resort," Mikey clarified.

The warehouse door opened, then Eamon entered looking composed.

"Where do they come from?" Felony asked. "The Forsaken?"

Rosa looked at all the cold bodies littering the colder warehouse floor. "Mostly rejects from Stonefall."

"We were on our way there," Eamon said, now at the edge of the group.

Rosa nodded. "Your friends were telling me."

He extended his hand and she shook it. "I'm Eamon."

"Rosa."

"Thanks for charging in when you did. We'd probably be dead if you hadn't."

Rosa laughed, shaking her head. "I'm not sure about that. Looks like you guys know how to handle yourself fine."

"The final few inches'll get you," Eamon said with grateful eyes. "So, what do you know about Stonefall?"

"Probably not much more than you, mostly just what we've heard on the broadcasts. But we have been there, and we did meet Gleeson."

"The Father of Stonefall," Felony said. "What's he like?"

"A tough, God-fearing Bible thumper. He didn't care for me or my girlfriend Rebecca much when we dropped by the first time, but I figure he won't remember me now, especially with different traveling companions. He refused to help us, but that doesn't mean he made the wrong choice for his community. He keeps his people in line, and they have supplies. Stonefall seems strong for the most part. That's why we're going — we need medicine. How about you? What are you hoping to find, and what did you do before all of this?"

Felony barked a laugh. "How much you want to know?"

Rosa looked around the warehouse and shrugged. "We're here for the night. How about all of it?"

"You ever hear of the Quinn Family?"

Mikey and Paul both shook their heads, but Rosa nodded. She'd heard a few stories.

Felony nodded at Eamon. "That's Eamon, Jack's son. Liam was his eldest."

"Ah," Rosa said, trying not to notice Eamon's gaze on the floor.

"That's Sherry. She's from Billings, same as us. We met her right after Astral Day."

"I was just happy the aliens were getting me away from my mother," Sherry cut in.

"I know exactly how you feel," Rosa said.

Mikey grunted.

"I was a sort of lieutenant for the family. Ironically, I was more of a bad guy before all of this." Felony laughed, as if only now realizing the absurdity.

"How did you get your name?" Paul asked.

Felony grinned. "For a long time, people looked at me and saw only what they wanted to see. Didn't think I was smart. Thought I was a walking felony. So I kept my mouth shut and fed my brain on the down-low while embracing the idiot thug persona to better surprise my enemy. You probably thought gang banger when you saw me, am I right?"

Rosa felt her face flush. "Maybe. And I'm sorry."

"It is what it is. No worries. Like I said, I embrace it. It helps me."

"Have you always worked for the Quinns?" Rosa asked.

"Except when I was in the military."

"Oh?" Rosa raised her eyebrows. "And what did you do in the military?"

"I was a medic."

"No shit," Mikey said, taking Rosa's line. "We've been looking for a medic."

"He's right. We've been looking for people to bring into our community, and needing a doctor for a while. You interested in coming back with us to The Reserve? We could really use someone like you."

"Thanks, but we've got a place, and we'll head on back to it once we've done what we need to in Stonefall."

"But you don't need to go there," Mikey said. "We can give you whatever you need."

"Your friends are welcome, too." Rosa looked at Eamon and Sherry. "Of course."

"I know how to stitch a wound on the battlefield. It's not like I could open my own practice." Felony gave her a self-effacing laugh. "I'm sure I'd be a disappointment. A doctor without medicine. That's why you're headed to Stonefall?"

"We're hoping there's medicine there, but we've also heard Gleeson has some sort of miracle child." Rosa laughed, shaking her head, wanting them all to know she wasn't nuts. "I normally don't believe in stuff like that, but things are different now, and I don't know … maybe it's true."

Eamon and Sherry were both suddenly alive, trading glances that looked pregnant with hope.

"Miracle child?" Eamon repeated. "What have you heard?"

Rosa told them about Gleeson's broadcasts from the last week, about how God had given His Grace to Stonefall and blessed them with a miracle child who was able to heal the sick and informed.

"The last broadcast said he healed someone with depression. Gleeson was going on and on about how the Good Lord could see inside our souls, and that through this child, he can heal what's hurting us most. You know, a lot of religious puffery. I'm sure there's nothing to it. Gleeson's just found a way to keep his people believing and the outside wanting to know. It's like an old-time revival, and those have been around forever."

Felony, Eamon, and Sherry had grown graveyard quiet. Sherry was leaking tears, and it looked like Eamon would be too if he hadn't emptied his eyes in the snow.

"Is everything okay?" Rosa asked.

"That's why we were on our way to Stonefall," Felony explained. "His son … *their son* … he was stolen away."

Sherry spoke, her voice brittle. "Do you think it could be him?"

"I'm wondering a whole lot of shit right now," Felony

said, his dark face darkening with rage. "Like whether the people who stole William knew what he is, and if so, how in the fuck did they find out? Did Gleeson send someone to our cabin? Or did someone come, take the baby, figure out what he could do, then take him to Stonefall?"

"We'll head out first thing in the morning." Eamon said. "Until then, tell us everything you know."

Chapter Thirty-Five

Kirk slowed the Behemoth, not the largest, but one of the bigger vehicles in Stonefall's growing fleet.

It was impossible to see. The sky was too dark and the blizzard was picking up. There were only ten miles between the warehouse and Stonefall, but on a night like this, it might as well have been a hundred.

"You see it?" Kirk asked Beckett.

His passenger squinted, and made a few other useless faces, but then didn't so much as grunt in response.

"Fuck. I know the turnoff is right around here, but I can't see shit."

They lost another half of an hour to the same mess, with Becket shifting in his seat the entire time. "You have to take a shit?"

"No," Beckett said. "Guess I'm just anxious to get back, which we can't do until after we finish with Braxton."

"Gleeson won't even notice we're gone," Kirk said.

"He notices more than you think."

But Kirk only shrugged. Then he smiled. The warehouse was hard to see, sitting behind a wide pall of white, but he made it out.

"What the fuck?" Kirk muttered, mostly to himself as he pulled to a stop then killed the engine. He hopped out of the Behemoth and into the snow, at the very edge of the warehouse parking lot.

Beckett's door slammed then he circled the Behemoth, looking at litter of fallen bodies. "What the hell happened here?"

"I have no idea," Kirk said, pointing. "But those are our men. Maybe they got hit by a crew from The Reserve."

"What makes you think that?"

"Braxton said they came needing medicine and wanted to exchange painkillers for antibiotics. He took their pills and told them to fuck off. This looks like retaliation to me."

"Not necessarily."

Beckett was becoming increasingly argumentative, more regularly forgetting his place. Kirk would have to deal with it soon, but there was a proper time and location for that business, and now wasn't it.

Kirk studied the battle site instead of responding to the bullshit. No, it didn't look like a large crew had been there. There weren't enough prints in the snow to support it, and there definitely hadn't been any bears.

"You see Braxton anywhere?"

"Nope," Beckett said, "but it looks like there's a vehicle gone. So where to now? You're not thinking of heading out to the Slums, are you?"

"Would it be a problem if I was?" Kirk stared, waiting for Beckett to flinch.

It took two seconds longer than it should have. "No. Of course not."

"I want to finish looking out here, then go inside the warehouse."

"What if whoever did this is still inside?"

"Then we kill 'em all," Kirk said.

He didn't wait for Beckett to answer, already crossing the long lot toward the warehouse, staying low.

Kirk planted himself against the wall and gestured for Beckett to get the hell down, even though he shouldn't have to do anything of the sort. The guy was becoming less reliable all the time. He peeked through the window and saw something he didn't expect in the shadows.

It was hard to tell in the darkness, but it looked like there might have been another half dozen bodies of fallen Forsaken lying dead on the warehouse floor.

There were also horses, and people talking. He spotted a large black man, at least as big as Gleeson, sitting in a chair with a gun in his lap.

He ducked back. "Nigger has a gun."

"Good thing we parked all the way out there," Beckett whispered, a bit too loud, though any volume was deafening when he should be keeping his fucking mouth shut.

They continued to listen.

He heard a woman talking about needing to get medicine from Stonefall, how Braxton had turned her and Rebecca down.

So, this is the Reserve!

Kirk considered for several long moments, thinking until he finally had a plan. Then he turned without a word and started walking back toward the vehicles.

"We're not going to kill them?" Beckett asked.

"Did you not hear me? Nigger's got a fucking gun. He shoots and it's Alien Fucking City up here. And who knows how many of them are in there? They took on a bunch of our men and they're still kicking? No, I don't like the odds.

We need to regroup, get with Braxton, and see what's what."

"So, we're gonna do nothing?" Beckett asked.

Kirk glared at him. "You wanna go in there?"

"No, just … I don't like leaving like a pussy."

"It's not being a pussy. It's called strategic thinking, you dumb cunt."

He looked at the vehicles then pulled out his knife to slash their tires.

"You're gonna slash our tires? What's the point?"

"To slow them down."

"Why?"

"If the Reserve's best and brightest are here, then that means The Reserve is undefended now. We head to the Slums, see what's what, and then launch a counter attack while they're sleeping tonight."

Beckett smiled. "So we hit them while they're expecting us to be licking our wounds? That's fucking genius."

Kirk smiled, hoping that Braxton would agree with his plan.

Chapter Thirty-Six

Eamon could only stare straight ahead, his eyes fixed to the solace-teasing horizon.

Stonefall could be seen in the distance. Wooden spires painted gray, perhaps to make it look more like a castle or to match the tall concrete walls. But in the black and white of winter, it was a dull stain on the landscape.

They woke to flat tires, meaning their trip took longer than they'd hoped, being relegated to riding on Rosa's horses. He rode with Rosa, Sherry was on Mikey's, and Felony on his friend Paul's, who was the smallest of their rescuers.

His surroundings were a blur. He couldn't focus. Eamon hadn't slept and was feeling like he might be coming down with a fever. He buried Liam alone, not because no one offered to help — everyone did, and obviously meant it — but because he needed the time to grieve. Eamon said his name over and over and over, not sure if he couldn't feel how freezing it was because he was numb inside or out. Maybe it was frostbite. How would he know since he'd never had it — maybe Eamon didn't feel cold because he no longer could.

"We'll be there soon," Rosa said, stating the obvious.

"How much longer?" Eamon asked, realizing how hard he was working to stay awake.

"A half hour or so," she answered.

Eamon expected a question, even if only to kill the quiet.

Do you think they'll let us in?

Do you think we'll find the baby?

Do you think the Father of Stonefall might kill us?

Anything would be better than a heavy silence still bearing the weight of last night's misery.

"Are you okay?" Sherry asked from one horse away.

Eamon lied by nodding then stared at Rosa's back. Then there was nothing but the clomping of hooves in snow after that.

His mind wandered until it ran into something he should've remembered before. The aliens stacking those rocks. It gave Eamon a chill just to think about it. The kind that stayed in his toes for a while.

What were they building, and why?

And why there ... in that place?

"Have you ever seen the aliens stacking rocks?" Eamon asked.

"Stacking rocks?" Rosa repeated. "You mean like those big boulders they drop everywhere?"

"Sort of, but these were flat. I saw some titans stacking them when I left our shelter to check out a noise. It looked like maybe they were building a bridge or a monument or two tall towers. I have no idea what, but it was something."

"The big rocks affect our brains," Rosa said. "We don't understand it, we just know a psychic connection can form within a certain proximity."

"What do you mean *can form?*" Sherry asked.

"Exactly that. It doesn't happen for most people, but we have evidence that it has happened."

Sherry muttered something to herself that Eamon couldn't hear.

"Are you one of those people?" Eamon asked.

Rosa shook her head. "No. But I think it's some sort of alien bluetooth pulling thoughts from all our brains, and some other people are obviously picking up on the signal. I guess my brain doesn't get that particular channel."

"She thinks they're eavesdropping on us," Mikey added.

"Because they don't get *The Beam* on their mother-ships." Paul laughed.

"They sure seem interested in what we're doing," Rosa continued. "Remember the cubes?"

Silence stretched for a moment. And not because they'd forgotten. No one could ever do that.

Eamon said, "We were in our Cottage during the first couple of weeks after the invasion, but we couldn't get anything on TV, so we only heard about it. Never actually saw any footage."

"I saw one in person," Rosa said, her voice sober enough to scare him.

"I never saw anything," Sherry said. "What are they like?"

Paul talked fast, like he was trying to beat everyone else to the story. "One of those shuttles comes down and opens up, then this cube comes out. It's like an old crushed car. It hangs there by a beam of light, then the light disappears and the cube is just *there*. That was the footage from some-where in Europe. Some little village."

"There was a display on the cube," Mikey cut in. "But

it wasn't digital like something we'd have, it was moving parts, so the face kept shifting."

"I'm not sure I know what you mean," Sherry admitted.

"It looked like it was working," Mikey said.

"Like it was trying to figure something out," Rosa added.

"Tell them about the one you saw in person," Mikey suggested, his voice somber.

Rosa sighed, swallowed, then said, "Rebecca and I went to a small community of survivalists. Actually, I don't know that the word *small* is even appropriate. It was maybe two weeks into the invasion, and they had already amassed a few hundred people. They were friends of Rebecca's, so it seemed like a logical place for us to start gathering people into The Reserve, or at least establishing the relationship. We stopped to survey the situation ahead about a mile outside their camp. Thanks to a clear day and excellent binoculars, we could see what looked like most of the camp crowded around one of those cubes, and an alien shuttle just hovering there."

Mikey looked heavier. This was Rosa's story, but it was obviously harder on him for some reason.

"We were riding for another two minutes or so when the sky went suddenly bright. It was like we all turned our heads and stared right into the sun, even though we were looking ahead. We made it to what was left of the camp a few minutes later, but the place was in ashes. Same for most of the people. Three children, including the oldest girl in camp, Katrina."

"Your girlfriend?" Felony said, looking at Mikey. "The one who's sick?"

"Yes," he said, his eyes on the snow.

"Why did the children survive?" Felony asked. "Any theories?"

"Of course," Rosa said. "There are always theories. We were calling them Judgment Cubes even before Rebecca and I saw what happened at that camp, but we might've even picked that up from some earlier news reports, I don't really remember. But the pattern wasn't unique. It was the same with all of the cubes. Cities were either spared or obliterated. This camp was surprisingly small. With only a few hundred people, I'm not even sure why the aliens would bother."

"Maybe they were trying to scare us but don't understand how our news works."

"Being in the sky is plenty enough to scare us. I think the aliens have reasons for everything they do, and we don't have enough context to understand it. Or *any* context," Rosa added at the end.

"Did you hear about Austin?" Felony asked, since he apparently had.

Rosa nodded, along with Paul and Mikey.

"What happened in Austin?" Eamon asked.

"One of the cubes," Rosa said.

Sherry gasped. "Oh my God? Is Austin gone?"

Rosa shook her head. "No. The aliens spared the city."

Talk of the cubes turned everyone thoughtful. No one spoke again until Rosa stopped her horse and the other two followed. She dismounted then turned to her brother. "I need you to stay back. We're—"

"No way," Mikey said, shaking his head. "You can't leave me here, I'm going, too."

Rosa turned from her brother to Paul. "You guys are going to stay back in case shit goes south. We need backup, and our endgame has now changed. We have company."

She glanced to Felony, Eamon, and Sherry in turn. "And different objectives. We still want the medicine, but the way I see it, Gleeson has more on the line. If things go bad and we don't come out, I need you two back at The Reserve, gathering our people to launch an assault."

Paul nodded. Same for Mikey.

Eamon turned to Sherry. "You should stay back with them."

"Absolutely not." She shook her head.

"It's safer," Felony said.

"I don't care. If William's behind those walls, then that's where I'm going."

"If she gets to go, then we should to," Mikey argued.

"One has nothing to do with the other," Rosa said, staring hard into his eyes. "Can I count on you or not?"

"Of course." Mikey nodded, looking almost sorry he'd spoken at all.

He and Paul stayed with the horses while Eamon and the other three walked to Stonefall, discussing their possible scenarios on the way.

"I wish I had a better idea about what to expect, but Gleeson is unpredictable," Rosa said.

"Unpredictability is predictable in itself," Eamon argued.

"What do you mean?" Rosa asked.

Felony explained. "He means that even wild behavior has rationale behind it. Really, he's talking about his old man. Everyone thought Jack Quinn was erratic, but those of us who knew him always saw the rhyme and reason in his supposed psychosis. It's probably the same with Gleeson. We're too much on the outside to figure out how the guy ticks, and I bet it's the same inside Stonefall. But I also bet there are a few people inside who would be able to help us figure out exactly how the man thinks. That should be one of our objectives while inside."

"You're right," Rosa agreed. "But it's also a tall order. Why would anyone in Stonefall trust us?"

"Because," Sherry said. "The person we're talking about might be looking for a way out."

They arrived at the gates a few minutes later, greeted by two guards wearing all black, armed with sheathed swords.

"What's your business in Stonefall?" the taller of the men asked without preamble or introduction. He had a thick beard and looked much rougher, and tougher, than the younger wide-eyed man with him.

"I'm Rosa Lopez, and these are my friends Eamon, Frank, and Sherry." She sounded like a diplomat, and was smart enough to give Felony a name that didn't sound like a violent crime.

"State your business," the bearded man said, his hand finding the hilt of his sword.

"You have my son," Eamon said.

"I'm sorry?"

"You have my son. The kid with the glowing scars. Ring a bell?"

"I don't know what you're talking about," the guard said, though his eyes told Eamon differently.

"We want to speak with Gleeson." Eamon wouldn't move until the man gave him an answer.

But instead, he nodded at Eamon. "He's here for some kid. How about the rest of you?"

"Frank and Sherry are here with Eamon," Rosa said. "I'm from The Reserve and would like to speak to Gleeson about a trade."

The man looked surprised. "You're from Yellowstone and you've come here alone?"

"I'm with them."

"I see," the man said, looking like he actually might. "Stay here. We'll be back."

Moments later, a slot in the gate opened and a pair of eyes glared out at them before it slid shut again.

Eamon and Felony exchanged a glance — shit was about to go south.

Chapter Thirty-Seven

Gleeson kept stepping toward the Light.

This was what healed and filled and fueled him. It's what made life what it was, not just for Gleeson, but for all of Stonefall. For anyone willing to see through the veil draped across humanity's eyes, and into the Truth. It had become more than habit, but not an addiction. A passion and perhaps an obsession, pure and undiluted devotion.

As always, Gleeson drifted without using his feet, crossing the expanse like an angel gliding over the clouds.

But this time he didn't stop at William. Now Gleeson found himself drifting farther than ever before.

The child was gone, same for the withered old man that was one and the same. Gleeson didn't long to know more because in this moment, he knew everything there was to know.

Everything He knew.

And this wasn't William, it was a vessel through which the Lord had chosen to speak.

The undulating shape kept getting brighter and brighter. Gleeson could feel its power radiating through his body, warming his blood and massaging a mind that was suddenly one with everything, his thoughts like seeds inside a melon shared with the world.

He felt its radiance, understood the power, and knew God.

Gleeson was humbled, head bowed as he hovered in front of pure Divinity, knowing he was but moments away — eternal as each of them might have been — from the angels' song which still rang in his head while fading in the face of His booming voice and from the ancient yet everlasting wisdom that would be falling like heavy rain from a pregnant cloud.

But Gleeson waited and waited. Maybe for minutes, though it might have been years. It was impossible to peel back the layers of time when everything around him was eternal.

Finally, unable to take a cold shoulder from the warmth of Jehovah himself, Gleeson looked directly into the Light and opened his mouth.

"What do I do?"

Gleeson was penitent and waiting, willing to do whatever God said.

But the Lord said nothing.

"You ask and do not receive because you ask with wrong motives, so that you may spend it on your pleasures," Gleeson said. "If I regard wickedness in my heart, the Lord will not hear."

And still he waited, knowing that to prove himself persevering was to manifest triumph in Heaven.

Gleeson kept looking into the Light, unwilling to flinch even though it was now burning his eyes.

He gave the Lord another line of scripture, "If my people, who are called by my name, will humble themselves and pray and seek my face and turn from their wicked ways, then I will hear from Heaven, and I will forgive their sin and will heal their land."

And, finally, the Light began to glow. The Good Lord was about to answer back.

But a terrible pounding like the rolling of boulders and snow down a mountain, ripped him out of his reverie.

Gleeson opened his eyes and turned toward the door.

"Who is it?" he called, his euphoria rotting to a misery of rapture missed only by inches.

"It's Kirk. I need to see you."

Gleeson sighed and started his approach toward the door. He opened it up, motioned for Kirk to take a seat on the sofa across for him, then collapsed onto the couch, surprised by how drained he felt after that last meditation, especially considering the fatigue was only in his shell. Gleeson's mind, so close to God, had never been sharper.

"What is it?" Gleeson asked.

"William's father, or at least a man proclaiming to be him, is coming to take him away."

"What?" Gleeson tried not to roar, holding his fading euphoria like driftwood a mile from shore.

"Apparently the man has rounded up some supporters from Yellowstone, if he isn't from the Reserve himself. There are a total of four intruders at the gate. Two men and two women."

Gleeson leaned back, exhaling with a sigh as his irritation at Kirk receded like bubbles in boiling water left to cool. Processing, saying nothing, watching Kirk and working to ignore Roy, who looked at him from the corner, one leg crossed over the other, biting his lip as he smiled and tried not to say what he always did. Something about his not trusting Kirk.

He had asked God for an answer, and while the Light might have remained silent, Kirk knocking on his door was a Heavenly response. The Lord wanting to protect William from a life outside Stonefall.

"I thought the child's parents were dead?"

Kirk gave Gleeson a solemn looking shrug. "I thought so, too. But this man is telling people that *you* stole his child."

Gleeson was suddenly standing, patting his chest with two meaty paws. "*I* stole his child?"

"Yes, Father."

He puffed air out of his nostrils and started to pace. "Do you think the child is his?"

Kirk shook his head to follow a moment of thought. "I have no way of knowing. The people inside the cabin were dead when we got there. Maybe he was out hunting or something, then came back to the cabin after it had been attacked."

"Surely the child will remember his father."

"Not necessarily," Kirk said.

Gleeson stared at him, waiting for him to retract his idiocy — of course the child would remember his father — but instead he added, "But even if he could, so what? He's a baby. He—"

"William speaks, Brother Kirk. And besides, Angel will remember the child's father. We cannot lie."

"And the Lord wouldn't want you to," Roy chimed in from his seat in the corner.

Gleeson went to his window and looked outside at Stonefall's citizens milling about in the morning. Everything was going so right, he couldn't stand the thought of them suddenly going wrong. His Flock was safe and God-fearing. The Brothers protected them with daily patrols and filtered news. Their stores had grown. Pantries were packed with more than anyone realized or should perhaps even be possible in a time such as this.

God had given them His Grace, and Gleeson couldn't afford to put it in jeopardy. This man might change everything.

"Do you have any orders for me, Father?"

"I'm thinking."

He couldn't allow William to leave Stonefall. Not under any circumstances. Not only was he the miracle Gleeson had asked for, the child was his conduit to God. He had helped to unify their community already, but more importantly for the future of their tiny little city, Sweet William gave him a direct line to the Lord.

Gleeson would rather die than give that up.

"You can't trust him," Roy said into the silence.

No one asked you, he thought, but said nothing, not wanting to indulge Roy's paranoia.

After another long minute of Gleeson thinking, Kirk cleared his throat. "Would you like me to stay, Father? Is there anything I can do?"

"No. Thank you. I just need a moment. One of the best gifts we can ever give ourselves is time alone with God."

Kirk bowed his head. "Yes, Father Gleeson."

He stood by the window, looking out a few long moments after the door closed. Then he walked back over to the couch and sat, waiting for Roy to join him.

"So, what're ya' gonna do?" he asked, taking a seat beside Gleeson.

"What do you think I should do?" Gleeson asked, genuinely needing to hear Roy's perspective, despite — or maybe because of — them recently not seeing eye to eye.

"Do you really want my advice, brother? Or do you just like to ask?"

"I'm sure you're sitting on plenty," Gleeson answered. "Why keep it to yourself?"

"Because I'm sensible to know when it's best, like when the strain of our friendship might not be able to take it."

"Is that what this is?"

"Friendship is born the second one person proves they can keep the other from feeling lonely. Don't I make you feel less alone, brother?"

"I don't want to argue," Gleeson said.

"Conflict can rip you apart or stitch you together. It's all in the attitude. How's yours, brother?"

"I'm scared," Gleeson admitted.

"Of what?"

"Losing the child."

"Because you know it's the right thing to do," Roy said. "You need to give the child back. It's not just the right choice. It's the only choice."

Gleeson shook his head. "I can't do that. The babe has provided for Stonefall. He is healing the sick and giving hope to the Flock."

"But that's not why you want to keep him, is it brother?" Kirk asked with a knowing smile.

"Of course it's the reason."

"It's *part* of the reason. Now why don't you tell me the rest. Go on and say it out loud."

"He's connecting me to God, Roy. I can't give that up … Why are you shaking your head?"

"Because, brother. That baby isn't your connection to God. It's a distraction *from* Him."

"No." Gleeson shook his head, not understanding why Roy would want him to believe something like that. "Stonefall's child is a blessing."

"Have you considered that he might be a curse?"

Gleeson ignored him, shaking his head as he stood from the sofa and walked over to the table where he kept his walkie. He picked it up, turned it on, then called Kirk.

"I want you to let them in. Take their weapons, then bring them directly to the prison. I don't want anyone to see them. Do you understand?"

"Yes, Father."

With Kirk gone, Gleeson renewed his meditation. And in it, the Light revealed things to him about Eamon.

Chapter Thirty-Eight

Melinda didn't like the way Ophelia was looking at her.

It wasn't unkind, but it was sort of condescending, which Melinda was trying to understand rather than resent. She wouldn't like that sort of look from anyone, but it hurt coming from a girl as young as Ophelia, especially considering how much Melinda had done to help her, and Percy before he was taken.

But then again, she also understood. If Melinda hadn't been the one to experience the unlikely situation, she might have had a hard, if not impossible, time believing it herself.

"Maybe just explain it to me again." Ophelia smiled. "How did William *speak* to you about Percy."

Melinda shook her head. "I already told you, that's not what I meant to say. William wasn't talking to me about Percy. I think he was trying to reach me through the child."

"You mean Percy, who is no longer with us, is speaking to you through William … a baby?"

"A baby who can heal," Melinda said, irritated. How could Ophelia so easily believe the child was a miracle, yet find it so unlikely Percy could be talking to her just because he was dead? The girl had faith in Heaven and angels. Each of the pieces were individually there, but she refused to put them together.

"Of course William can heal. But he can do that for everyone. You're the only one hearing Percy, right?"

Again with that condescending expression.

Melinda wanted to drop it. The discussion wasn't getting them anywhere. But she couldn't help it.

"Maybe other people are having experiences they don't want to talk about on account of people not believing them or thinking they might be crazy."

"I don't think you're crazy."

"I didn't say you did." Melinda sighed. She really should let it go. "No, you never said I'm crazy, but you don't believe Percy is trying to tell me something, even though I've tried to explain it a dozen times. And you're looking at me like you feel sorry for me."

Ophelia reached out to take Melinda's hand. "I don't mean to make you feel that way. It's just …"

"Just what?"

"It's just that I can understand. How you would be missing Percy and wanting to hear him through William. The baby is a miracle, after all. I miss my parents, too. And I can see how much I would want to believe they were talking to me through William, being as close to him as you have been."

Melinda finally understood. She should have got it before. Ophelia had been near the child as well. Several times, thanks to her relationships with both Melinda and Kirk. If she felt nothing when something was possible, then what did that say about how much her parents might love her?

Melinda shrugged. "You don't have to believe me. It's

really not important. But Percy *is* trying to tell me something."

"Maybe God is trying to tell you something." Then Ophelia gave her a smile; a wink at the truth shared between them.

"Well, God or Percy, it looks like the baby is trying to tell me something. I'll let you know what happens when I get back."

Ophelia nodded. "Good luck. And tell whoever it is I said hi."

Melinda left her quarters, grateful to be out in the fresh air despite the bitter cold. She was on her way to Angel's. After the last healing, Gleeson asked her to include William in the next selection. She didn't understand what he meant at first, and Gleeson had to explain.

The child had remarkable insight and, the Father of Stonefall insisted, a direct line to God. Melinda liked to think he was right. Because regardless of what Ophelia believed, or refused to, if William could talk to God, he could sure as hell talk to her Percy.

"Your list doesn't have to be long, but give Sweet William some choices," Gleeson had said. "Even if he points to one out of three and it seems like an accident, trust the Lord has placed the boy's finger righteously."

Melinda found herself lost between wanting to laugh everything off and dying for it all to be true.

She knocked on the door and waited.

Angel opened the door, then Melinda stepped inside. She glanced into the empty living room, wondering if Gleeson was home but not hard enough to ask. He was usually bolted to the living room floor.

"Minda!" William called out the second he saw her, jumping up and down in his crib.

It was hard to look at him without either staring or

wanting to flinch. It reminded Melinda of the time she saw her father without any hair on his face. She'd just turned ten, but for the decade before that he'd always had a beard. One day he came into the kitchen before breakfast after shaving it all off. Melinda couldn't look at him for more than a few seconds at a time. He was suddenly a stranger to her eyes, with his misshapen face and the unfamiliar lip of an obvious imposter.

William was like that, the child looking somehow different whenever she saw him.

"Hello, William." Melinda turned to Angel. "May I?"

"Of course."

Melinda scooped William out of the crib and into her arms. He was getting so big. More than twice the size of Sophia, though the little girl might have been older.

Are you in there, Percy?

She set him on the floor then sat beside him and took out her list. "Are you ready to help make someone better?"

William nodded. "Yes."

"I made a list of people I think could use your help. Would you like to see it?"

He nodded again. "Yes."

Melinda unfolded the paper and pointed to the three names, saying each one out loud as her finger brushed it. "Samantha Jacobs. Bob Runyon. Paul Roberts."

Percy, please. I'm here, waiting.

Angel looked over at Melinda, smiling, her eyes curious.

William studied the paper. Then he held out his hand.

Melinda gave him the sheet and watched as he focused even harder, as though the baby could actually read the words.

I need you, Percy. I know you have something to say, and I need to hear it. Please, I—

"Run one."

"Can you please repeat that?" Melinda said.

Angel pointed to the second name. "I think he means Runyon."

William vigorously nodded. "Run one."

Melinda wondered if there was anything to that. Did the child actually know who needed help the most, or who was most deserving? Because if not, then it was crazy to let his finger and a giggle decide on was supposed to get the most help. Bob Runyon was the last one she would've chosen herself. Eczema wasn't that big of a deal no matter how itchy his skin got in the winter. She placed him in the middle for a reason, knowing that would be William's most likely choice, statistically. She was hoping he picked Samantha, who was first on purpose and hardest to say.

I'll have to leave soon. Please, I know you're in there.

Melinda hated begging the silence but would keep on doing it until she was shoved out the door.

"Can I tell you a little about Bob before you meet him?" Melinda asked.

"Run one!"

"Right. Bob Runyon." Melinda smiled at William, then turned to Angel. "Would you mind getting me something to drink? My mouth feels so dry."

"Of course." Angel stood then left the room.

Melinda could tell William all about Bob Runyon, but she didn't need to. She wanted the baby to herself. Maybe that's what he was waiting for.

PLEASE, Percy.

"I'm here."

Percy! Is that really you?

"Only pieces."

But pieces of you?

"Yes, Galahad himself."

She wanted to burst into tears, but kept it together.

Why are you here?

"Because I need you to know two things, Melinda. Everyone's lives will depend on you listening and obeying every word."

Tell me everything.

And he did.

Chapter Thirty-Nine

EAMON TOOK Sherry's hands as they were led through the bowels of Stonefall.

It felt like they were prisoners being marched to their cells. Every step felt somehow worse than the one before it, his instincts clanging with the certainty that his friends were feeling it, too. They were taken around the wall and through a rear entrance, then nowhere near the new construction and over toward the bones of an old penitentiary.

Eamon wasn't surprised when they stopped in front of what was obviously a holding cell. They were being led by who seemed to be the man in charge, at least under Gleeson, a walking asshole named Kirk. Everything about the man's demeanor — from the way he looked at them, to the way he spoke, to his sharp commands — reminded Eamon of the worst of the weasels he'd ever met. The guy was a weak-minded, power hungry dick who wielded what tiny bit of influence he had like a petulant child.

"You'll wait in there until Father Gleeson is ready to see you."

"Are we prisoners?" Eamon asked.

"Of course not," Kirk said.

"Then why are you locking us in a cell?"

"You are strangers in Stonefall. Do you expect me to let you roam around?"

"Not at all," Rosa answered. "But we wouldn't lock up a visitor who came to The Reserve."

"Maybe that's because you don't have any miracles to guard. Between you and me, I felt it was a mistake to broadcast word of our miracle. It only attracts people who might want to steal this child for themselves. People who would claim all sorts of things just to get their hands on his power. What proof do you have that these are his parents?"

Sherry said, "He was born the day the aliens came. It's not like we have a birth certificate."

"As you'll soon see, Father Gleeson can see into your soul. He will know if you're lying."

"Why don't you just let us see our baby," Eamon said. "He'll recognize us."

"I'm sure Father Gleeson will be happy to do that, but it's his decision. Not mine. I'm sorry."

Nothing about Kirk made Eamon buy his apology. He enjoyed saying no. More petulant behavior from a wannabe tyrant.

Rosa said, "We're not a threat to you."

Kirk shrugged and gestured toward the empty cell. "We can't be too careful, but as you can see, we're not in the business of collecting prisoners. There are a lot of people outside of Stonefall who see Father Gleeson as a threat. They would love to depose him or harm the child. You wouldn't believe how many wicked people there are beyond these walls."

"How do we know you won't leave us in here to rot?"

Kirk shrugged. "You don't. But if you want to see Father Gleeson, you have no other choice."

Eamon entered the cell without another word, then waited for his friends to follow. Felony was the last inside, and about the same distance behind Rosa as Sherry was behind Eamon.

The door closed and locked, then Kirk turned around and walked down the corridor, leaving the four of them alone. Eamon immediately started to pace. Felony studied the cell, from corner to cranny. Sherry and Rosa traded whispers, chatting fast but working to keep the conversation quiet, all of them working to maintain their calm facade.

"Do you think Gleeson really might have William?" Sherry asked Rosa. "And if so, do you think he'll give him back, or do you think we're prisoners for good?"

Rosa said, "I don't trust Gleeson, but I don't see how keeping us prisoners will help him."

"Right," Felony agreed. "So, if he does have the baby, he'll probably want to kill us. We'll need to think fast and be ready to move."

"How do we know we're not being eavesdropped on right now?"

Eamon was glad Sherry asked. He was wondering the same thing.

"We don't," Felony and Rosa answered in tandem.

That was an invitation to shut up. No one wanted to, or even seemed willing to, speak after that. A pall of silence lay upon them, refusing to leave. But surprisingly, and true to Kirk's word, they weren't forced to wallow in the quiet for long. It was maybe a half hour before Kirk was back and unlocking the door to their cell.

Eamon didn't like the look on their jailer's face. It

seemed as if Kirk would've been thrilled to leave the lot of them rotting inside their cell.

"Come with me," Kirk said, once the door was all the way open. Everyone shuffled toward the exit, but then he held out his hand and gestured toward Eamon. "Just him."

"Why?"

"You're the child's father?"

Eamon nodded.

"Then you're the only one Father Gleeson wants to see. At least, for now."

Kirk stepped aside to make room for Eamon, then closed the cell door once he passed.

Without a word, Eamon began to follow Kirk down the long corridor. He didn't even get to say goodbye, and he could very well be marching toward his death. Wasn't this what it would probably be like? And how could he possibly know if he wasn't? His heart was pounding, his palms were sweaty. Dank walls reeked with a brew of fungus and disinfectant he could practically taste, and flickering lights turned the short walk into a strobing horror show.

They stopped at another door, a lot like the one they left, then Kirk knocked four times, decisive and hard.

The door swung open. Eamon found himself looking at a large man with a giant's face. Square and oversized. A bit like a human boar. The man stuck out a hand for Eamon to shake, and he swore it was the size of a ham.

"You're Eamon?"

"That's me," he said from his side of a vigorous shake.

"Strong, proud name, but with a softness to it. Irish, am I right?"

"You are," Eamon agreed.

"I'm Gleeson Crowe. Father of Snowfall. It's good to know you. Care to come in?" Gleeson gestured into the room. It was much larger than the cell he just left, with a giant round table sitting in the center, and several chairs outside it.

"Thank you." He nodded, and entered the room while Gleeson thanked Kirk and asked him to please stay outside until they were finished.

The Father of Stonefall was pleasant. But that didn't assuage Eamon's nerves. His father invited people to dinner. Laughed with them through every course, then slit their throats as their eyes rolled into the backs of their heads during dessert.

Eamon chose a chair, then Gleeson took the one opposite him.

"So," he started before his ass had settled into the seat, "you say the Child of Stonefall is yours?"

"Yes, Father Gleeson. He was stolen from us."

That bothered him. Made his nose twitch as his face flared with an expression, wrinkled with what might have been guilt, but was more likely something else. An existing irritant he'd been working to remove.

"He was stolen from you, but you are here alive. Did you see the thieves who took your child?"

"No. We did not."

"*We.* Is William's mother one of the girls who came with you today?"

"Yes … but not his biological mother. We're raising William as ours."

"Ah … like I've been doing here at Stonefall."

"Yes, but I'm his biological father … sir."

"So you say …" Gleeson took a breath to control the moment, staring at Eamon as if daring him to break the silence and talk out of turn. "You do understand why I can't just take your word and you hand you our child?"

"Of course, Father."

"How am I supposed to believe that you are who you say?"

"We were living in the woods. Me and Sherry. Our other friend, Frank, wasn't with us at the time. He went back to Billings, hoping he could help my brother, Liam. He did, and they both came back. But then Liam was murdered by The Forsaken."

"I am sorry to hear that," Gleeson said, seeming and sounding genuine.

"While he was gone, we were living with this old couple. Great people. They were watching William while Sherry and I were out hunting. We came home to find them murdered and William gone."

"And you think I stole your child?"

"No, Father. At first, we thought it was this crazy lady who had an army of kids dressed like circus freaks, but that didn't pan out. I don't know how he came here, nor do I care. We just want our son back."

"*We.* Where is his mother? Should I expect someone else to come pounding on the gate demanding an audience?"

"No, Father. His mother died during childbirth … on the day the aliens came."

"That is not the story I was told," Gleeson said. "And if the child is yours, you have my word I was not behind his capture or the murder of your friends. My men were coming to your cabin after God showed Sweet William to me. They were coming to invite you here."

"How do you know his name?"

"An Angel told me." Gleeson smiled. "My daughter. I assume you know her."

The truth crashed onto Eamon like a pile of rocks. It had been Angel, just different than he would have thought.

"But Angel only gave me his name. The Lord showed

me his Light. The truth is, I have seen you Eamon, since long before you came into this room. I believe you are his father because except for the story of coming home to the cabin, everything you say agrees with what I know. And I have seen more than you've told me. The boulder that crushed his mother. Your father being such a difficult man to love. And your brother, the Cain to your Abel."

Eamon said nothing so Gleeson continued, spitting scripture.

"The rain came down, the streams rose, and the winds blew and beat against that house; yet it did not fall, because it had its foundation on the rock." Then he took a breath and finished like the more regular person he had been just a moment before. "You were meant to come here and live with us, Eamon. To have your thousand years of peace, which your child will help to usher in. God brought you here to us. You followed His Light to our gate."

"No." Eamon shook his head, unable to stop what he was about to do, even though it would likely unravel the hope he'd only just started to feel. "There was no light on our road here. It was filled with darkness and—"

"It is always darkest before the dawn."

"I appreciate the platitudes, Father, but we've been through hell. It doesn't feel like God has much of an interest in us."

"How can you say that?" Gleeson was looking at Eamon in genuine awe. Wonder in his eyes. A total lack of understanding. "God has given you a miracle."

Gleeson had a point. William was a wonder. But the Lord had still taken more than he had giveth.

"Yes, he has," Eamon agreed. "But the world is also a shit show. There's no peace out there. Bandits, yes. Gangs of men who will take whatever they want, and by any means necessary. The good guys among the bad guys because there's also The Forsaken and all the other homicidal nut jobs. Oh, and the aliens. If there is a God out there, he stopped caring a long time ago. And if I had to guess, I think my son being born while there was an alien ship beaming light onto his body made Sweet William the way he is."

"Do you hear yourself?" Gleeson was smiling, like he knew a secret that Eamon did not. "You say that Light from the Heavens made your son what he was, and—"

"That's not exactly what I said."

"And the terror you speak of lies outside Stonefall. Here we're building a future, preparing for a thousand years of peace, with the Good Lord pulling every string. We may not know our purpose, but we all have our part to play. You and William included. You're supposed to be here, same as your son."

Gleeson was still smiling, still amiable, but Eamon was understanding the truth. The Father of Stonefall had no intention of ever letting him leave. He could be the child's father, if he stayed behind and played his part. But he would never let him walk away with William in his arms.

Eamon was trapped, and so were his friends. For now, there was no way out. But of course, they could always escape later. Once William saw him and Sherry and was back with his parents again, it would be harder for Gleeson to keep them imprisoned without losing face.

"Maybe you're right," Eamon said after a long sigh. "Everything bad that's happened to us has been away from Stonefall. And we've been hearing about this place for a while."

"What took you so long? Why not come before your son is spirited away?"

"We felt safe. We had shelter and a cabin, and we could make our own rules." Another long sigh, Eamon playing the game that he needed to. "But look where that got us. Besides, The Forsaken stay away from here."

He started talking lower, almost mumbling, as though the Eamon's words were only for himself.

"Maybe it would be best to stay here."

Gleeson stood, and delivered another flummoxing line. "Behold, I stand at the door and knock. If anyone hears my voice and opens it, I will come in to him and eat with him, and he with me. Welcome to Stonefall."

He held out his hand. Eamon stood and shook it again.

"I'll arrange for you to meet with Angel. If everything checks out, you can live here with us. We'll provide a home for you and your friends, so long as you allow William to continue his healings."

It sounded like a sideshow and felt like a kick to the stomach, but it wasn't like Eamon had much of a choice.

"Of course. Whatever is best for Stonefall."

Gleeson walked Eamon to the door. Kirk was waiting outside as ordered.

"Please take Eamon back to his friends," Gleeson said. "And bring me the ranger."

Chapter Forty

Rosa was ushered down a long hall by Kirk, who was eyeing her up and down like a drunk frat guy.

She wondered if he remembered her, that she was with Rebecca when they came seeking medicine. That she was gay. Would he even care?

He stopped suddenly in a tight hall with no doors.

He smiled. "I remember you. You're the dyke from The Reserve, right?"

She glared at him. Had he already told Gleeson? Would this lead to yet another rejection? She had to bite her tongue, not take his bait. Yet a part of her could not lie, could not hide who she was. She spent too many years hiding her sexuality.

She nodded.

"So, you've never been with a man?"

"I'm not talking about who I've been and not been with."

"How about your lover? What was her name … oh, yeah. Rebecca."

There was a look in his eye, a familiarity that didn't make any sense. That, with his leering grin, sent a chill through her.

"I bet Becky is an animal in the sack. Bet she loves anal, huh?"

If she were anywhere else, if she didn't need the medicine so bad, she would deck this fucker right in his face. Maybe shove her palm into his Adam's Apple.

She said nothing.

He reached down and grabbed his cock through his pants, squeezed it like he was remembering the best sex he'd ever had.

Was this him trying to come on to her? Him just fucking with her? Or was he going to try and rape her?

He might try, but there was no way in hell he'd get far, not as long as she had a breath in her body.

Then he winked and resumed walking in front of her. "This way."

He led her into a small room with a large round table where Gleeson was already waiting.

Did he remember her?

He reached out and shook her hand.

"It is good to know you," Gleeson said, a genuine-looking smile on his face. "What you all have done at The Reserve is remarkable, at least from what I have heard."

"You're welcome to visit at any time."

"I wouldn't want to trouble you."

"It wouldn't be any trouble. These are hard times, and we need as many allies in this world as we can get," Rosa said, hearing Rebecca in her head. "It's us against people like The Forsaken."

Gleeson bowed, and when he raised his head, she saw sorrow in the man's eyes. "It pains me to know they are out there, harming innocents."

"Same to you. Stonefall seems to be thriving. Your leadership is impressive, Father Gleeson. But even a community as well tended as yours surely has a few holes. Perhaps we could make a trade if I know what you need."

"How did you come to know Eamon?" Gleeson asked, ignoring everything she said.

"I ran into them last night. After they were attacked by The Forsaken."

Gleeson's face withered into itself. "They are a blight upon our land. Woe to those who call evil good and good evil, who put darkness for light and light for darkness, who put bitter for sweet and sweet for bitter. They are a stain upon our planet, but it is good that there are people like us."

You wouldn't think that if I were here with my girlfriend.

"True," Rosa said. "We must crusade for what is right."

"Tell me more about the medicine you need. How many are sick?"

"Quite a few of us, and unfortunately it's spreading. Without medicine, we'll lose a lot of people."

"Practically speaking, and as awful as it is to say, resources are scarce. And the more people there are, the further those supplies need to go. Perhaps this is natural selection in action. Or at least the Good Lord's version of it."

"Maybe, but I doubt you'd be saying that if pneumonia were running through Stonefall."

"Is it possible that God has spared us because we attend to our Sins and Transgressions?"

"Of course. But it's also possible you were spared because the moment the first person came down with pneumonia, he or she got the antibiotics they needed to throttle the infection. Our medicine was stolen by The

Forsaken, and the illness spread fast once we were out. Do you think you can help us?"

"I can," Gleeson nodded as he stood. "Follow me."

She stayed three paces behind as Gleeson left the room, dismissing Kirk before leading her to a sharp turn, then down a hallway to another identical door. He unlocked and opened it, then gestured for Rosa to enter.

"What is this place?"

"It's our pharmacy, I suppose. But it's kept under lock and key. Trust in God, but tie your camel." Gleeson smiled. "What do you need?"

He gestured to the many shelves of medicine. Rosa was having a hard time believing her eyes, expecting the Father of Stonefall to start laughing before having her Kirk drag her off somewhere for torment and torture. But there he was, watching her stare at the shelves. She stepped closer, almost as if drifting.

Amox, Doxy, Levo, Ceftriaxone, Quin, and Zosyn.

These shelves could save The Reserve.

"So," Gleeson prompted. "Do you see anything you can use?"

Rosa was overwhelmed, and something about the fully-stocked room made her want to cry. Katrina would be saved, and so would everyone else still suffering at The Reserve. Assuming she could pack up the medicine and make it back without getting accosted or losing her spoils.

"Of course. I don't know what to say. You've saved us. How much can we take, and what would you like in return?" She was still waiting for the trick.

Gleeson looked from the shelves to Rosa. "Please, take whatever you need and consider us The Reserve's greatest ally. We are God's chosen people, holy and dearly loved, but we do wish to help the less fortunate. Please, clothe yourselves with the compassion and kindness of Stonefall."

He handed Rosa an empty box and she began to fill it with medicine, still expecting his kindness to expire at any second. But it never did. Instead, he patiently waited for her to make her selections, without seeming to care which bottles she pulled from the shelves or how many she gently set into her box. Maybe medicine mattered less when you had a miracle child who could do all the healing for you.

Had he forgotten who she was? That she was the sinful lesbian he had turned down before? Or did he have a sudden change of heart? She wondered about his conversation with Eamon, suddenly certain that Gleeson's kindness was a direct result of whatever had happened between them.

Once the box was full, Gleeson asked her if he could help with anything else, like a valet awaiting his tip. She needed nothing else, so he said, "Then let's get you back to your friends."

Still the gentleman she never expected, Gleeson led her out of the pharmacy, then back to the cell where her friends were waiting. He opened the door and gave them their freedom. Walked them outside, beyond the gates where the Father of Stonefall turned to Eamon. "You're welcome back inside at any time. And to the rest of you, good luck."

Then he left them alone to talk among themselves.

"What does he mean?" Rosa asked.

"I'm staying here," Eamon explained. "It's the only way I can get William back. Gleeson's offered me a home, and I have to take it for now. I don't have any other choice."

"I'm staying with Eamon," Sherry said.

"And I'm heading back to The Reserve with you," Felony added, looking unsure of the situation.

Rosa knew exactly how he felt. Despite Gleeson's

generosity, it all seemed a little too perfect. Free medicine and lodging, ample help from a man who had so readily turned her and Rebecca away before.

"I don't plan on staying long. Just until we can get William and find a way out of here. If we're not back in two weeks, that means we're being kept here against our will."

"If you're not back in two weeks, then we'll be back for you," Felony promised him.

She leaned in and whispered to them, "Be careful of that Kirk dude. He was eye raping me the whole time, saying some pretty vile things. Gleeson was nice as cake, but that Kirk is a snake. I wouldn't leave Sherry alone with him for even a second."

Eamon turned back to Sherry, grabbed her hand, and squeezed it. "I won't."

They said their farewells, Felony hugging Eamon and Sherry long and whispering something to them, probably words of encouragement. Then they headed outside, where Kirk was waiting with their horses.

"Back to The Reserve, eh?" he said, smiling that sick fucking smile like he knew something they didn't know. She wondered if this was all some trap, if they were going to ride ten minutes then get felled by sniper shots or something.

"Yeah," Felony said, eying the man up and down. "Thank you again for the supplies."

"Best of luck. I hope you're able to keep your folks healthy."

They began to ride away.

As they were almost out of earshot, Kirk called out, "Give Becky a kiss for me."

Rosa resisted the urge to flip him off.

Felony looked at her and could read that she wanted to say or do something. He shook his head subtly and said, "It's not worth it. Another time."

They headed off to find Paul and Mikey.

Chapter Forty-One

SHERRY WASN'T sure how to navigate whatever was wrong with Eamon.

He was quiet, back in the cell after his conversation with Gleeson. That made sense. Her man was probably staying silent because he figured they were being listened to and didn't want to tip his hand. But the silence continued even outside, when the four of them were alone and bidding one another farewell. Even now, something seemed off.

"Why did you tell them two weeks?" Sherry asked. "That feels like forever. How do you know we won't both be dead by then?"

"We'll be fine," Eamon assured her.

"How can you possibly know that? That Gleeson guy is obviously crazy."

"Of course he is. But that doesn't mean that he's going to harm us. He gave Rosa all the medicine she needs and is willing to offer us a place here as long as we want it. I actually think he means well."

"He's only giving us a place here if we let him keep our child!"

"Not so loud," Eamon said, shushing Sherry, pissing her off. "He's not keeping William, he just wants us to stay in Stonefall."

"Are you hearing yourself? What did he say to brainwash you so fast?"

"Nothing, but I don't see that we have any other choice. We'll figure a way back out. But until then, isn't this what you wanted?"

It sure as hell didn't feel like it. "I guess."

Sherry held her hand out for Eamon. He took it, then together they approached the gate. There were still no guards, but this time it opened wide, and Gleeson was waiting on the other side with a smile and a small congregation of people who seemed so perfectly happy to see them that Sherry couldn't help but feel herself starting to ever so slightly relax. Maybe it was because that creepy guy Kirk was nowhere in sight.

"Let's give our guests some space," Gleeson said to the small crowd. "We'll have plenty of time to properly greet them during tonight's ceremony."

Of course no one would argue with the Father of Stonefall, so they finished their greetings and shuffled off, then Gleeson told them both to follow.

"*Do you really think everything will be okay?*" Sherry whispered.

Eamon looked at Gleeson walking several steps ahead then whispered back, "*I do.*"

For now, that had to be enough.

They both fell silent, observing their surroundings as Gleeson led them through his hamlet. There was construction everywhere, and people working, most of them smiling. Sherry somehow expected to see only varying degrees of misery once they made it behind the wall, but this was nothing like she expected.

Maybe she was wrong. Gleeson seemed reasonable, and his loyal subjects or whatever seemed content. Safe from bandits outside, even if they remained as vulnerable when it came to the aliens as everyone else.

It wasn't much of a tour. Gleeson didn't speak, at least not to them, though he did keep mumbling to himself and turning his head to mutter at the air beside him. Sherry didn't dare ask Eamon who he thought Gleeson might be talking to, though she could feel him wondering and knew they'd be discussing that later.

They were walking for around ten minutes or so when they finally turned onto a narrow trail that took them down what looked like a sort of Main Street, past the rows of small frame houses to the one at the end.

"It isn't much," Gleeson said once they were all standing outside, "but this is my home. William is here, with Angel and Sophia. You're welcome to make your home here as well."

Sherry was surprised to see there were no visible locks on the doors or guards posted outside the house. Still, it was difficult to imagine living with Gleeson would make it easy to slip out of Stonefall unnoticed.

He opened the door and gestured for them to go inside.

Angel was waiting on the other side and yelped with joy when she saw them. "Sherry! Eamon!" She hugged them both, starting with Sherry. Then she pulled away and finished her thought. "I thought I'd never … when I saw William here … I assumed the worst."

"For God has not given us a spirit of fear, but of power and of love and of a sound mind," Gleeson said. "You need never assume in Stonefall."

Sherry wasn't sure, but it seemed like Angel might have wanted to roll her eyes. And thinking back to all she said about her father, there was a wide chasm between the man standing before them now, and the one who had been absent by way of incarceration throughout her childhood.

"I didn't think we'd ever see you again, either," Sherry admitted.

"Where is Felony?"

"Felony?" Gleeson repeated.

"Frank," Eamon said, sounding slightly embarrassed. "We weren't sure his nickname would go over well in a place like Stonefall, so we went with something a little less eyebrow raising."

"Ah …" Gleeson said, turning to make a face at no one.

"So, where is William?" Sherry asked, looking at Sophia sitting with some sanded wooden blocks in the corner.

"He's napping, but he's *always* sleeping, so I'm sure we can get him up." Angel left the room, and returned moments later with William in her arms.

She squeezed Eamon's hand, about to jump out of her skin.

Angel handed the child to his father first. Sherry was both surprised and disappointed to see William's muted response. Maybe was just waking up, and it had been a while since the baby had seen them. And despite his obvious gifts and abilities, a baby wasn't a dog, ready to lick its master's face the as he came through the door, regardless of how long he'd been gone.

Besides, it wasn't like Eamon was William's mother. It would be different with her. Sherry had nursed him from just moments after his birth. He would smell her, know her as the person who kept him alive. All those feedings in the middle of the night, in the earliest morning, and all through the day. Sunup to sundown. Surely he'd remember that, somewhere in his lizard brain.

But after holding her son for a few minutes, Sherry wasn't sure he did. His indifference made her want to cry. She couldn't have been any more excited, even after his muted display with Eamon. But in her arms, he wasn't just unemotional. The child seemed almost detached.

"Hi, Daddy," he said to Eamon without any emotion.

"Hi, Mommy." His words were well beyond his age and sounded horridly robotic.

The scars on his cheek burned brighter than she remembered and looked a bit longer to match his growing face.

Sherry didn't know what to do. She had so many questions, but here in this living room they all felt wrong. The wrong query could prove she didn't believe what Gleeson expected her to while staying in his home. She was dying to get Eamon alone, longing to talk about it. Because this was all wrong. William was changing too much, too fast. Sherry was a good mom, but no longer able to prove it. Her baby was a creature of silence and sorrow, a child she no longer knew.

Taking care of William was the only thing she'd ever been good at. Redemption from a childhood spent in an emotional gutter. The reality around her now was devastating, but Sherry had no choice but to hide it.

Her stomach swam in acid, and she felt herself wanting to drown. The truth was obvious. She failed to protect her son from being stolen, and now she had failed to prevent his brainwashing by Gleeson's cult.

That's what this was. What it had to be.

"He's just waking up," Angel said, looking embarrassed.

"Many are the plans in a person's heart, but it is the Lord's purpose that prevails. Your son has not been in Stonefall long," Gleeson added to Angel's excuse, "but his time with us has been significant. Please, do not take his mood to heart. Soon you'll meet everyone. We'll have a feast, and you will see for yourselves how much the community loves him."

"But does he still love us?" Sherry asked, placing a hand over her suddenly aching stomach.

"William will learn to honor his mother and father, so he may live long in the land the Lord his God is giving him. He simply needs a little time." Gleeson turned to Angel. "Would you please make our guests comfortable? They will be staying here with us."

"Of course," she said.

Angel led them to their rooms. Separate, and neither one with a crib.

Chapter Forty-Two

GLEESON LOOKED out at his Flock, then up at the night sky.

He closed his eyes and thought about everything.

They were under the stars and God. The universe like a blanket above them. He stood at the front of the crowd.

His closest friends and allies, along with William and his parents, were in the front row. Everyone was standing.

Stonefall was swaddled in God's grace, their planet a babe to Her breast. God had sent his sentries, and even though Gleeson could not see them in the night, he could feel them in the sky, hovering somewhere and everywhere, whistling through the depths of their heavens.

Angels and humans were rarely so close. It hadn't been like this since the last time the Lord sent his angels to judge the planet. Soon, a decision would be made, and those in Stonefall would see its other side. They would survive the Extinction and be there for the Resurrection.

Gleeson had been longing for this night without even knowing it. He had been shown a miracle and was now awaiting its delivery. He hadn't realized the miracle was complete. Jesus had Mary and Joseph. Sweet William had

Sherry and Eamon. The child would grow up and in the time of Judgment would die for the sins of Stonefall. He'd seen it in his visions. He wondered if the boy had seen it as well. He must have, Gleeson figured, though he'd never admitted as much.

In order for humanity to continue, the boy would have to die.

Because humans were sinners. Even Gleeson, righteous as he was, still wanted his drink, same as he wanted his women, even if he abstained from them both. His violent streaks. All flaws Roy gave him regular reminders about.

And the Lord said, "My Grace is sufficient for you, for My power is made perfect in weakness." You know it, brother. God is upon you, even though you're a human mess like the lot of them.

Stonefall was full. He had Angel and William, Eamon and Sherry. The gates would close. They had plenty of space and nearly three-hundred people. Twice the number Gleeson had originally wanted. Yet, the place still felt empty, giving the families inside plenty of space to multiply in God's Light until judgment was upon them all.

Everything was finally perfect. Gleeson could—

Except Kirk and you know it. He should not be here.

He shook his head to clear Roy out of it. He wasn't even there. Or invited. Gleeson didn't want him around because Roy kept questioning his judgment. But he didn't need to do that. Brother Kirk had been reborn under Gleeson's watchful eye. Roy was remembering the man he was instead of the man he turned out to be.

William would warm up to his birth father and Sherry. But hopefully not too much. He had been cool with them so far. It had surprised Gleeson to see it, though he had to admit feeling pleased. Eamon was a function of bringing William into the world, and God placed Sherry in his path to keep them both alive. Every part of that child's tale was yet another part of the miracle. Further proof of His Holy Existence. A Gospel to one day be written.

Gleeson thought about how grateful he was for all of it. And for the opportunity to be redeemed before God judged the planet. That he, a wretched sinner, had been chosen to save humanity, spoke to God's good grace.

Soon, a new world would be upon them, and Stonefall would serve as the cradle of this new world and the thousand years of peace that would follow. A thousand years without death. A thousand years of God's good glory until Gleeson could finally ascend into Heaven.

He opened his eyes and spoke to the Flock.

"Work itself is a victory, and yet our toil since Heaven's angels anointed our land has yielded a harvest none of us could have imagined. Tonight, we close the gates of Stonefall for good and call our family complete."

The Flock nodded, fire lighting their eyes and gratitude warming their faces.

"There is much to tell you before we start our sermon. I promised you justice, and tonight Stonefall shall have it. We've located The Forsaken. Justice will be paid for Percy's murder and their scourge across this land."

They had not found The Forsaken, but he felt he was close. His visions had told him all would be revealed soon, so it wasn't a lie, and yet it offered so much comfort to his people.

Grateful applause rolled through the Flock, but it wasn't as it had been before. Violence no longer steeped in the crowd because the Father of Stonefall set the tone, and violence no longer boiled in Gleeson's blood. Yes, The Forsaken would pay, but he would imprison those who surrendered, not murder them.

"Justice brings joy to the righteous but terror to evildoers, yet that is an ugly discussion, and though necessary and saintly, it is also borne of the darkest of humanity and no longer welcome in what we are celebrating tonight."

Gleeson enjoyed their curious faces, even though most of them knew or had heard the whispers rippling through Stonefall like a winter wind on everyone's breath. His hulking frame stood center-stage, arms spread wide like a prophet.

He looked at Eamon and Sherry, with William between them, holding their hands. Gleeson invited them onto the stage with a nod. "I would like to welcome the two newest members of our community home to Stonefall."

The trio stood to his right, leaving room for Melinda on his left.

"This is Eamon and Sherry, William's parents."

Gasps and cheers, pleasant yells and mannered applause, from all those who knew and all those who didn't.

"We believed they had been killed, leaving our Sweet William an orphan," Gleeson continued. "But God has chosen to save the Child of Stonefall's earthly parents."

More cheers and pleasant applause.

"Thank you for having us," Eamon said.

"And for being so welcoming," Sherry added. "Every-one's been really nice."

William said nothing, though he studied the crowd with curious and unflinching eyes, soaking it all up while he could. His parents seemed unsure, especially Sherry. But Gleeson would earn their trust, eventually. They would come to understand how good they had it in Stonefall, that sharing would make them better people. They had been touched by God. It was his responsibility to make sure their blessing was met with respect.

"I am so glad you have found us." Gleeson was surely glowing with joy. "Thank you for making Stonefall your home. Please, let us continue to welcome you. After tonight's feast, tell everyone how we may help you."

"We will." Sherry smiled, but the corners of her mouth were working against her.

Gleeson turned to Melinda and gestured her onto the stage.

She had a knowing smile that somehow felt like a handful of rocks. It made him instantly wary. His muscles tensed and posture tightened — a towering giant looming over his flock, like an idol staring down from atop a mountain. He probably looked an inch taller.

Melinda was only a few feet away, the knowing smile now wider.

Gleeson knew he should say something else, stray from the script before the devil in Melinda's eyes slithered its way inside him. But the original words came out anyway, and in the exact order they were supposed to.

"Do you know who William shall be healing tonight?"

"I do," Melinda said, stepping in front of Gleeson. "But first I have something important to say ..."

Gleeson's heart was already pounding. Roy appeared from nowhere, standing in the front row with wide eyes, waiting to see what was about to go down as Melinda held the moment.

She finally let it go and said, "I'd like to call your attention to something wrong."

Gleeson had to stop this, whatever it was. He was about to step in front of Melinda, shut her up however he needed to, but Roy yelled, "No, brother! Let her speak."

Even if that only stopped Gleeson for a moment, that was enough for Melinda. Her mouth was already open. Once the words were out, he wouldn't be able to muffle, mute, or murder them.

"There *is* no enemy," she announced. "Kirk and his

men *are The Forsaken!* They are a tool to keep us imprisoned here, in constant fear. We are no safer in Stonefall than we are beyond the walls with the bandits."

Melinda jabbed a finger into the crowd.

Gleeson followed her pointer, and it landed on Kirk, who was standing beside Angel and Sophia.

The Flock's eyes were all on him. Gleeson yelled, "She's lying!"

"No, she isn't!" Roy yelled back.

"Now, now …" Gleeson raised his hands to calm his Flock. Eamon and Sherry looked upset, and William had an expression he'd never seen on the child before. It looked almost like anger, but a sophisticated breed, much too old for his innocent face. "Let's all calm down. I'm sure Melinda can explain herself."

The crowd was getting upset, restless and muttering. Soon there would be shoving and shouting. The grief had finally gotten to her. Melinda had gone out of her mind.

This was beyond shocking. Why would Gleeson ever want to fake something like The Forsaken?

For control, like she said.

Gleeson could no longer hear Roy yelling over all the commotion, so his old friend was taking the direct route, whispering right into his mind. But Roy had to be wrong, Melinda was projecting her thirst for revenge on Kirk because she needed someone to blame.

He's the snake in your grass, brother.

"We have all at one time or another witnessed Kirk's cruel inhumanity. A wicked barbarism encouraged by our so-called Father of Stonefall. What have we done, putting men like this in charge of our lives?"

Kirk was shrinking under the weight of so many stares, the hardest coming from the stage. Melinda, of course, but she knew this was coming and her eyes were steady. Eamon and Sherry's were wild, trying to reconcile what they were hearing, but the child's were the hardest of all. Fixed on Kirk as though they were boring through him.

Angel looked frozen, like a deer in the headlights, unsure what to do.

He wanted her to move away from Kirk but couldn't find the words to warn her without possibly exciting the crowd even more.

"Liar!" William yelled, pointing his tiny finger at Kirk.

Kirk looked past the child and his parents, over Melinda's head and into Gleeson's eyes, hoping that the Father of Stonefall would give him salvation from stage.

But he finally heard the truth in William's words, and saw it in Kirk's dilated eyes.

Gleeson yelled to the crowd, sorry it had taken him so long. "Melinda is right! That man is not our brother! But I swear, I had nothing to do with this!"

Kirk suddenly had a gun at Angel's head.

Angel cried out, her baby erupting into tears.

"She's a fucking liar!" Kirk yelled. "She's a fucking nigger liar!"

"You are the liar!" Melinda yelled, drawing a gun from nowhere then aiming it not at Kirk, but at Gleeson himself. "You and the Father of Stonefall, both liars!"

Gasps and shouts from the Flock, not only knowing the threat of either gun going off but also the threat of such violence drawing the aliens.

Everything was out of control, and Gleeson couldn't do a single thing to fix it.

"Please," he begged Kirk, ignoring Melinda's gun for the moment. "Please, let them go and we'll figure this out."

Kirk looked terrified, his eyes wild. "She's a fucking liar!"

Kirk took aim and fired at Melinda.

She fell back, firing two shots into the air as she hit the ground.

And then chaos erupted.

Drones soared through the air. Tracer fire darted into the crowd.

Gleeson screamed out, trying to run for Angel and his granddaughter only to see them evaporate into red light and ashes in front of him.

The crowd dispersed in screams, but Gleeson was only peripherally aware of the movement as he could not take his eyes off of the spot where Angel and Sophia had been only seconds ago.

Gone.

Forever.

Kirk racing away into the crowd.

Then something else caught his attention — William, with his arms spread wide, bathed in a bright white light.

Why is he smiling?

Eamon scooped the child into his arms and started running with Sherry a moment behind him.

Explosions of light and burst ash all around him.

A ringing in his ears.

He was frozen in his spot, and, surprisingly, terrified.

Chapter Forty-Three

Eamon was like a jacket around William's burning body.

He ran hard, searching for escape into one of the nearby buildings, Sherry by his side.

But every time they attempted to turn one way or another, someone, or something, exploded in front of them and they had to pivot.

People around him were quite literally turning to ash. Swallowed by light, brilliance filling every pore before it was too much for their bodies, reducing them to cinders that scattered in the wind. Drifted into his nostrils and coated his tongue.

Eamon ducked into an alcove between buildings. A narrow recess he hoped might keep them alive for another few minutes.

"What's happening?" Sherry was working hard to sound only panicked instead of hysterical. "Why is William burning up?"

"I don't know!" Eamon shouted, not meaning to shout. He put William down then studied him head to toe and back.

The boy's eyes were rolled back into his head, a stupid smile spread over his face, his body burning even brighter. It wasn't like last time, when he turned red like a lobster. This time it looked like the light from his scars was filling his entire body and might burst forth at any moment.

He shook his son, "William. William!"

The boy was unresponsive.

Stuff and people still exploded around them.

Screams and cries and the trampling like a stampede of buffalo surrounded them. The people not being destroyed by the drones were covered in the same white light William was bathed in. Everyone except him and Sherry.

They were frozen to the spot, neither willing to move just yet. Where did you run when the world was falling apart?

"We have to go," Eamon said suddenly. He didn't know where, but he knew it in his gut. Staying meant dying.

They looked down at their son, then back up at each other. Sherry turned her eyes to the sky and stared as if lost. Finally, she stood from her crouch. "Okay, let's go."

"Gleeson." William pointed toward the Father of Stonefall, who was standing stunned and frozen, staring into the sky.

The man was the only other person not bathed in light, though the significance of that was lost on Eamon. The only person other than Melinda, who was on the ground, looking as if she'd been trampled in the rush of people to escape.

She was bruised and bleeding, confused.

Her gun was gone.

William's brightness was more intense, as if his skin might rip apart at the seams. Eamon wanted to hold him to stop him from being ripped apart by the light, but the boy was burning hot.

"Melinda, Gleeson, Mommy, Daddy. Save them."

Then, as if he weren't surprising the hell out of Eamon already, the baby added, "Gleeson first. It *hurts*."

Eamon ran without thinking, three of them racing toward Gleeson.

Two things happened a few feet away. William began to cool down and Gleeson's gaze surrendered to awareness as he looked at them and then William.

He burst into tears, "Angel and Sophia ... they're gone."

"Come," Eamon said, guiding him toward Melinda.

Now that all of them were together, the entire world around them began to glow bright white — everything but the area immediately around them.

They were in a dome of darkness, save for the light inside of William. And even if Eamon couldn't explain it, he suddenly understood just fine. William was keeping them alive in a bubble outside of everything else.

A family ran past them, screaming "Go, go!"

The parents turned to embers in a second. The child, left unharmed, kept running, unaware of his parents' fate.

The world was dying around them, and the only thing protecting them was William holding the bubble.

People must have recognized what he was doing.

They ran towards the bubble for safety.

A big bearded man and a woman behind him were racing toward them.

The moment they touched the bubble, they flew back, bouncing twice before exploding in a blast of ashen noth-ingness.

A high-pitched piercing sound erupted around them as the light grew so bright, it was as if they were looking into the sun. Its pitch rose like an unholy tea kettle signaling not that the tea was done, but the world was.

William's body burned brighter still as the bubble began to dim, succumbing to the light.

His body shook violently.

Drool bubbled at his mouth.

His eyes were nothing but white.

His scar split open. Light bled through.

How long could he hold it before they all perished in the light?

A young teenage girl ran toward them, a silhouette in the brightness.

Melinda called out, "Ophelia! Let her in! Let her in!"

But it was too late.

She exploded into dust that hit the bubble then bounced off it, scattering into the breeze.

Melinda screamed.

The piercing sound rose to such a loudness, they all covered their ears to keep their eardrums from exploding. The light brightened further, a blinding brilliance they had to close their eyes to.

The whistle reached its climax as the world exploded around them.

Silence.

Darkness.

Stillness.

Chapter Forty-Four

Eamon's ears still rang when he opened his eyes.

The sky was clear. The drones were all gone.

It was hard to see how many survivors there were. Lots of people slowly rose, dazed, confused. Some of them bleeding, most of them covered in the ashes of those destroyed.

An entire carpet of ashen remains covered much of the snow. The world around them was gray, just like the walls. Every surface caked, cinders sticking to everything and freezing in place immediately.

Melinda stood there, staring at them, dazed. She looked around as if seeing the world for the first time.

Sherry asked, "Where is he?" Then she screamed, "Where is he?!"

Eamon looked toward her, saw the horror on her face, then followed her gaze to the empty spot where William had been standing just before the ball of light exploded.

"William!" Eamon yelled, over and over, in chorus with Sherry. But their miracle was nowhere to be seen.

Had he exploded?
If so, he wasn't the only one gone.
Gleeson was, too.

Chapter Forty-Five

Oddly, Felony was making Rosa think a lot about Rebecca.

She liked him. A lot. He was the sort of guy she would normally never have talked to before. He looked like a thug. It wasn't just his size or tattoos, or even his name. Felony seemed like the sort of person who got her mom into the kind of messes she had been in for Rosa's entire life. Part of the problem instead of the solution she spent her life trying to be.

And yes, before Astral Day, Felony was apparently all of that. But that wasn't even close to *all* he was. And in a post-invasion world, what Felony had was a helluva lot more valuable than whatever all the lawyers and accountants Rosa saw lying slaughtered before the first snowfall apparently had.

Rosa hadn't liked a lot of the changes she'd seen in Rebecca during the last several months. But Felony got her thinking that maybe she'd been wrong. Rebecca was only being practical, behaving like a good leader should. It was hard work, looking into the future and figuring out who you would have to be to keep everyone alive. Rebecca had done an admirable job, and Rosa hadn't been fair. She was glad they were almost home, grateful for the chance to make it up to her.

"So, how did you two meet?" Felony asked after Rosa mentioned Rebecca for what might've been the seventeenth time.

Rosa laughed. "There isn't much of a story there."

"Is she lying?" He called up to Mikey and Paul, riding in front of them. "There's gotta be a story. There's always a story."

Mikey said, "If there's a story, it'll probably put you to sleep."

Paul laughed.

"See," Rosa gave him a smile. "No story."

"There's always a story," Felony repeated, though this time he mumbled it to himself.

"We worked together. We were both rangers. She was the director and my boss. Now she's one of The Reserve's leaders."

"Well sacrebleu, I didn't know I was dealing with someone fancy. And inappropriate, with you fucking your boss and all. I have to assume you spent most of the day licking each other."

"I have to assume you watch too much porn."

"Not anymore." Felony dramatically sighed.

"You'll like her," Rosa said. "Rebecca, I mean. And I think she's going to like you."

"I'm looking forward to meeting her."

Felony smiled then they fell into a light silence, anticipation swelling in the final stretch.

They knew something was wrong about a mile away. Smoke drifted from the direction of their village.

A mile from the main gate, they found Garvey nailed to an upside town cross.

"What the fuck?" Rosa cried out.

They raced the rest of the way and arrived to the rest of the crosses. A hundred or so just outside the main gate.

There were still glowing embers of their homes and structures, and a few survivors milling about, some of them in a daze and others working to clean the grounds — moving bodies and sweeping ashes. But otherwise, The Reserve had been burned to the ground.

Rosa was on her feet and running. She crashed into Solomon, the one person alive who couldn't tell her what happened. He looked down, then quickly back up. His eyes were brimming but no tears had fallen.

He gestured for her to follow him. So she did, heart pounding, the taste of ash in her mouth, swallowing hard in pregnant expectation as an awful anxiety fluttered like a coked-out hummingbird and seemed to get worse by the step.

She crashed into the sight like plowing right into a wall.

Rebecca lay broken on the ground, the word *DYKE* painted across her body in what Rosa had to assume was her very own blood. She'd clearly gone down fighting, there was too much blood around her. And there was one other body that had obviously come from the Slums — a stray hand that didn't belong to either corpse.

She didn't get a cross. Instead, Rebecca was staked to the ground.

Rosa fell down beside her, and clutching the empty shell to her chest, sobbed until she was empty.

And then she thought of Kirk's knowing smile. And it hit her — he did this.

Six Months Later

Chapter Forty-Six

EVEN WITH PERCY gone from Melinda forever, it was a lot easier to call Stonefall home with Gleeson still missing.

There were sixty or so survivors after the alien attack that night.

Melinda had never been more scared. It was like living outside her body. She remembered seeing the fright in her eyes, the round O of her open mouth, unable to make any words. Only screaming. She could still sometimes hear as though her shrieks were being bellowed from someone standing behind her.

But miraculously, Stonefall had the right survivors, if such a thing could be said. If Melinda were to have made an inventory of those most deserving, that list would be similar if not exactly the same.

She didn't believe it when Percy told her through William, but every word was true. Kirk was behind it all, and the aliens saved the righteous.

Gleeson was anything but. He was saved by the child. Melinda had no idea why William wanted to spare a monster like that, and she never would. The child sacrificed himself. He was gone, even though word of what happened had spread enough to draw both the faithful and the desperate to believe.

In the six months since the attack, Stonefall had blossomed. Even before the snow finally thawed, people came from all over to knock on the gates, request entry, and promise to help build this new and vibrant community.

The vetting was kind and efficient. Nothing like Gleeson's and having zero to do with religion. Survivors of Rosa's Reserve had been absorbed into Stonefall.

Rosa, Eamon, Felony, and a few others had gone to scout the Slums to retaliate against Kirk and Baxter, but the Slums were empty. The Forsaken had left in a hurry. Where they'd gone, nobody knew. But they weren't far. Their crosses, and victims, could be found dotting roadsides every now and then, a constant reminder that human evil still existed in their world.

Life wasn't anything like Melinda had imagined it could be last spring, and it was a lightyear away from anything she ever imagined before Astral Day. Lately, she was surprised to find herself almost happy. Crops were thriving, and the people felt safe. Even better, Melinda liked her new friends, Sherry most of all.

Melinda didn't like interruptions, but they were always welcome if they were coming from Sherry. Three knocks followed by a flat slap against the wood told her who was at the door.

"Come in!" Melinda called.

The door opened and Sherry entered. "They're back!"

Melinda dropped her clipboard and followed Sherry outside, then all the way to the front gates so they could both be waiting when Felony and Rosa returned.

They drove through the gates and over to the garage.

Felony parked, then jumped out of the cabin with Rosa. Sherry ran over to hug them.

"How do you like them pomegranates?" Felony asked, beaming as he opened the back of an armored truck, requisitioned in early spring and used for runs through the summer.

"See." He pointed inside at the stacks of boxed firearms, bullets, and grenades.

"Is that Kevlar?" Rosa asked.

"It is," Felony said, still grinning.

Recent reports said the aliens weren't as invulnerable as they previously thought, and the same reports claimed their friends in the sky were spending a lot more time on the ground. And apparently, the days of them responding to gunshots were seemingly over.

"Wow. Well done." Melinda laughed out loud, surprised she could feel so happy about a truck full of guns. Something she once tolerated but never enjoyed.

"Any word on William?" Sherry asked.

The guns were of interest, but her son was the most important thing in the world.

"No," Felony shook his head. "I'm sorry."

"And Gleeson?" Melinda added.

Felony kept shaking his head.

No one knew what had happened to the child or to the Father of Stonefall. Most people believed he snuck away and the child drowned in too much of alien light. Melinda thought he was dead but wasn't willing to destroy Sherry's hope. Her's and Eamon's, both.

"What about Kirk and the rest of The Forsaken?"

Rosa said, "You'll know when we find him because I'll be carrying his head in my lap."

Her brother ran toward the truck.

"Hey, Mikey!"

But Miguel wasn't coming to see his sister, or at least not Rosa alone. "You've got to come," he said to them all. "Someone's at the gate!"

"Who?" Rosa asked.

"Just come. Now."

Then he turned around and started racing away.

"Hey, Miguel!" Felony called after him.

He turned.

"Go get Eamon!"

"I'm already on my way." Miguel turned back around and raced away.

"Do you know what he's talking about?" Melinda asked.

"No," Felony answered, "but whatever it is, Eamon's gonna want to know."

The four of them paraded into the bottom floor of the lookout tower then peered through the slats while waiting for Eamon.

"No shit," Felony said.

"What the hell is he doing back here?" Melinda demanded.

Gleeson was standing outside the gates with what appeared to be a young man or a woman in a jacket, a hat pulled low over his face.

Melinda turned away from the slat as one of the guards approached her.

"What do we do?" he asked.

"Open the door," she ordered.

Despite having few violent thoughts in the seasons since the alien attack, Melinda planned to shoot the man between his eyes.

"Let me in!" Gleeson roared. "You have kept the Father of Stonefall waiting too long. I have something you will all want to see."

Eamon entered with Miguel behind him.

But then they left, following the four friends and two guards on their way to the gate.

It swung open, then Gleeson started marching toward them.

"Where is my son?" Eamon demanded, taking Sherry's hand.

Guns were drawn.

Rosa and Felony walked up to Gleeson, Felony ordering the man down onto his knees with the barrel of his guns while Rosa went to cuff him.

She was right. They should interrogate the fucker before they killed him.

The teen with Gleeson raised a hand as if to stop them from harming his father figure, or whatever Gleeson was to this adolescent in oversized clothes. His body began to tremble.

"No, William!" Gleeson called out.

Miguel grabbed the boy and yanked him back.

The hat fell off his face and got lost in the shadows. They all saw the glowing scars on his right cheek, and everyone gasped.

Eamon and Sherry were staring, tears already leaking from both of Sherry's eyes.

"William?" They said, tentatively yet together.

"Hi, Mom and Dad," he said.

About the Authors

Avery Blake doesn't want you to know where she lives, or what she does. She travels the world, moving from place to place quickly to ensure she can't be tracked. It's safer that way.

When she's not looking over her shoulder, you can find her in the corner of a cafe, facing the exit, typing as fast as she can.

David W. Wright is the co-author of edge-of-your seat thrillers including the best-selling post-apocalyptic series *Yesterday's Gone*, the paranoid sci-fi *WhiteSpace* series, and the vigilante series, *No Justice*, as well as standalone thrillers *12*, and *Crash* which was recently optioned for a movie.

David is an accomplished, though intermittent, cartoonist who lives in [LOCATION REDACTED] with his wife and son [NAMES REDACTED.]

He is not at all paranoid.

He is "the grumpy one" on the *The Story Studio Podcast* with fellow Sterling and Stone founders, Sean Platt and Johnny B. Truant.

David writes about books, TV shows, movies, and video games he enjoys; his struggles with anxiety and OCD; writing; and posts the occasional drawing at his personal blog at davidwwright.com

You can email him at david@sterlingandstone.net

We swear, he almost never bites. Unless you feed him after midnight.

For a full list of his most recent books visit sterlingandstone.net.

~

Please join the Invasion Universe Facebook group for the latest news and discussions, including excerpts of upcoming books.

If you'd just like to be told about new releases each week, join our new release mailing list.

Thanks for reading!

Also By Avery Blake

The Invasion Series

Longshot

Invasion

Contact

Colonization

Annihilation

Judgment

Extinction

Resurrection

Save The City Series

Save The City

Save The Girl

Save The World

Stonefall Series

Alienation

Stonefall

Snowfall

Downfall

The Taken Saga

The Taken

The Changed

The Hidden

The Saved

The Next Evolution

Transition

Convergence

Evolution

Stand-Alone Novels

Analog Heart

Family Royale

Ruthless Positivity

Vicarious Joe

Also By David W. Wright

Cold Vengeance

Cold Vengeance

Cold Reckoning

Hidden Justice

Hidden Justice

Hidden Honor

Hidden Shame

Hidden Virtue

No Justice

No Justice

No Escape

No Hope

No Return

No Stopping

No Fear

Karma Police

Jumper

Karma Police

The Collectors

Deviant

The Fall

Homecoming

Yesterday's Gone

October's Gone

Yesterday's Gone Season One

Yesterday's Gone Season Two

Yesterday's Gone Season Three

Yesterday's Gone Season Four

Yesterday's Gone Season Five

Yesterday's Gone Season Six

Tomorrow's Gone

Tomorrow's Gone Season One

Tomorrow's Gone Season Two

Tomorrow's Gone Season Three

Available Darkness

Darkness Itself

Available Darkness Book One

Available Darkness Book Two

Available Darkness Book Three

WhiteSpace

WhiteSpace Season One

WhiteSpace Season Two

WhiteSpace Season Three

Stand Alone Novels

Crash

Emily's List

Threshold

The Secret Within